Seeking the Smart One

Twenty-four-year-old Jen Reid had her life in good shape: an okay job, a tiny-cute Seattle apartment, and a great boyfriend almost ready to get serious. In a flash it all came apart. Single, unemployed, and holding an eviction notice, who has time to remember trying out for a reality show? Then the call comes, and Jen sees her chance to start over—by spending her summer on national TV.

Luckily *The Fishbowl* is all about puzzles and games, the kind of thing Jen would love even if she wasn't desperate. The cast checks all the boxes: cheerful, quirky Birdie speaks in hashtags; vicious Ariana knows just how to pout for the cameras; and corn-fed "J-dawg" plays the cartoon villain of the house. Then there's Justin, the green-eyed law student who always seems a breath away from kissing her. Is their attraction real, or a trick to get him closer to the $250,000 grand prize? Romance or showmance, suddenly Jen has a lot more to lose than a summer . . .

Books by Laura Heffernan

Reality Star Series
America's Next Reality Star

Published by Kensington Publishing Corporation

America's Next Reality Star

Reality Star Series

Laura Heffernan

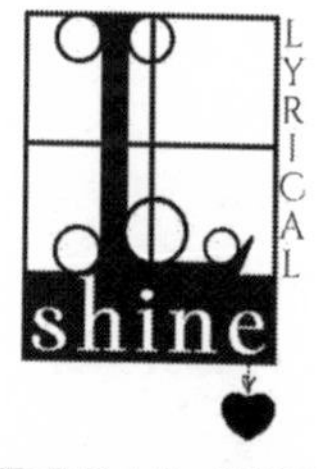

LYRICAL SHINE
Kensington Publishing Corp.
www.kensingtonbooks.com

Lyrical Press books are published by
Kensington Publishing Corp.
119 West 40th Street
New York, NY 10018

All Kensington titles, imprints, and distributed lines are available at special quantity discounts for bulk purchases for sales promotion, premiums, fund-raising, and educational or institutional use.

Special book excerpts or customized printings can also be created to fit specific needs. For details, write or phone the office of the Kensington Special Sales Manager:
Kensington Publishing Corp.
119 West 40th Street
New York, NY 10018
Attn. Special Sales Department. Phone: 1-800-221-2647.

First Electronic Edition: March 2017
eISBN-13: 978-1-5161-0153-5
eISBN-10: 1-5161-0153-7

First Print Edition: March 2017
ISBN-13: 978-1-5161-0154-2
ISBN-10: 1-5161-0154-5

Printed in the United States of America

To Steph

Duh.

Acknowledgements

First and foremost, I'd like to thank my darling husband for his unwavering love and support, even when I locked myself away in my office for hours (days??) at a time. Thank you to Stephanie Thornton for coming into my life at exactly the right time and being the friend I needed (Then and now. You're the best.). You also gave me a peek into an exciting new world. This book literally could not exist without you.

A huge thank you to my amazing agent, Michelle Richter, for everything (especially your endless patience), and to Jen Karsbaek for seeing something special in my Jen's story. Thank you to my editor, Wendy McCurdy, for helping me see what this story needed to be. Thank you to my publicist, Michelle Forde, for all your hard work (and putting up with my barrage of questions).

A book really is written by committee. Thank you to my priceless critique partners for their help: Carey O'Connor, Kristin B. Wright, Mary Ann Marlowe, Marty Mayberry, and Kara Reynolds. A special thank you to Michelle Hauck for picking *America's Next Reality Star* for her query and first page critique workshop (and the zillion other things you've done for me since).

Also, thank you to Deana Anker, Kimberly Ito, Kellye Garrett, and all the PitchWars mentors for helping to keep me sane during this long and sometimes difficult journey (And Brenda, of course, for inviting me into the community). I love you all.

Finally, I'd like to thank the good people at Cadbury for fueling this journey. Thank you for making mini-eggs available year-round in Canada, and thanks to my husband's family for keeping me supplied. <3

I hope you enjoy A*merica's Next Reality Star*. Writing it was a lot of fun. The best thing for a writer is to know that readers liked their book. If you did, please consider leaving an honest review on Goodreads or referring it to friends. A recommendation is the greatest support a reader can give an author.

Chapter 1

DO YOU WANT TO WIN $250,000? ARE YOU OUTGOING, VIVACIOUS, AND ENGAGING? DO YOU ALWAYS HAVE TO BE RIGHT? DO YOU LOVE PUZZLES AND TRIVIA? DO YOU USUALLY FIND YOURSELF SURROUNDED BY LESS INTELLIGENT PEOPLE? WE'RE LOOKING FOR SMART, SPUNKY 21 TO 25-YEAR-OLDS, FOR AN EXCITING NEW REALITY COMPETITION FILMING THIS SUMMER! E-MAIL STEPHANIE WITH YOUR NAME, AGE, 2-4 PICS, AND A LITTLE ABOUT YOURSELF FOR MORE INFORMATION.

I huddled at my desk, wrapping a blanket over my hoodie. Maybe one day management would trust employees to turn the heat above sixty degrees. Until that glorious day, I held my caffeine molecule-painted mug close to my body, futilely trying to gain warmth from the steam pouring off the top. The coffee tasted like pencil shavings and feet; drinking it wasn't an option.

With my right hand, I scrolled through my Facebook newsfeed, scanning the jokes, cartoons, and mindless banter. It was against the rules, but everyone did it. "Marketing assistant" apparently was code for "exhausting bursts of activity punctuated with lots of sitting around." The irony wasn't lost on me. After working insanely long days all week to include last-minute changes on a major project, I appreciated a few hours' break while my boss reviewed it. The craziness would start again soon enough. I turned up the volume on my computer to project my music over the howling November storm. My toes tapped the linoleum floor.

A message popped up at the bottom of my screen, informing me of a new e-mail. I hit alt-tab to switch programs, expecting the feedback I needed before starting my workday.

No such luck.

It was Seattle General Hospital's billing department. "Dear Ms. Reid, Thank you for your payment. . ."

Silently, I cursed them for the reminder.

If only the debt could be erased with the same easy click that sent the message to trash. I'd been in perfect health during my high school and college years. So, naturally, my ankle broke a week before my insurance with McCain & Webster kicked in while showing off my impression of Miley Cyrus's latest MTV Music Awards performance. When I slipped on the wet grass and fell, they'd laughed until my tears started. No one realized the fall wasn't part of the act.

Despite my efforts to tough it out ("Unless the bone sticks through the skin, it's fine!"), my boyfriend had dragged me to an Urgent Care facility. Dominic swore it would be affordable. He was half-right: urgent care might have been cheaper than an ER, but the necessary surgery to reset the bone cost a lot. My eyes crossed at the first bill. With my salary, this stupid thing would haunt me until my unborn kids graduated high school. To add insult to (literal) injury, I couldn't figure out how to turn off the automatic e-mails they sent every month.

I peeked at the empty desk behind me. My officemate would've told me to pretend to work until I got my next assignment. However, he'd left to bond with his newborn daughter. For the next eleven weeks, three days, our tiny office belonged solely to me. I'd been freed from Pete's obnoxious laughter, disapproving looks, and fried fish lunches. With my hall monitor gone and nothing work-related to do for the moment, I checked the bankruptcy qualifications—again—before clicking back to Facebook.

Wait a minute. What was that?

An old college drama professor posted an ad that caught my eye.

A reality show designed for smart people? How intriguing.

Voices buzzed outside my closed door. I glanced nervously over one shoulder. Being located next to the kitchen had its perks, but sometimes I couldn't tell if people were about to burst in on me or just picked an unfortunate spot to gossip.

After deciding my coworkers had gathered to make an early lunch, I read the description again.

DO YOU WANT TO WIN $250,000?

It sure beat filing for bankruptcy. There would probably be enough left to go back to school and get a degree in something more interesting. Or maybe put a down payment on a place bigger than a shoebox.

ARE YOU OUTGOING, VIVACIOUS, AND ENGAGING?

Well, I liked to think so. All through grade school, I took it upon myself to reach out to new students and make them feel welcome. Now, I hosted parties to celebrate big and small holidays. And I had no problem striking up conversations with random people on the Metro.

DO YOU ALWAYS HAVE TO BE RIGHT?

Hmm. I didn't *have* to be right, but I frequently was. I happened to have a good memory. Being able to repeat anything I'd heard came in handy during trivia, mostly. And basement bar debates. Maybe I'd found another use for it.

DO YOU LOVE PUZZLES AND TRIVIA?

Did owning four themed copies of Trivial Pursuit or spending Metro rides playing Pic-a-Pix and Hashi on my phone count?

DO YOU USUALLY FIND YOURSELF SURROUNDED BY LESS INTELLIGENT PEOPLE?

I didn't judge other people. But, I competed on the math and science teams in high school. Some people (those who'd met me) would've said I was kind of a geek. I hoped the show considered that a bonus, since it did nothing for my social life. I didn't go on a single date until my junior year of college.

WE'RE LOOKING FOR SMART, SPUNKY 21 TO 25-YEAR-OLDS.

I was a twenty-one to twenty-five-year-old. Twenty-three, to be exact, turning twenty-four in a few weeks.

As I read through the ad yet again, the little voice in the back of my head piped up. *You should do this*, it said. *E-mail them.*

What? That was silly. I wasn't an actress—marketing and academics were my bag.

The little voice spoke again. I did love puzzles. I was good at them. The money would be extremely useful. Plus, I couldn't remember my last vacation.

My boyfriend worked as a traveling nurse, which made him less-than-enthusiastic about taking trips with me when he wasn't away on an assignment. I understood. Still, it would be nice to get away, even on my own. What was the time commitment for something like this?

I needed more information before making a decision.

Before I could chicken out, my fingers opened a new e-mail and began to type as if of their own accord.

Dear Stephanie,

My name is Jennifer Reid, and I'm writing to request more information about your puzzle-based reality show. It sounds like something right up my alley. I'm 23 years old. I live in beautiful Seattle, Washington. It's important to me to live life to the fullest and to grab opportunities when they present themselves.

Since I was a little girl, I've loved puzzles. I chose a career in marketing because I like figuring out what the consumer wants and how to give it to them.

Can you send me more information about the show and when you're looking for someone? Thank you for your time.

Best,
Jennifer Reid

Next step, pictures. Which ones to attach? Something showing my face, obviously. But also something fun.

Thanks to the Internet, essentially every picture of me taken over the past six years sat at my fingertips. Thanks to my older brother, Adam, some older and more embarrassing pictures were also there. I bypassed those. The casting director didn't need to see me, at ten, with chocolate cake smeared across my face or four-year-old me waving a cape as I pranced around in Wonder Woman panties, a pink tiara atop blond hair that hadn't yet darkened with age. Thanks, Adam. Twelve-year-old Jen's first attempts at wearing makeup also didn't need to be shared with the world. What had made me think purple eye shadow smeared up to my forehead brought out my blue eyes?

Thanks, Adam, for posting my diving meet pictures where anyone can see them.

It only took a few minutes to find what I wanted. A few years ago, my friends and I went bungee jumping. Someone under the bridge snapped each of us as we took the plunge. My picture showed me falling through the air, head tilted back, arms spread, pure joy on my face.

I had no idea how they caught that expression. I'd been terrified, thought I was going to pee my pants. My breakfast had climbed into my throat, and I'd tamped it down using sheer willpower.

There must be a split second of bliss a person experiences between "Oh, please God, I don't want to die!" and "Why am I doing this?" They happened to click the picture at exactly the right time.

Another great one showed the mess I created trying to cook Dominic dinner for his twenty-fifth birthday (before ordering birthday takeout), but the image focused on the burnt paella, not me. Then I found the perfect shot. While on a trip to New York City, I'd found a sign reading, "This is a library. Quite, please!" My head tilted toward the sign, mouth twisted into a grimace. One hand underlined the word "quite."

I attached it to the e-mail, along with the bungee picture and a regular close-up. Before stopping to consider any potential consequences of my actions, I took a deep breath and hit "send."

* * *

A few hours later, my keys jingled as I struggled to unlock my front door. Rainwater dripped from shopping bags balanced on one raised knee. My purse dug into my armpit as I pushed against my apartment door. It stuck. Again. I braced myself against the jamb. One good shove usually did the trick.

My phone, cradled between my chin and shoulder, beeped, startling me. Bags, purse, and umbrella crashed to the floor. An orange rolled out of one bag and down the hall.

Ugh.

As I scrambled to pick everything up, the door swung open. I tensed for a second before my boyfriend's voice sounded from the doorway.

"Oops. So. . .you got my text?" He crouched beside me and gathered bags.

"Only if it said, 'Hey! Drop everything!'"

As always, seeing Dominic brought a smile to my face. Although we still crouched in the hallway, I leaned over and kissed him.

When we separated, garlic and basil scents wafted by my nose.

Dominic stood and pushed his wavy black hair out of his face with one hand. "Actually, it said, 'When are you going to be home? I have a surprise for you."

A grin stretched across my face. He knew how I loved surprises. "You know, you're not supposed to use your key to jump out and scare me."

"What? That's half the fun." His hands now full of my stuff, Dominic stepped through the door, holding it open as he nodded toward the interior. "After you, gorgeous."

As soon as I entered my four-hundred-square-foot apartment, I spotted the surprise. Freshly baked garlic bread steamed on the two-person wooden table, next to a tossed Caesar salad and spaghetti with homemade meatballs. My mouth watered.

I popped on to my toes and planted a kiss on his cheek. "You are the best boyfriend ever."

"I know. I'm having a T-shirt made."

Dominic's lips hovered over mine. My arms wrapped around his neck, and I rose up to meet him before allowing myself to sink into the kiss. After a moment, he picked me up and spun me on to the kitchen counter. My legs wrapped around his waist as his hands cupped my face.

God, I loved him.

We'd met my last year in college, when he was a graduate student. I'd been attracted to his rugged good looks and liked that he wasn't clingy or demanding. We had fun together, but he didn't complain when I worked overtime or spent time with my girlfriends. A year later, I'd already caught myself looking at engagement rings.

Er. . .just the one time, though. We had plenty of time for that later.

Dominic's hand found the clasp to my bra—we hadn't seen each other in more than a week. However, my body interrupted the kiss by emitting a sound that was less a growl of hunger and more the howl of a wild animal being murdered. Dominic pulled back, gave me one last kiss, then set me on to the floor.

I gazed at the tiles, hoping he didn't see the mortification on my face. "Sorry. I took an early lunch."

"Don't be sorry." With a sweeping bow, he indicated the table. "Your feast awaits."

A piece of garlic bread disappeared into my mouth as I sat, surveying the table. "This looks amazing! Thank you!"

"You're welcome." A slow, lazy smile spread across his face. My stomach flip-flopped. "You've been working so hard, I figured you probably weren't eating right."

I speared a meatball with my fork. "You're a smart man. It's been mostly canned tuna or Lunchables in my office at ten PM."

Dominic shuddered. "Lunchables?"

"Eight days in a row. Luckily, I get a few days' reprieve before it picks up again."

"Ew. You poor thing. Well, I brought a ton of food and Tupperware, so you're set for at least a week."

Reaching across the table, I took his hand in mine and squeezed. My skin tingled at the contact. "Thank you. That helps a lot."

We didn't talk about it, but Dominic knew I couldn't afford to eat well. The fact that he'd gone out of his way to make me lunch for several days sent butterflies fluttering in my belly.

"You're welcome, babe. Next time things get crazy, promise you'll call me so I can bring you a real meal? Or have one delivered so I don't interrupt you?"

Cheesy-noodle-and-marinara-saucy-goodness glued my mouth shut, so I nodded. His twinkling brown eyes captured mine. A spark of lust sent my thoughts away from dinner and on to a more interesting path. Dominic's dilating pupils told me his thoughts followed the same route. I chewed faster as a familiar thrill of anticipation spread through my body.

Dominic's hand wrapped around mine. I pushed the plate away and stood. Our lips met. We didn't quite make it to the bedroom.

The reminder that I had a good thing with Dominic in Seattle pushed my reality show application out of my mind. There were other ways to make extra cash. I arrived at work the next morning dreaming about the next step in our relationship. We'd been dating for over a year, and he'd had a key to my apartment for months. I'd have his, too, as soon as I figured out where it had disappeared to, hours after he'd given it to me.

Lost in thought, I walked to my desk and opened my e-mail. A new message appeared from someone named Stephanie Long. Who? I didn't know anyone named Stephanie.

Subject: Re: Casting call.

Oh. My. God.

My heart beat faster.

Dear Jennifer,

Thank you so much for your interest in our new series. The Fishbowl *is a fast-paced reality show with physical and mental challenges to push the contestants on every level. What makes this different from other shows is that viewers vote on aspects of the game. With things always changing, you'll never know what to expect!*

Filming will start at the beginning of June. We estimate that contestants could be on the show as few as a couple of days or as long as ten weeks.

Our team is interviewing applicants across the country now. We'll be in Seattle next week and would love to meet you. Please call my assistant at 323-555-1258 to set up an interview.

Best,
Stephanie

The viewers would tell us what to do? On live television? Huh. What if they made us eat bugs? I'd have to ask the interviewer. But otherwise—up to three months in LA? New people and new experiences? It sounded interesting, but I wasn't sure I could afford to take that much time away from work. Or my boyfriend.

On the other hand, it would be fun to surprise Dominic if I made the show. And our relationship had never been stronger. We could handle time apart. Between my overtime and his traveling to care for patients, we didn't exactly hang out every day.

Hey, honey, your girlfriend's going to win loads of money on a reality show so we can buy a house. . .

I reached to call Stephanie's assistant practically before I finished reading.

* * *

On Wednesday morning, I showed up at the address they'd given me. Peeling paint, boarded up windows, and several "Space for Rent" signs against a backdrop of drizzle and gray morning light welcomed me. Trash spilled out of the can next to the front door. A rat scurried away down an alley. It seemed odd to think my fate might lie within this dilapidated building.

Sure, Jen, lots of women's fates lie in old, run-down buildings. But is that the way you want to go?

I double-checked the address on my phone. Google informed me I stood in the right spot. As I hesitated, remembering that guy who picked up women on Craigslist and murdered them, the front door opened. A girl about my age walked out wearing red tights and a blue shirt that didn't look as much like a dress as she must've thought. Sunglasses covered the top half of her face, so I couldn't tell if she noticed me as she tottered past on five inch turquoise heels, chatting on her phone.

"Yeah, I just left the interview. It's totally not a beauty contest. . ."

Was that what I should've worn to the interview?

My black pants and red button up shirt with matching red and black polka-dotted ballet flats were appropriate for going to work when I finished, but now they made me look boring. My own heels lived in a drawer in my desk, to be taken out upon my arrival at the office. Were the producers looking for people who dressed more colorfully?

Only one way to find out.

Taking a deep breath, I smoothed my hair and entered. A layer of dust on the empty sign-in desk suggested no one had welcomed visitors to this building since the Reagan administration. A curved staircase stretched ahead of me. A hand-lettered sign next to the mailboxes informed me that ABC Casting could be found on the second floor. It didn't seem worth looking for an elevator.

My foot caught almost immediately on a missing step. Awesome.

I clutched at the decrepit-looking metal railing. It wobbled, but thankfully held.

I hadn't been cast yet, and already someone was trying to kill me. Were there cameras in the stairwell?

I righted myself and let go before the railing snapped beneath the unexpected weight. Then I peeked behind me. Nothing else dangerous lurked in the dim light. The darks corners of the ceiling probably didn't hide cameras.

It was probably an old building, not a trap. Sometimes, I had an overactive imagination. Still, I proceeded carefully to the stop of the stairs. Thankfully, no other missing steps or holes in the floor jumped into my path.

The procedures must have just set up the room for these interviews. Nothing hung on the white walls. Someone had shoved a lumpy beige couch against one wall with a couple of armchairs overturned on top of it. End tables piled in front of the couch dissuaded anyone who might have considered clearing it. A card table stood in the middle of the room, buried under stacks of paper. Extension cords snaked around the industrial beige carpet.

A guy in his late twenties, medium build and height, with floppy brown hair and a wrinkled shirt greeted me with a grin. His unkempt appearance made me feel better about not dressing like a fashion model.

He looks so normal. Definitely a serial killer. Like John Wayne Gacy.

"Hey! I'm John," he said, shaking my hand before settling into a folding chair behind the table.

Wayne Gacy? I asked myself before I could help it. Then I shoved those thoughts aside. That line of thinking wouldn't lead to a productive interaction.

"I'm Jen. It's nice to meet you." I moved a laptop off the only other chair. Unsure what to do, I offered it to him.

"Sorry. Thanks. We're casting for a brand-new show here, like nothing you've seen. There will be puzzles, physical challenges, and more. Contestants will push themselves on all levels. It's not a beauty contest, and it's not for the faint of heart."

I nodded. I'd learned all that from the ad and Stephanie's e-mail. "That's exactly what I'm looking for."

"Excellent! So, why do you want to be on television?"

"My personal hero is Eleanor Roosevelt. She said that life is for living, for grabbing on to each new experience and savoring it. I believe that. So, for me, it's more about wanting to experience new things and explore every opportunity. This seems like a great way to meet new people, and I love puzzles, trivia, and games. Plus, I'm broke. I could really use $250,000. So when I read the ad, it was like it was shouting, 'Jen, come be on our show.' It's exactly what I need right now."

He consulted his clipboard. "You said you like games. What was your favorite toy as a child?"

Some people might have had to think before answering this question, but I'd done a lot of research and prepared my answers. "My older brother's Erector Set. I used to sneak into his room to build pyramids when he played baseball." I laughed. "He never figured out why pieces sometimes went missing."

John smiled. "Sounds like he should have let you play with him. Did you go to college?"

"Yup! University of Washington, Class of 2012! Go Huskies!"

"Okay," John said. "Tell me this. If you were out in Seattle at a bar with your friends and a guy sat down to talk to you, what is the one thing he would be absolutely shocked to find out about you?"

Without missing a beat, I offered a big, sweet smile. "I'm an assassin."

John showed me the whites of his eyes. Then he pushed his chair back from the table and shivered in exaggerated fear.

We both laughed. "Okay, I'm not. I'm pretty normal." I let my mind roam for a moment. "You may not believe this because I'm fairly small, but a few years ago I won a hot dog eating contest."

"What? No way!" He gasped in mock disbelief.

"Absolutely!" I flexed my biceps, preening for a moment. "Of course, the only other person who entered was seventy years old; he ate three. Grandpa might have let me win."

"A win's a win, right?" He consulted his papers. "Okay, that's everything I needed to ask you. Do you have any questions for me? Questions about the show, the process? My favorite color?"

"I did wonder about one thing. The e-mail said the viewers would tell us what to do?"

"Right. They'll vote on things like which mini-challenge to do, which player deserves to be up for elimination, and things like that."

"Okay, so they're not voting to make us do bizarre or disgusting things?"

"Like what?"

"Like. . .eating bugs? Cleaning the toilet with our toothbrushes?"

He laughed. "No, no. Nothing like that. This isn't *Fear Factor*."

My shoulders sagged with relief. "Awesome. Then it's all good. I'm excited."

"Great! We're excited, too! I need a four to six minute video by the end of the week, telling me who you are, what you do, your hobbies—basically, why we should pick you. If you Google it, you can find audition videos from other shows to get an idea of what we're looking for. Do you have any other questions for me?"

I consulted the list on my phone, although I'd memorized it three days ago. "Can you tell me about the casting process?"

"People who make it to the next round will fly to Los Angeles for a screen test, IQ tests, a medical exam, psych tests, etc. Then we'll do background checks on the people we choose. The finalists will be notified a couple of weeks later. It's pretty straightforward. The hardest part is waiting."

"Makes sense. Thanks."

John stood and shook my hand. "Great. Thanks for coming in, Jennifer. We'll be in touch."

I thanked him, and that was it. The whole thing took less than half an hour.

After carefully navigating the stairs, I left the interview with a smile on my face and a spring in my step. Since I'd taken the entire morning off work, I decided to walk to the office. Most likely, I'd need to stay late; a new project could hit my desk any minute.

Regardless of the dark and gloomy skies, a beautiful day peeked from behind the backdrop of the old buildings. My feet danced around the puddles, oblivious to the rain streaming around me. When the wind fought to steal my umbrella, it didn't faze me.

Rather than rush back to the grind, I stopped at a coffee shop to read the application John gave me. I'd told my boss I had an appointment and didn't know how long it would take. When I implied I needed personal time, he'd assumed that meant a gynecologist appointment. He wrung his hands and prohibited me from sharing any details before rushing me out of his office. Men.

Reading the application made me laugh at how thorough the producers were. They asked about everything.

What kind of people did I dislike?

Mean people, bigots, and people who text during movies on giant phones that light up the theater.

What would I do with an extra five grand?

Owe five grand less to Seattle General? Or buy a new purse and owe $4,980 less.

How do other people see me?

With their eyeballs, usually.

What would I do if I knew no one would ever catch me?

Break into Fort Knox. Or maybe Buckingham Palace.

How would I describe myself in twenty-five words or fewer?

I'm a twenty-three-year-old marketing assistant, completely unchallenged. I make no money and live in the world's smallest apartment. Being an adult sucks.

Hmm. . .Maybe I should go back to that one later. I kept reading. What clubs or organizations did I belong to? If I could have plastic surgery on any part of my body, which one and why?

Any part? Like, could I walk around with giant earlobes or add fingers to my elbows? That would be a conversation starter.

What was my height/weight? My dress/ring/shoe/hat size? Hat size? I had no idea. I had to measure my head. How cool was that?

It was like completing the world's most interesting job application. Still, after the ninth or tenth page, I expected them to ask my favorite brand of dental floss or whether I preferred one- or two-ply toilet paper (For the record: Oral B, and two.) My favorite part was the self-portrait.

Luckily, the coffee shop provided crayons for children and, apparently, reality-show hopefuls. Since my eyes were my best feature, I started with the blue crayon. Some quick brown strokes filled in my hair. How realistic did this have to be? I mean, I could give myself a button nose, right? Maybe soften my chin?

After a few minutes, I leaned back and scrutinized my work. Hmm. I may have gone overboard. Or maybe Cartoon Jen wears Wonderbras. I added an asterisk.

NOTE: NOT TO SCALE.

Then for good measure, I sketched a party hat on my head and some board games in the background. A red crayon added a smile I hoped looked friendly, not manic. Perfect.

I hoped that, next time I applied for a job or promotion, they requested a self-portrait enclosed with my resumé. Maybe I'd add one. I pictured the cover letter: "I have attached a resumé for your consideration, along with a self-portrait of how happy I'd be in this position."

When I reached my office, I was still laughing at the silliness of the whole process.

Chapter 2

Excerpt from Jennifer Reid's Audition Video:

Hi, my name's Jen. I'm twenty-three years old, and I work in marketing for a large multi-national corporation. Check out my fabulous studio apartment in Seattle. It's only steps from all the excitement and restaurants of downtown, so I'm in a great location. Look at my view of the Space Needle! I love to entertain here. My friends and I do a rotating monthly dinner club. Everyone brings food that fits a theme. My last one was "Food Starting with the Letter Q." We ate quiche, quinoa, quince pie. . .I know it sounds weird, but everything tasted delicious.

Anyway, I built this cupboard myself. It's full of games and puzzles. One thing I love to do, at least once a month, is have friends over for Games Night. We play board games, video games, charades—everything!

This is the best part of my apartment: the closet. I added the shelves and these cubbies, which tripled the space. That was a fun project.

Hmm. Is my landlord going to see this? Don't worry, Mrs. Perez! I'll put it back when I move.

My smile broadened when I arrived at my desk. A gift basket sat on my chair, covered with pink and purple cellophane. What a nice surprise! Peeking through the wrapping, I saw about a dozen chocolate-covered strawberries and a bottle of red wine. *YUM!* What brought this on? Was it from the casting people?

No, that was silly.

Papers and clutter covered every inch of my desk's surface, so I carried it to Pete's before reaching for the card taped to the wine bottle. No reason not to utilize the extra space while I had it. My smile faded as I tore open the envelope and read.

Hey Babe,

I'm sorry to do this to you. Work told me this morning I have to be in San Francisco today. Headed to the airport at 11. Call me?

Love,

Dom

Uh-oh. I shouldn't have wasted so much time getting back to the office. It was 11:17 AM I might catch him in the cab. While dialing, I bit into a strawberry. Chocolate crumbled on my tongue as sweet juice filled my mouth. Chocolate strawberries were my favorite.

He answered on the fourth ring, right as I started worrying the call would roll to voice mail. "Did you get my message?"

The roar of road noise in my ear said I'd caught him just in time. "I did. And the consolation prize. They're delicious. Thank you." I hoped he didn't hear the defeat in my voice.

"I'm sorry. I was supposed to be within driving distance of Seattle for at least a couple of months, but my boss needs me to cover a patient in Portland at the last minute. My co-worker was supposed to go, but his daughter got the chicken pox. He can't risk infecting the patient. They just told me. I have to cancel our date tomorrow night. I don't even know my schedule yet."

"Oh no! Any idea when you'll be back?"

"I'm not sure, babe. Looks like at least three weeks. I'll keep you posted. May not be home for a while."

"What about our Book of Mormon tickets next weekend?" I'd eaten ramen and boxed macaroni and cheese for two months to afford them.

"You'll have to take someone else. Or you could sell them?"

No way I'd miss a show I'd been waiting to see for years. One of my friends might want to go. Or maybe my mom could visit for the weekend.

"Yeah, I guess. . ."

Maybe he heard my disappointment, because his tone changed. "Wait. I'm sorry. You should go. You've been looking forward to this for months. I'll pay you for the unused ticket if you can't find anyone on short notice."

Taking his money wasn't an option, but I appreciated the offer. "You don't have to do that. If I can't find someone, I'll go by myself."

"Sorry, babe, I'm about to go through a tunnel. Gotta go."

"Okay. Have fun. I love you."

"I love—" The roaring in my ear stopped, and he was gone.

* * *

The oven chimed.

I giggled. "Why, what's that?"

This whole thing was so over-the-top I couldn't stop laughing. It was Thursday night, and my friend Brandon had come over to help film my audition video.

I led him from the closet into the kitchen, narrating. "Well, I just finished baking my fantastic secret recipe chocolate chip cookies!"

Brandon walked to the trash, and bent low, still filming.

"Why are you shooting my garbage?" I hissed.

He laughed. "Honey, I'm showing them your 'secret recipe.'" The empty Toll House bag perched atop the can for the world to see.

"Ha!" I waved the bag in front of the camera. "You caught me, America. This is my secret recipe. But, hey, if you cast me on the show, cookies for everyone!"

"Hey, Jen?" Brandon sniffed the air. "Don't you want to take them out of the oven?"

"Oh no!"

Yes, I wanted to do that. I yanked the handle. With an oven mitt in each hand, I waved smoke away and grabbed the smoldering tray. The cookie sheet clattered on to the cooling rack. Still fanning the air, I turned off the oven. The remaining batches could wait.

When I stepped back, the black knob stayed in my hand.

A camera lens entered my field of vision, reminding me I had more important things to do than fume over a broken oven. An awesome video could fix my financial woes.

"Brandon! What are you doing?"

"I'm showing America what an excellent baker you are."

Blackened lumps lay on the tray. I poked one with a spatula, and it crumbled. Maybe I liked them that way.

Or maybe it had to do with the oven dial in my right hand.

Brandon turned the camera toward himself. "Don't you want to eat those? Mmmmmm!"

I swatted his arm. "This was a test batch. You distracted me."

The fire alarm blared.

"Oh, shit!"

I raced to the door and yanked it open. Then I ran around the room, opening the windows, while Brandon waved a dish towel in front of the smoke detector.

"And this, America, is the beautiful sound of my fire alarm. That's right! Every time anyone burns microwave popcorn, these dulcet tones fill my ears."

Blissfully, the blaring stopped. Brandon stepped closer to the window and peered out.

"Hey, Jen, can we talk about your 'view of the Space Needle'?"

"What about it?"

"Well, I mean, technically it's there. Did you want me to put binoculars on the camera lens? Or maybe a periscope? Because that's what it would take if anyone wanted to see it."

I put my hands on my hips and made a face at him, but he ignored me.

"Oh! I could film you hanging out the window to get a glimpse while I white-knuckle the back of your shirt?"

"Just what I need. Hey, America, here's my ass!"

"That's not a bad idea. Turn around."

"What?"

"You want people to want to watch you on TV, right? You've got a great ass. Let's show them!"

"Brandon, you've lost your mind."

He lowered the camera and stepped toward me.

"It's still on! The red light's blinking."

"That's the off light." I glared at him. "Fine. Just walk toward the door. I'll follow you."

"Does Mark know about your fixation with my ass?" I grabbed a spoonful of cookie dough and warded him off with it.

The laughter on his face died. "Actually. . .He doesn't know it yet, but Mark and I are done."

My face dropped. The spoon clattered to the tile floor. They'd always been my example of the perfect couple everyone wanted to be. "I'm sorry, Brandon. I didn't know."

He put one arm around me. "No worries, honey. I haven't told anyone yet—and you can't, either. But we've drifted apart since graduation. I pretended everything was fine, but we can't go on like this. I'm looking for my own place."

Words caught in my throat. I couldn't respond.

"Seriously, cheer up. No way you could've known. Hey, why don't we order—" He sniffed the air. "Go out for dinner? Somewhere less pungent? You've got enough footage. The casting people will love your burnt cookies and our banter."

"You want to be in the video?"

"Duh! Why do you think I dropped everything and rushed over here instead of watching *The Millionaire Matchmaker* while reading my Torts assignment?"

I popped up on to my toes to kiss his cheek. "Good point. Plus, having a golden Adonis of a man in my audition video can only help. Maybe they only want people with super attractive friends."

He flexed into a bodybuilder's pose. "Want to grab the camera? I could take my shirt off."

I threw a cookie at him. He swatted it away. "It's a good thing I know you're too modest to do that, or I'd wonder why we're friends."

"And it's good I know you don't usually burn the cookies. Grab your coat. I'm starving."

* * *

Dominic returned from his business trip two days before my birthday. He surprised me Saturday morning by picking me up for a mysterious "getaway." I waited in the living room while he packed a bag for me, trying not to scream out instructions about which clothes hadn't fit in months. When he finished, he led me down the stairs to the front of the building.

"Is this blindfold really necessary?" I asked as he helped me into his car.

"It's not a surprise if you can see where we're going, is it?"

Instead of answering, I crossed my arms and leaned back into my seat. The seatbelt clicked around me.

"If you'll stop glaring at the window," Dominic said, "I'll hand you your coffee."

"Oh! Yes, please!" A moment later, a warm cup entered my hand. Dominic's lips touched my forehead. "Thank you. So where are we going?"

He laughed, a low gravelly sound that sent a tingle down my spine. "Nice try. You'll have your answer soon." He turned up the radio to discourage further questions. My mind raced.

Was this it? Did he plan a romantic weekend so he could propose? We'd been dating a long time; cohabitation or engagement was the natural next step. I let myself dream about what he would say, how it would make me feel until the car stopped.

The music faded away, and Dominic finally spoke. "Wait here. I'll be back in a minute."

Tapping my foot, I gathered clues without doing the obvious and removing the blindfold. I wanted to guess the surprise, not ruin it. When Dominic opened the door, cold air rushed in, carrying a whiff of burning wood and evergreen trees. Nearby, tires crunched as a car's engine drifted by. Where did Dom take me that wasn't on paved roads? A few yards away, a car door slammed.

Maybe we were somewhere in the mountains. Hopefully not a picnic, considering the chill in the air and the frozen ground.

Before I narrowed down our location, Dominic returned, helping me out of the car and leading me through a room where my footsteps echoed. A ding sounded, metal whooshed, and we entered what had to be an elevator. A moment later, he led me across plush carpet, trying not to stumble and fall. The blindfold was a little exciting at first, but my fingers itched to remove it. Walking was much easier when I could see ahead of me. Something scraped against metal, gears turned, and a door handle rasped. We were in a hotel. Had to be.

When he removed my blindfold, my jaw dropped. A king-sized bed dominated the room, buried under a stack of fluffy pillows. Real pillows, not those doll-sized hotel ones. My fingers sank into the top one. When I sat on the mattress to remove my shoes, a cloud embraced me. My bed at home would never feel the same.

Next to the bed, a sitting area waited, complete with one of those expensive couches that looked nice but felt like a rock. In the corner of the room, gleaming wood caught my eye. My hands clapped over my mouth.

"Oh my God! We have a fireplace!"

Dominic's muffled voice came from the bathroom. "Did you see what's in here?"

"Um. . .What are you about to show me? Because when I mentioned taking our relationship to the next level—"

"Ha ha." Dominic pulled me into the room. "Come see the tub."

Gold and white marble glinted in the lights. The shower hid behind a smoky glass door tucked into one corner. Next to it, a similar enclosure concealed the toilet. On the other side of the room sat a bathtub roughly the size of my entire apartment. You could fit a basketball team in there. A peek inside confirmed it had jets. We had our own private hot tub.

I spun around, bouncing on my toes. "Oh, Dominic! It's beautiful. I love it! Thank you!"

"You're welcome. Happy birthday."

After a brief kiss, I went to change into something without coffee stains from the trip. When my shirt hit the floor, warm hands caressed my belly from behind. Dominic's hot breath touched my ear.

"We don't need to ski today, right? We can just stay, here, order room service, and. . ."

I turned into him. "Mmmmm. I like the sound of that."

Things were heating up when a buzz sounded from Dominic's pants. "Ignore it," he muttered, trailing a line of kisses down my neck. I obliged, one hand unbuttoning his shirt. The other hand cupped the back of his neck.

Dominic's pants buzzed again. And again. I couldn't focus on what we were doing. I stepped back.

"Unless part of your surprise is a new toy, maybe you should answer that."

He cleared his throat. "No, it's just the woman taking my patient this weekend. She tends to overthink things. But if the phone's bothering you, I'll turn it off."

"Thanks."

Frustration twitched across Dominic's face as he looked at the phone. "Sorry, babe, one second."

"Okay. I'm going to run a bath."

My apartment didn't even have a bathtub. The second I'd seen the hip-level marble and the jets, I'd wanted to sink into the tub and let steaming water pound my cares away.

Dominic scrolled through his phone, probably not really listening. "Sure, sounds great."

In the bathroom, hot water poured from the taps while I dug through the provided toiletries. I'd just found one labeled "Relaxing Bubbles" when Dominic stuck his head through the doorway. "Hey, babe, I'm going to go get some champagne. I'll be back in a few."

"We don't need champagne! Let's enjoy the tub. . .and each other."

"I'm not a bath guy. Have fun, relax. You won't even miss me." Before I could protest, the door closed behind him.

Stupid job, always running him ragged. Poor guy. He needed a permanent position at one of the local hospitals.

I piled my hair on top of my head before climbing into the tub. The steaming water eased stress I hadn't realized I'd been carrying. Lavender-scented bubbles settled on to my skin. I folded up a nearby hand towel to create a pillow. With a contented sigh, I leaned back against the edge of the tub and closed my eyes, letting the jets do their job.

Only a glass of champagne could've made the moment more perfect. Or my boyfriend.

Sometime later, I sat up with a start. Jets of hot water no longer pounded against my back. No bubbles floated on the surface of the water. My teeth chattered in the cool air. My mouth reminded me of an old sweat sock, the unwelcome taste of falling asleep without brushing my teeth.

I stretched and rubbed my eyes. No sounds reached me from the rest of the suite. "Dom?"

No one answered.

"Are you there?"

Silence.

Weird. I stood, wrapping a thick white bath towel around my body. After my own threadbare towels left over from college, I wished these mini-clouds were complimentary, like the shampoo. How many years would I have to save to buy a couple?

My phone sat on the bedside table. Dominic's voicemail answered my call.

Now he turns it off. . .

Inside the closet, I found two waffle-print bathrobes. I slid into one, marveling at the softness against my damp skin. The sleeves hung well below my fingertips. Still, I wrapped it tightly and tied a bow, rolled up the sleeves, then dropped my room key into a pocket and went to find my boyfriend.

It didn't take long to find him. When the elevator doors opened, Dominic exited, holding a bottle of champagne. "Where have you been? I thought you only went downstairs for a minute."

"So sorry, babe, I ran into this guy from college. He just got engaged. Insisted I have a shot with him. I figured you wouldn't mind, since you were taking a bath. But I should've come right back." He dropped to his knees and held up hands clasped around the bottle, bottom lip trembling. "Please forgive me? Pwetty pwease, with a cherry?"

I giggled at his exaggerated contrition. My irritation evaporated. After all, I'd been asleep. Not the most exciting date. I leaned forward and kissed his forehead, bringing my breasts inches from his face.

Dominic peeked inside the neckline of my bathrobe. "Wait a minute. Are you wearing anything under this?" He wiggled his eyebrows at me.

I helped him to his feet. "Come find out."

* * *

We spent the next day skiing. Dominic persuaded me to leave the bunny trail behind and helped me on the more advanced slopes. I only fell a couple of times. He dropped me off at home after dinner, exhausted but happy.

My thoughts consumed me as I ninjaed my apartment door open. Something brushed my shoulder where it braced against the door. A piece of paper fluttered.

Distracted, I opened the letter, letting the door fall shut behind me. The happy aura lingering from the weekend evaporated.

The words NOTICE TO VACATE jumped out at me.

What?

As I read the full text, my heartbeat slowed a touch. The property owner was converting the building to condominiums. If I wanted to stay, I could sign a purchase and sale agreement by the end of April. Otherwise, I needed to leave on May 31. Plenty of time to make a decision.

No way I could buy this place, unless they'd accept a five-hundred-dollar down payment. That would be. . . let's see. . . about one-quarter of one percent of the purchase price. I had a nice overtime check coming, but even if I didn't need it for other bills, it would barely cover a down payment on one of those tiny houses on TV with a toilet in the kitchen.

A vision swam before my eyes. I saw myself in Dominic's kitchen, baking cookies (in a working oven). He sat at the island, chatting with me. Waking up in Dominic's king-sized bed every morning. Talking until late at night, the way we had at the hotel. Snuggling when we woke up together in the morning. Maybe getting evicted wasn't so bad after all.

Moving in with Dominic would be perfect, and the notice provided me with the motivation I needed to make the suggestion.

Chapter 3

THE FISHBOWL APPLICANT QUESTIONNAIRE

PLEASE ANSWER "YES" OR "NO" TO THE FOLLOWING STATEMENTS. IF NECESSARY, WRITE AN EXPLANATION IN THE SPACE PROVIDED:

HAVE YOU EVER BEEN CONVICTED OF A CRIME?

HAVE YOU EVER BEEN CHARGED WITH OR PLEAD GUILTY TO A CRIME?

DO YOU LIKE SHRUBS?

HAVE YOU EVER BEEN INVOLVED IN A FISTFIGHT?

HAVE YOU EVER HIT SOMEONE IN SELF-DEFENSE?

DO YOU HAVE ANY ALLERGIES?

HAVE YOU EVER BEEN A PARTY TO A CIVIL LAWSUIT OR OTHER COURT PROCEEDING?

HAVE YOU EVER SET A FIRE INTENTIONALLY, OTHER THAN A CAMP OR COOKING FIRE?

The following Tuesday, my phone rang. A number flashed on the screen. Where was area code 714?

"Hello?"

An unfamiliar female voice spoke. "Is this Jennifer Reid?"

"Yes."

Hopefully it wasn't someone from the hospital's billing department. I meant to start making bigger payments, really.

"Hi, Jennifer! This is Stephanie from ABC Casting."

Oh. My. God. It had to be good news. They didn't call to reject people, did they?

"The interviewer loved you! And your video was fantastic! We'd like to schedule a screen test. Can you come to Los Angeles next week?"

Holy crap. It's really happening!

"That's amazing, thank you! I'd love to go to LA." Something prickled the back of my mind. "If I'm cast, how long will I be gone? I'm not clear on the whole process."

"The series will last ten weeks. The tentative schedule has the contestants arrive in Los Angeles on June 11. The winner will be announced near the end of August, and the finalists should be home a couple of days later."

"What about the eliminated players?"

"Eliminations are weekly, and people can go home after their episodes air. But you don't want to be one of them!"

"No, of course not. Just curious."

How could I afford to take ten weeks off work? While saving first and last month's rent, plus security? Without filing for bankruptcy if the hospital sued? And did I really want to leave Dominic for all that time?

"Do we get paid anything if we don't win?" I calculated how much overtime I'd need to work before leaving. There'd been rumors management planned to limit our hours. That made me both nervous and more determined to find another solution.

"There's no salary," she said. "But you'll get a per diem. People who stay more than a few weeks wind up with at least a couple thousand dollars. Plus, we cover all expenses while you're in the house."

I wondered how long I'd have to stay on the show to make it worth not getting paid while I was gone. This required a pen and paper. "Thanks, Stephanie. Can I check my schedule and call you tomorrow?"

"Sure. Also, the casting process is confidential. We ask that you not discuss it with anyone who doesn't absolutely need to know, like a spouse. If you're cast, we'll tell you when it's time to make the big announcement."

That made sense. I hadn't mentioned it to anyone yet because I didn't want to jinx myself. "Okay."

"Perfect!" she chirped. "I'll talk to you tomorrow!"

I thanked her again, and we hung up.

They wanted me for ten weeks. I didn't have ten weeks of vacation time saved. Maybe I'd have three weeks by June, since I didn't take a vacation last year. That meant, if I went to the end but didn't win, I'd lose seven weeks of pay. Which may or may not include overtime.

Then again, if I moved in with Dominic, I wouldn't need as much for the summer. I needed to raise the subject, but he wouldn't be back from Tulsa until Monday night. My budget would change significantly if we shared expenses.

"One thing at a time, Jen," I said.

No point worrying about time off and summer living arrangements before the show picked me. Moving in with Dominic presented the perfect solution, especially after almost a year together. It was time.

* * *

The next Tuesday, for the first time in my life, a man met me at the airport, holding a sign with my name on it. Maybe life wasn't exactly the way I'd envisioned it, but someone thought I might be interesting enough to be on TV, and they sent a car to welcome me to Southern California. I threw my shoulders back and held my head high as I strode to the car.

My parents had taken me to Disneyland as a kid, but I hadn't seen much of the area besides the hotel and the park. I pressed my face against the car window, taking in the palm trees, bright sun, and skyscrapers in the distance.

After about an hour, the car stopped at a hotel much nicer than expected after the building I'd interviewed in. It wasn't like the place Dom took me, but the rooms smelled like cleaning products, the toilet paper folded into a point, and the TV dwarfed the one I had at home. Good enough for me.

A fast-talking woman with blond highlights led me to my room. "We've rented out the entire floor. You're not allowed to talk to anyone other than staff. You can't leave your room without an escort. We have the only key. If you leave, you're locked out. We've stationed staff at the ends of the halls. If you need anything, call them. They'll help you. Ice, aspirin, whatever—we'll take care of you. They'll also take you anywhere you need to go. Got it?"

I nodded, too surprised to say anything. No one had mentioned being imprisoned in a hotel room, but all the cloak and dagger stuff just made me more curious to find out about this show.

"You can keep your phone and laptop. The Wi-Fi is free. The TV has HBO and Showtime. We'll be back to get you for dinner in a couple of hours. Here's a waiver we need you to bring with you tomorrow." She opened the door with a flourish but stayed in the hall. "Enjoy your new home."

With nothing else to do, I examined my surroundings. The king-sized bed looked inviting. The flowered navy bedspread matched the closed curtains. I pulled one panel aside to peek out the window. Below, people milled around the parking lot like ants. Not the most exciting view. Oh, well. The mountains in the background were pretty. Was that snow? In Southern California?

Yes, Jen. It snows in the mountains, even in Southern California. Especially in January. Silly.

After unpacking my tattered duffle bag, I looked at the clock. Four and a half hours to kill before dinner—and, presumably, the entire evening. I flopped down on the bed, turned on the TV, and opened my laptop.

The next morning, after a continental breakfast appeared outside my door, a van transported me and about a dozen other people to the interview site. The driver admonished us not to talk, so I pulled a book from my bag. I'd come prepared for down time. Considering my excitement, it was hard to focus on the words. After I read page forty-seven for the third time, I gave up and shoved it back in my purse.

Maybe we couldn't talk, but they couldn't stop us from looking around. I smiled at the people sitting behind me. Neither smiled back.

It's like the Metro, Jen. Avoid eye contact, and you'll be fine.

The guy to my left reminded me of a stork, all arms and legs awkwardly folded into his seat. He wore a faded, patched black jacket, and his stretched skin was so thin it was practically translucent. Purple stains on his fingers suggested he was an artist.

Across the aisle, a redhead whose beehive hairdo made her look about forty stared straight ahead. She looked past everyone else, lips pressed together in a thin line. Apparently, Ms. Red Lips was too good to be on the bus with the rest of us. Beside her, a girl about my age chewed her lower lip and stared out the window. I didn't want to turn around again and get more strange looks, so I examined the backs of the heads in front of me. As we pulled up to what looked like a giant warehouse, I admired the boldness of a woman's long blue and green hair. How would I look if I did that?

Unemployed, probably. My job expected us to look "business

professional" at all times. Multi-colored hair didn't fit the dress code.

Dozens of people with headsets and clipboards plus what looked like hundreds of contestants milled in all directions. It felt like Black Friday before the stores opened, but sunnier.

First, one of the headset women took my waiver, checked my name off a list, and handed me a clipboard full of papers to fill out. I gave my medical history, agreed to let their doctors examine me, answered a psychiatric assessment, took a personality test, and answered what felt like a thousand questions.

I read the questionnaires with fascination. Were they trying to cast shrub-loving, fire-starting fighters? Or were they trying to weed those people out? If I wasn't a shrub person, was I out? My mom banned me from her garden years ago because I forgot to water things for days, then overwatered to make up for the neglect. And drowned all her plants. Does lack of skill mean I'm not a shrub person? Maybe I should go home and learn to appreciate my nice, ordinary life where no one would set me on fire or judge me by the greenness of my thumb.

The paperwork took almost two hours. Around me, people scribbled furiously. After I handed in the questionnaire, my eyes scanned the room. One of the other applicants watched me. He was cute, with short, wavy blond hair and full lips. When our eyes met, he smiled and waved, beckoning toward the empty seat on his left.

We weren't really supposed to interact with the other applicants, but it would be a lonely summer if we all shunned each other. Plus, I had to sit somewhere. I waved back and approached shyly.

"This seat taken?" I asked.

He shook his head. When I sat, he addressed me out of the side of his mouth. "Thank God you saw me. That dudebro over there's been eying this seat, and I wasn't sure how much longer I could hold him off."

The dudebro in question stood about fifteen feet away, glaring at me. He towered over the sea of applicants, moving around the room with a permanently affixed sneer. He wore loud plaid shorts with a clashing Hawaiian shirt and, for some reason, a snorkeling mask around his neck.

Nearby, another contestant cleared her throat. I couldn't see who it was, but remembered we weren't supposed to talk to each other.

"Is there a swim test?" I whispered to the guy beside me. Up close, he was even cuter than I first thought, with piercing green eyes and a crooked nose, like it had been broken and never healed right. Some people might think it was too big for his face, but it gave him character.

He chuckled and leaned closer. "Maybe he took the whole 'Los Angeles is full of sharks' thing literally? Whatever. He was loudly harassing the girls on the bus on the way here, and he thought I'd want to join him. Thanks for saving me."

"My pleasure."

With one hand, he reached toward me. "This is where I'd normally introduce myself, but that's forbidden. So let's say, I'm J from F."

"J from F, huh?" I shook his fingertips quickly while rolling that one over in my head. "Jeremy? John? Jimmy?"

He shook his head, but offered no more information. Nearby, a production assistant narrowed her eyes at us. No one in the room was talking other than staff on their headsets.

"Well, J from F," I said. "I'm J from S."

"S?" He asked, and I nodded. "That's intriguing. There aren't any states starting with S. I guess that means you're from Saskatchewan? Saturn?"

I bit my lip to keep from giggling. For the first time since I'd landed in LA, I didn't feel tense or nervous. This was fun! "Sure. Probably one of those. Or not. And Florida is too boring, so I'll assume you're from. . . Finland? France?"

"You've got me," he said, adopting a terrible accent. "Je m'appelle Jacques. I am from France."

I giggled. "That's the worst accent I've ever heard!"

The production assistant who'd been hovering turned to walk toward us, so I hurriedly diverted my attention to the packet before me. The last thing I needed was to get disqualified for having a conversation during the audition process.

The first page just wanted contact information. Names of three friends or family who might be willing to host the show if we made it to the final round. My mom was a no-brainer. I wished I could put my brother down, but I suspected the show wouldn't be willing to foot the bill for a visit to Montreal, where he'd stayed after falling in love with a fellow college student. Instead, I wrote Brandon.

Relationship? the form asked.

BFF.

Name?

Dominic Rossellini. Even though he traveled a lot, he'd probably be excited for me if I made it far enough for television crews to come to his house. He'd love to be on camera. Or maybe they'd do a special where loved ones came to visit the remaining contestants—didn't that happen sometimes?

Relationship?

Boyfriend. If only I could put down fiancé, but we weren't there yet. Instead, I added a caret and wrote *Serious* above *Boyfriend.*

Before moving on to the next page, I peeked to find that our PA had vanished into the crowd. She must be stopping other contestants from getting to know each other. I leaned toward J, but he'd turned away from me and hunched over his paper, blocking the page with one arm. Ah, well. Better to focus on the paperwork, so I could eat when I finished. My stomach reminded me I'd been too nervous to do more than pick at my breakfast.

My second packet contained an IQ test. I've always done well on standardized tests and this one wasn't all that tricky. A few minutes later, I whispered a good-bye to J before handing the test in with a confident smile.

"Good luck," he said, offering me a flash of dimples.

I didn't glance over my shoulder to see whether he watched when I left. But, just in case, remembering what Brandon said about my "assets," I swung my hips on my way out of the room. Being off the market doesn't mean I can't appreciate a little harmless attention from other guys.

Chapter 4

***THE FISHBOWL* CONFIDENTIALITY AGREEMENT**

BY APPEARING AT THE AUDITION, THE UNDERSIGNED, ______________________, (HERE-INAFTER, "THE APPLICANT") AGREES TO THE FOLLOWING TERMS AND CONDITIONS:

1.THE APPLICANT AGREES NOT TO DISCUSS THE APPLICATION PROCESS FOR THE FISHBOWL (HEREINAFTER, "THE SHOW"), THE AUDITION, OR RELATED MATTERS WITH ANYONE WHO DOES NOT HAVE A STRICTLY NECESSARY NEED TO KNOW THE APPLICANT'S WHEREABOUTS.

2.THE APPLICANT AGREES NOT TO POST ABOUT THE APPLICATION AND AUDITION PROCESS ON THE INTERNET, INCLUDING, BUT NOT LIMITED TO: FACEBOOK, TWITTER, INSTAGRAM, MYSPACE, TUMBLR, OR OTHER BLOGS. . .

. . .THE APPLICANT UNDERSTANDS THAT THE SELECTION PROCESS FOR THE SHOW INCLUDES TRADE SECRETS AND OTHER PROPRIETARY INFORMATION. THE APPLICANT AGREES THAT THE SHOW WILL BE IRREPARABLY HARMED IF THE APPLICANT VIOLATES THIS AGREEMENT AND THAT IT IS DIFFICULT TO CALCULATE IN ADVANCE HOW EXTENSIVE DAMAGES MIGHT BE. THEREFORE, THE APPLICANT AGREES THAT, IN THE EVENT OF A BREACH, THE SHOW IS ENTITLED TO INJUNCTIVE RELIEF, A PENALTY OF TWO HUNDRED AND FIFTY THOUSAND DOLLARS ($250,000), AND REASONABLE ATTORNEY'S FEES.

After leaving the sea of plastic chairs, my next stop was the lunch room. One of the casting assistants directed me to sit alone at a small table, then brought me coffee and a sandwich: turkey and Swiss on white with packets of mayo and mustard. Not terribly exciting, but the scent of fresh tomatoes made my stomach growl. The sandwich tasted better than expected.

With nearly an hour to kill before my appointment with the psychologist, I sipped my coffee and surveyed the room. Unfortunately, J was nowhere to be found. Some of the other applicants glared at those sitting around them, trying to be intimidating, so I would've welcomed a friendly face. One girl, with long, silky black hair, flawless caramel skin, and eyes such a bright turquoise they had to be contacts, glowered at me. The intensity of her expression made me burst out laughing.

She tossed her hair with a sneer and focused on another victim. I mentally shrugged. Trying to psych out other contestants this early in the game made no sense to me.

After lunch, they directed me to a small room where I met the show's psychologist. "Jennifer! It's nice to meet you. I'm Doctor Hernandez."

"Nice to meet you."

"It's nice to meet you, too. Let me tell you, we don't usually get contestants who score this high on the IQ test."

Her candor surprised me. "Really? The ad said the show's casting intelligent people."

Dr. Hernandez consulted papers in a manila folder. "Maybe—I don't get that information. But I do have your psych test. Nothing out of the ordinary there."

I sat up straighter. "Does that mean I got the shrub question right?"

She laughed, but I wasn't kidding.

"There aren't right and wrong answers. The test is designed to give us a profile. You didn't choose any of the answers that set off alarms."

"Well, that's a relief." I started to relax into the chair, but Doctor Hernandez stood. I tensed until she spoke.

"That's it."

"Really?" This sounded like a trick. It was too easy. Like maybe they were testing to see what I did when the psychologist left the room.

"Yeah. My job is to go over IQ test results and the psych test. You passed both with flying colors. Time for hair and makeup for your screen test. And I've got ten minutes to get coffee, so thanks." She left me alone in the room. Not knowing what else to do, I followed her until a middle-aged man in a headset pointed out my next destination.

Hearing that I'd done well on the tests put a bounce in my step. I hadn't realized how much I wanted this until it sounded like it might happen. I could go on television. I might win a quarter of a million dollars. No more sixty-hour workweeks or stocking up on pre-packaged foods for children when they went on sale. Dominic wouldn't need to pay for all our dates. Maybe I'd even be able to go out with my friends once in a while.

This show could give me my life back. Restore me to the pre-medical debt Jen. The fun Jen.

* * *

The stylist finished my hair and picked up her makeup brushes, surveying my face. "You have perfect skin. No, seriously, I'm jealous."

"Thanks, Angela. I try to take good care of it."

"Make sure you do," she said. "Too many girls your age spend so much time in the sun. When they get older, their faces look like handbags. Don't let that happen. Wear sunblock and moisturize."

I smiled at her reference to "girls my age." Angela couldn't have been more than about five years older than me. "Always. . .I burn like crazy without SPF 50, at least."

"Good. Close your mouth."

She applied more makeup than I usually wore, so my fingers tapped against the arm of the chair while I fretted about whether she'd overdo it. I reminded myself the show wanted normal people, not actors. She wouldn't do anything too out there. Still, when Angela finally put down the brushes, butterflies fluttered in my stomach.

"Ta-da!" She spun me around to face the mirror.

My jaw dropped. I inhaled sharply.

I looked absolutely stunning—the best I'd ever looked in my life. I tended toward a pretty healthy self-image, but I'd no idea someone else had the ability to make me look so fantastic. Usually, I blow-dried my stick-straight hair and let it cascade down my back. Angela had somehow given it body. Loose, gleaming waves framed my face.

Shadow and eyeliner made my ordinarily pale blue eyes huge and gave them dimension. When I put mascara on the top and bottom, I gave myself spider lashes, but Angela had made it work. I usually didn't wear blush because I wound up with pink splotches, but she'd given my entire face a healthy glow.

"Wow." I blushed. "Sorry. I don't want to seem conceited, but you did an amazing job!"

"Hey, if you think you look good, I'm happy. It means I've earned my paycheck. Luckily, you gave me an easy palette to work with. I just brought out your natural beauty." She put out a hand to help me stand. "Go knock 'em dead."

Another ten minutes passed before the producers summoned me into the room for my screen test. Bright lights illuminated the front wall, shining in my face. I squinted at what looked like two men and a woman in chairs along the back wall. The man in the middle sat in a taller chair and held a larger clipboard than the others.

Cameramen stood on both sides of the room. One of the producers pointed to a spot in front of the lights. I walked to the center of the room and introduced myself, trying not to squint. The man in the middle directed me to repeat their questions in my answers. Then, they fired questions at me. I couldn't tell who asked what. Everything blurred together.

"What role do you play among your friends?"

My head tilted to one side. "I'm the Secret Keeper. I'm always the first to know when someone is getting married, applying for new jobs, pregnant, or breaking up."

"Oh, yeah? Then who do you tell your secrets to?"

The corners of my mouth curved upward in a way I hoped looked mysterious. "I don't tell my secrets to anyone."

"Try to include our questions in your answers. Are you a people person?"

This answer had been practiced. "I'm very friendly and outgoing. I love surrounding myself with people and making new friends. So, yes, I'm a people person."

"Would you say people either love you or hate you?"

"No, I wouldn't say other people either love me or hate me. I think those kinds of extreme statements are a bit much. There's a huge range of emotion between love and hate. Plenty of people like me well enough or don't have much of an opinion. Most people aren't the kind of person you either love or hate."

"What would you do with the money if you won?"

"A little over a year ago, I broke my leg—and I didn't have insurance. So, if I won I'd finish paying the hospital first. Then I want to take my mom on a weekend away somewhere; she works hard."

"Just your mom?"

"Yeah, my parents split when I was pretty young. I've always been closer with Mom. Anyway, then I'd put a down payment on a condo, and use the rest to get by until I find a new job. Maybe it's not that exciting, but the money would change my life."

"If you are cast on the show, who do you think your fan base would be?"

Another answer I'd practiced after watching audition videos for other shows. "Primarily, gay men will root for me. They're the exception to the love me or hate me rule. Most of my male friends are gay, and I bonded with each of them instantly. Also, I hope smart, successful women will cheer me on if they see a positive image of a young career woman living in a big city."

"What is your strategy for staying on the show if you make it?"

A small smile crossed my face. "My strategy? I can't tell you. It's a secret."

One of the producers chuckled. A couple others smiled. He stood and shook my hand. "Thanks for coming in, Jennifer. That's all we need. We'll call you."

When I left the test, I couldn't help it. I took five seconds to do a mini dance of joy in the hallway.

Before heading back to the hotel, I stopped in the ladies' room. As the tepid water poured over my hands, I marveled once again at Angela's handiwork. When the water stopped, sniffles escaped from the stall behind me.

"Hey," I knocked softly on the stall door. "Is everything all right in there?" Only a sob answered. "Do you need anything?"

Someone drew a deep breath, followed by a long sigh. "Umm, do you have any toilet paper?"

Sensing what the unseen woman really needed, I went to the counter and grabbed several facial tissues out of a box. Then I passed them under the door. "Here. Have some tissue. It's better."

"Thanks," said someone softly.

A moment later, the stall door opened. A girl about my age with long curly blond hair came out, staring at the floor.

"Really, are you all right?" I asked. "Is there anything I can do to help?"

When she looked at me, green eyes brimmed with unshed tears. A streak of mascara ran down the side of her face, and brown eye shadow smudged across her temples. "I'm sorry. This is so stupid. I don't want to be here. My brother talked me into it. But I don't want to be a reality TV star. I'm much happier at home reading a book. He knows that."

"I'm sorry." She looked so miserable that I wanted to offer her hot cocoa and a blankie. "You know, you should be doing this for you, not your brother. Tell the producers you don't want to go any further. You don't have to tell him. Let him think they cut you."

"He thought we'd have a better chance if we applied together. We're twins, which makes an impression, you know?"

"Well, sure," I agreed. "Twins are great. But only if both of you are voluntarily going on the show. You don't want the impression you make to be 'Look at how miserable this guy makes his twin sister!'"

She sniffled and blew her nose. "You may be right. I don't belong on TV, anyway. He's a lot more driven than I am. He'd do anything to win, and I'd be like, 'No, you take first place in the race. You earned it.'"

I smiled at her. "See? Just tell him the truth."

"Thanks," she said. "By the way, my name's Sarah."

"I'm Jennifer. Jen." Impulsively, I hugged her.

"My name's Skye." An irritated voice intruded into our conversation. An extremely tall, thin woman with green and purple spiked hair stood behind us. "You, Sarah, should go home and stop wasting people's time. You, Jen, are too nice for reality TV and will get eaten alive. Both of you are blocking the stalls."

"Sorry." I moved out of the way. Skye brushed past me, closer than necessary.

Sarah smiled at me before leaving. "I'll look for you after I talk to the producers. Good luck."

She wasn't on the van back to the hotel or in the shuttle that delivered a group of us to the airport. Wherever she was, I hoped she found the courage to follow her heart.

* * *

As I waited for my flight, I kept an eye on passengers walking to other gates, looking futilely for my new friends. LAX was crowded, though, even in the middle of a weekday. I had no way of knowing where Sarah was headed or even if she was flying out of the same airport. Los Angeles is a big place. I didn't see J, either, although I naturally wasn't really looking for him.

The plane didn't take off for another hour, so I leaned back in my chair. Might as well nap until boarding. My eyes drifted shut, and my mind wandered.

The plane is about half-full. It's a small, regional jet with only two seats on each side. As I make my way down the aisle, I see that my row is empty. I stow my carry-on and settle into my seat, watching each passenger walk by. When the stream of people ends, I'm still alone. I put the armrest up, planning to curl up across both seats after takeoff.

Wait. As the flight attendant reaches to close the door, she gets a call.

Another passenger showed up at the last minute! Footsteps pound down the bridge to the plane. Then, like magic, he appears in the doorway. It's J, also flying home to Seattle! He almost missed his flight.

The window seat next to me is now the only empty spot on the plane. I step out to let him pass, but our legs brush, sending a bolt of electricity up my thigh. As he settles next to me, the guy turns. His green eyes penetrate me. "Hi. My name's . . ."

I smiled dreamily to myself before the gate attendant's voice on the intercom shook me awake. "Last call for Flight 689 to Seattle. Everyone headed to Seattle should now be on board."

Grabbing my stuff, I raced down the runway, shoving the dream out my head. It was crazy the places a person's mind would go, especially after a couple of days in almost total isolation. One conversation with a stranger sent me halfway to Mile High Club dreams.

In actuality, an elderly man occupied the seat beside mine. He showed me pictures of his infant granddaughter until takeoff, then promptly fell asleep. Not quite as exciting as my fantasy.

Too keyed up to nap, I mentally reviewed the audition. It went well. I had a good shot at making the show. The time had come to share my plans with Dominic. I hated keeping secrets from him, and he'd be happy for me. Plus, if the show might take me away from Seattle for several weeks, he needed to know ASAP.

Instead of heading home, I took the Metro to my boyfriend's house. He'd asked me to call instead of dropping by so he could clean up and get his roommate out of the picture, but he'd understand when he heard my news.

Whirling thoughts consumed me while I walked up the steps to Dominic's house. As always, the pink welcome mat tickled me. A few years ago, Dom inherited the house from his aunt, including the decor. He hadn't changed a thing.

My hand poised to knock, but the front door stood ajar. That was odd. Was there a break-in?

I pushed the door open another crack and called Dominic's name softly. He didn't answer. The alarm panel on the opposite wall stayed dark. I opened the door further. "Hello?"

Dominic always kept the front door closed. And locked. And the alarm armed, whether home or not.

Something was wrong.

Chapter 5

WAIVER OF LIABILITY

THIS IS AN AGREEMENT BETWEEN THE PRODUCERS OF THE FISHBOWL (HEREINAFTER, "THE SHOW") AND _______________ (HEREINAFTER, "THE CONTESTANT").

THE CONTESTANT AGREES NOT TO SUE FOR ANY ACT OF THE SHOW, ITS EMPLOYEES OR OTHER CONTESTANTS, WHETHER NEGLIGENT, RECKLESS OR INTENTIONAL, THAT RESULTS IN PHYSICAL OR EMOTIONAL INJURY. . .

THE CONTESTANT HEREBY AGREES TO GRANT THE SHOW EXCLUSIVE RIGHTS TO HIS LIKENESS FOR THE PURPOSE OF PUBLICITY, INCLUDING PRINT ADS. THE CONTESTANT WILL NOT GIVE ANY INTERVIEWS WITHOUT THE EXPRESS WRITTEN CONSENT OF THE SHOW. . .

THE CONTESTANT WAIVES ANY RIGHT TO SUE FOR BREACH OF PRIVACY OR DEFAMATION OF CHARACTER. . .

THE CONTESTANT AGREES THAT THE SHOW MAY, IN ITS SOLE DISCRETION, USE LOOKALIKES. . .

THE CONTESTANT HEREBY WAIVES. . .

THE SHOW DISCLAIMS ALL LIABILITY. . .

THE CONTESTANT WILL NOT SUE. . .

I stood on the porch, my phone in one hand. Should I call the police? What if Dominic lay inside, hurt and unable to call for help? I needed to find him.

A quick peek around the door assured me there weren't any masked men with guns waiting in the hallway. That encouraged me. Squaring my shoulders, I thrust the door out of my way and entered. Immediately, my shoe collided with something hard.

Ow.

Rubbing my foot, I noticed a suitcase in the hall. Was Dominic going out of town again? Did he own a black and white plaid suitcase?

I hesitated. Laughter filtered down from the second-floor landing. Female laughter. I pressed myself against the wall and crept up the stairs.

When I neared the top, a woman's voice drifted through the air. "I'll be right back. Don't move a muscle." A door clicked shut, and a lock turned into place.

What. . .? Was his roommate home? No, his roommate was a guy. Of course, I'd met a guy once who had a really high-pitched voice. . .Or maybe his roommate had a girlfriend? Dominic might not even be home.

Without further delay, I bounded on to the landing. The bathroom door was closed. The bedroom door was not. I burst through that doorway. Dominic lay sprawled across the bed. His black curls tumbled across his forehead as he supported his head with one hand. His entire bronzed six-foot-two-inch frame lay fully visible in all of its glory. Every inch.

Odd, since he hadn't known I'd be dropping by. And since another woman was in this house somewhere. Realization dawned slowly.

For the first time since we'd met, the door in the far corner of the room stood open. I peered back at myself from the full-length mirror hanging on the door. A silk scarf trailed on the floor. A bar held what looked suspiciously like a rack of women's clothing.

"Jen! Hi!" Dominic's eyes darted around the room. He jumped to his feet and came toward me, speaking in a furious whisper. "What are you doing here?"

"I had some news, so I stopped by to surprise you. What's going on? Why are you naked? Who's here?"

"Yeah, so, funny thing, my sister showed up," He murmured, grabbing my elbow. "She lost her job. She's upset. Very fragile. We need some time alone. If you could—"

I didn't believe it. He was trying to turn me and move me toward the stairs. He wanted me to go. That jerk was cheating on me!

"Your sister," I repeated.

Right. How many women called their brothers "darling"? How many men waited naked for their sisters in their bedrooms? How dumb did I look?

"That's right." He kept trying to direct me not-so-subtly toward the stairs, but I dug in my heels and glared at him. When he tugged again, I dropped to the ground, crossing my legs. I wasn't going anywhere until I got some answers.

Waiting didn't take long. As Dominic essentially dragged me down the hall toward the stairs, the bathroom door opened. A tall, impossibly thin woman with red hair cascading to her waist stood before me, clad in a black lace teddy that left nothing to the imagination. Her erect nipples poked through the lace. The hem barely kept this encounter from becoming even more awkward, skimming the tops of her tanned thighs.

And she wore an antique-looking colossal diamond ring and a gold band on the third finger of her left hand.

"Dominic?" The woman's narrowed eyes must have mirrored my own. She cocked one hip and leaned against the doorframe. Her demeanor reminded me of a haughty high schooler in the cafeteria. "Why are you dragging a strange girl down our hall?" Her words may have sounded casual, but each dropped like an ice cube on my spine. Daggers shot from her eyes. "What's going on?"

Finally, realization dawned on me.

She'd said, "Our hall."

She wore wedding rings. Dominic wasn't cheating on me with another woman. He was cheating on *another woman* with *me*.

How could I have been so stupid?

It all clicked into place. Why he often couldn't see me for days—or sometimes weeks—at a time. The locked "attic door" in his room. Why he claimed not to have a Facebook profile (and when I found one, months later, why he pretended to think he'd deleted it. He swore he never used it). Why he spent so little time with my friends. Why I'd never met his "roommate" or his family. Why he didn't want to travel with me. All of those things made perfect sense if he didn't want his wife to find out he was seeing someone else.

That cheating, lying *asshole*!

I shook Dominic's grip off my arm and rose to my full five feet four inches.

"Hi!" I said brightly. "I'm Jen. Apparently, I've been sleeping with your husband for almost a year and a half. I'm sorry. I didn't know. But I absolutely promise, it won't happen again. He's all yours."

Shaking with rage, unshed tears blinding me, I turned, my head held high. Behind me, an outraged shriek sounded. Something thumped against the wall as I walked down the stairs and out of Dominic's life forever.

* * *

Six weeks passed in a blur. Having never had a serious boyfriend before Dominic, I didn't know what to do after finding out mine had a secret wife. I turned off my phone and gave myself two sick days to cry over *Desperate Housewives* reruns before forcing myself to return to work.

When I turned my phone back on, I had five texts, an e-mail and two voice mails from Dominic. Plus three Facebook messages.

Thought you didn't have an account, Dominic. You fucking liar.

I blocked him and deleted all the messages unopened. Then I threw myself into work. My boss still hadn't given me a new project to work on, so I volunteered to help on every other task I found. At the very least, I kept myself busy.

Each morning, I gazed wistfully at the empty desk in my office: Pete had decided not to return from paternity leave. Even though we'd never been friends, not being alone all day would've made things easier. Having to hold myself together for the benefit of another person in my office made it harder for me to slump into my chair and sulk all day.

As winter turned to spring, my workload tapered off. Overtime hours became scarce, and I had more free time each day. Rather than moon over my cheating ex, I devoted myself to researching reality shows. Turned out, there were a lot of seasons of *Big Brother* and *The Bachelor*. Cocooned in my office, door closed, many of them streamed, one after another, all day long.

Early one morning in April, a message from HR appeared in my inbox.

To our Marketing Employees:

This notice is to inform you that our Efficiency Team has spent several months evaluating the company's ongoing needs. Outsourcing the majority of our marketing needs would help McCain and Webster best achieve its objectives. As a result, we no longer require a large Marketing Department. If you have received this e-mail, your services for this company are unfortunately no longer required, as your position has been eliminated effective May 31.

An HR Representative will contact you shortly to discuss other employment opportunities within the company and any compensation package that you may be entitled to. Our employee services line remains open to any employee who needs to talk to someone during this difficult time.

We ask that you not discuss the contents of this e-mail with others before an official announcement is made. Thank you for your discretion.

The words swam before my eyes. My brain refused to process them. As understanding dawned, I slumped back into my chair, crossing my arms over my chest.

They're firing me? Seriously, does the universe think I don't have enough to deal with?

They didn't even have the courtesy to tell me in person. Or via an e-mail sent to me personally? All I get is this crappy mass layoff e-mail? It wasn't even signed!

A message popped up. "The sender of this e-mail has requested a read receipt."

Are you kidding me?

I clicked "NO" so hard the mouse jumped. If they wanted to know if I read their stupid e-mail, someone could come talk to me like a real human being.

Five minutes later, I was still staring out the window when another message came through. The subject said simply, "Severance Package."

Great. Rub it in, why don't you? "Dear Jen, you haven't been here long enough. Up yours, from HR."

My hand shook as I opened the message.

Dear Jennifer,

As you know, McCain and Webster prides itself on providing excellent employee benefits. Our severance package is no exception. Each employee affected by our downsizing will continue to receive health insurance for three months following termination. Furthermore, you will receive one week's pay for each quarter that you have been employed with us, based on your hire date and a termination date of May 31.

All accrued vacation time and sick leave will be paid on your last day. Again, we ask that you not share this information with anyone. Thank you for your discretion.

That wasn't nearly as bad as I'd expected. One week per quarter?

I scrolled through my calendar. I'd started right after college graduation. May 30. Two years ago. Which meant I'd get eight weeks of pay, plus somewhere between two and three weeks vacation/sick pay.

When I leaned back in my chair this time, my lips curved upward in a tiny smile. I'd just found a way to finance my summer.

* * *

On May 5, my phone vibrated while I walked toward my office. I answered without looking, expecting it to be my mother. She liked to call at random times to read the local newspaper or update me on people I hadn't thought about since childhood. I'd given up trying to explain phone etiquette and bosses months ago. Now that they'd fired me, I didn't care.

It wasn't her.

"Hi, Jennifer, this is Stephanie from LA Casting. Congratulations! I'm calling to officially offer you a spot on *The Fishbowl*!"

The phone nearly fell out of my hand. The rest of her sentence went in one ear and out the other. They'd picked me. They wanted me to be on their reality show. I couldn't believe it.

A small cheer escaped me before I remembered a group of coworkers stood about a foot away. They looked at me curiously. I ignored them, hurrying into my office to shut the door.

"Thank you so much for calling me, Stephanie! I'm so excited!"

She laughed. "We're excited, too! You're exactly what we want. I just need to e-mail you some contracts. Send them back as soon as you can so I can make arrangements."

"Contracts?"

"Oh, sure," Stephanie said. "It's all pretty standard stuff. There's a confidentiality clause, a release, some waivers, stuff like that. We have to do it with all the reality shows."

"Right. Okay."

The documents arrived minutes after the call ended. The legalese made little sense to me, but there had to be perks to a best friend in law school. I pulled out my phone and texted Brandon.

IF I SEND YOU THIS CONTRACT I GOT, WILL YOU LOOK AT IT?

The response came a few minutes later. *YOU KNOW I'M NOT A LAWYER YET, RIGHT?*

YOU'RE THE CLOSEST THING I'VE GOT. AND YOU ARE SOOOOO GOOD-LOOKIN'.

:) YOU KNOW I LOVE FLATTERY. SEND IT TO ME. YOU CAN BUY ME LUNCH, IF YOU DON'T MIND COMING TO CAMPUS.

The trip to his campus took more time than I usually got for lunch. Before answering, I pulled up my To-Do list for the afternoon.

1. Make To-Do List.
2.

Things had been slow before, but this was ridiculous. My calendar showed an "HR Check-In" at three. I'd be back long before that, not that I cared.

K. SEE YOU SOON.

* * *

"Okay." Brandon pulled a stack of papers out of his bag. We'd just chosen a table at an off-campus deli. "First, this contract is awesome. I want to write reality TV contracts when I graduate."

"Awesome, like it's super favorable to me?"

"Nope. Not in the slightest. Awesome in that you have no right to complain about anything. I'm not sure if you'd be able to sue if the show took out a hit man on you to boost ratings. It's an entertaining read. If you're kind of a dork, at least."

"Thanks. That's not helpful, though."

Brandon put the papers on the table and flipped through them. "Right. So, here's what I've learned during my one semester of law school. First, you can't sue the show for any reason. If you get so depressed that you kill yourself, you waive your family's right to sue on your behalf. You can't sue if you get hurt. If you're slicing a watermelon and you cut your finger off or whatever. No lawsuit, for any reason. The network is not liable for anything. Neither are the show, the producers, the casting company, or anyone associated with or working for any of them. And these are enforceable waivers, because you're engaging in a voluntary recreational activity and not, say, getting emergency medical services."

Better than anyone, I knew I couldn't afford to be injured, especially after I become unemployed. I made a mental note to see how the recent passage of the Affordable Care Act would affect my COBRA. Stupid Act that didn't exist when I broke my leg better help me now.

"See? Taking Contracts wasn't a boring waste of time."

"I learned that in Torts, actually." He paused while a pimply-faced teenager with pants falling off his hips brought our sandwiches. "If they want, they can hire a look-alike to play you. That look-alike can do whatever the producers want. For example, they can pay someone to pretend to have sex with people who look like the other contestants, letting the whole world think you're a sex addict. If you sign, you're okay with that."

Would they hire actors to make me look bad? Did I want to risk it? What were the odds?

"Interesting. Let's hope they won't. What else?"

"Those are the most fascinating provisions. You can't sue if you get an STI from another contestant. Since I'm failing miserably at getting you to leave Dominic's memory in a trail of used men, that seems unlikely. Most of the rest has to do with rights to use your picture, to market the show, to edit you however they want, etc. You have to get permission before giving interviews about the show. It's about ninety-nine percent stuff you'd expect to find in any contract like this."

I sipped my water. "Is there anything I need to worry about?"

"I don't know. The main one is probably people who get injured. Be careful. Some people might worry about the STI provision, but that's not your style."

I shuddered. "The last thing I want right now is to repeat my mistakes with Dominic on national television with a total stranger. No, thank you."

Brandon waved one hand. "Girl, you could do so much better than Dominic. You're better off without him—especially now. You're going to be a superstar."

"That's right! I'm going into this unattached and free! If I have to enter a kissing contest to win, I can. If I have to flirt to get ahead, I don't have to feel guilty. It's fine. Really."

I hoped I sounded sincere. After all, I'd been telling myself the same thing since Dominic's wife appeared in their bathroom doorway.

Brandon paused with his sandwich halfway to his mouth. "Wait. No one told me about a kissing contest. That would be awesome."

I shrugged. "We could be doing anything. No one knows."

"Right. So, say, hypothetically, if someone wanted to make a kissing contest happen, do you have a phone number for the producers?"

I stuck my tongue out at him. "Yes, but you're not getting it. Oh, but I need you to sign a waiver, too. Just a note saying you don't mind if they come to your house and film you watching the show."

"Oh my God, seriously? Of course I don't mind! That's so cool!" Brandon tossed his head back, ran his fingers through his hair, and framed his face with his hands. "I'm ready for my close-up, Mr. DeMille."

"Goofball." I tossed a French fry at him. He dove, catching it in his mouth. "I'll forward you the waiver when I get it. If there is a true and absolute emergency not related to my sex life while I'm on the show, my mom can reach the producers." My stomach rolled, remembering that I'd put down Dominic's name for the same purpose. Thankfully, I'd found out the truth before I'd asked him to sign the waiver. It would've been ten times more humiliating to spend the entire show talking about my amazing boyfriend and finding out the truth when I got home.

As soon as I got back to my office, I picked up a pen and signed every page of the contract. Then, I texted Stephanie.

HI, IT'S JEN. I'M IN! I'M SCANNING THE SIGNED CONTRACTS RIGHT NOW. WILL E-MAIL.

* * *

Preparing to put life on hold for up to two months was unlike anything I'd experienced. It wasn't something I'd ever thought about, but I couldn't walk away from everything and let the bills pile up. To minimize expenses, I asked my landlord to let me rent my apartment for an extra week and rented a storage unit to hold my stuff while I was gone. I'd stay with Brandon when I got back until I found a new place.

Two days before my flight to LA, the producers posted cast pictures online.

They'd listed the contestants in alphabetical order, so I found mine quickly. Wow! Thick, dark lashes framed my eyes, the bluest I'd ever seen them. Every hair lay smoothly in place, my clear skin glowed, and my white teeth gleamed. I wondered how much touching up they'd done.

After I processed the weirdness of looking at myself on the website of a national television network, I checked out the other contestants. There would be twelve people on the show, including me. One of them was the dark-haired girl who had scowled at everyone in the lunch room: Ariana. The rude woman from the bathroom, Skye, also made the show. Hopefully, the other contestants wouldn't be like them.

Then I spotted J, my friend from the audition room. When my eyes took in those gorgeous green eyes and full lips, my stomach flip-flopped. The site said his name was Justin. I'd always liked that name. "Justin." It sounded nice.

"Justin and Jennifer." I liked the sound of that, too.

None of the others looked familiar, although one resembled Rodrigo Santoro so much I did a double take. I wouldn't mind looking at him for twelve weeks. According to the website, his name was Eduardo. There was no sign of Justin's snorkel-wearing foe.

Next, I pulled up the promo videos. I'd seen myself on film before, of course, but there was something surreal about watching professional footage edited into a commercial. It was so cool. The videos were short; I watched all of them twice.

As I was halfway through my video for the third time, a message from Brandon popped up. He must've been scouring the website—I'd sent him the link the moment the cast page went live.

Brandon: Is this chick one of your cast mates? Ariana Sassani? Thought she looked familiar, so I did some googling. Looks like she wants to be an actress. A handful of bit roles in bad movies over the past couple of years. Dated lots of D-list actors.

A moment later, IMDB showed me a headshot of the woman from the cafeteria. Who I'd be living with the next few weeks. I'd thought the show was for "real people," but she was definitely an actress—even if her most prominent roles included "Waitress #3," "Cheerleader," and "Sexy Zombie Victim."

Did they hire an actress to ensure drama? Or was she doing the show to springboard her acting career?

Jen: Yes, that's her. Weird.

Brandon: Netflix streams three of her movies. I'm coming over. With ice cream.

* * *

The next day, I went shopping. I'd been surprised to learn that reality show contestants wore their own clothes. In the back of my mind, I'd half-expected they'd have a wardrobe department on the set. Which didn't make sense, once I thought about it. The "set" was a big house.

They had meticulous requirements for what not to wear: no visible brand names, no logos, no small patterns, etc. My closet contained some stuff that worked, but not enough for the whole summer. I also had to bring my own makeup, and my half-empty bag mocked me. The essentials were there, but I usually only wore mascara and lip gloss. My bargain drug store finds wouldn't let me compete with the model-beautiful women posted on the show's website.

Too bad they wouldn't send Angela to the house every day to help. Why didn't I have a personal makeup artist?

Oh, well. I could play around with makeup at the mall. Maybe I'd find some fabulous clothes at one of the consignment shops.

Five hours, eleven shopping bags, one makeover, and a couple hundred dollars later, I transferred my purchases from shopping bags to my suitcase.

I'd gotten some new jeans (no visible logos!), shorts, two swimsuits, a cover-up, several T-shirts and tank tops, a glittery green evening gown, and workout clothes. I'd spent more than I could afford, but almost a grand less than if I'd paid retail. Plus, the clothes were an investment in my future. I'd also begged a lot of makeup samples off the salesgirl at Sephora, telling her I was going on TV. That saved me close to a hundred bucks.

Looking good boosted my confidence. Confidence would make people want to vote for me. I needed votes if I wanted to win. And I was going to win.

Chapter 6

Jennifer in the School Room, Week 1:

This is going to be so much fun! I'm very excited and grateful to be here. A couple of months ago, I worked at a dead-end job, and now I'm living in an amazing house with a bunch of total strangers, having the experience of a lifetime.

The house is fantastic. I don't mind living with glass walls. I lived in a coed dorm in college, and people wandered around half-naked. No big deal. I'm not worried about privacy. The bigger issue is, we can't see the walls—I've already walked into them twice.

So far, most of the other contestants seem pretty cool. Joshua? You mean "J-dawg"? Yeah, he's different, I guess. It's almost like he decided to be a reality TV villain, but he watched Wile E. Coyote cartoons to prepare his act. I keep waiting for him to draw a fake tunnel on one of the glass walls and try to get someone to walk through it.

On the day we entered the house, a member of the production staff came to the hotel room I'd checked into the night before, blindfolded me, and led me outside to a waiting van. They apparently still didn't want us to see or talk to each other before the show started. Or maybe they didn't want us to be able to tell people where to find the house. Or both.

The drive felt long. Someone sang, a vibrant bass, but the driver hushed him. Too bad. I wondered who he was. The Brazilian hottie? The smiling Indian guy? Finally, I laid my head against the window and dozed until the van stopped.

Someone helped me out of the van and removed my blindfold. It took several blinks for my eyes to adjust to the blinding sunlight. We stood next to the driveway of a giant house. Pebbles covered the ground, with several larger rocks around the outer edges. Stone fish statues dotted the landscape. I recognized a blowfish and a clown fish scattered among the rocks. In the middle of the enormous curved driveway stood a fountain, where a dragon blew flames of water into a small pool. A fence extended from the edges of the house toward the horizon in either direction, separating us from the neighbors.

Directly in front of me, an oddly shaped house contrasted with the manicured landscape. The middle of the house stretched beyond the top and the bottom, which were the same size. The outer walls curved. It took a moment to realize the entire house was shaped like a giant fishbowl. All of a sudden, the name of the show clicked.

After I pulled my gaze away from the house, it only took a moment for my eyes to land on the guy who had crossed my mind more than a few times already: Justin. His gorgeous green eyes twinkled as he surveyed the other contestants. That smile made me glad to be locked into a house with him for the entire summer, and it wasn't even aimed at me. A traitorous part of me wondered briefly if we'd get coed bedrooms if I asked nicely.

Unfortunately, I wasn't the only one who'd noticed him. About ten feet away, I spotted Ariana. With her silky black hair, tawny skin, and full lips, she was even more beautiful than Dominic's wife—and she eyed Justin with a raw hunger that made me fidget. She looked like every man's wet dream. I took small comfort in the discovery that her eyes were now a deep chocolate brown. I *knew* she wore tinted contacts at the audition.

When Justin looked at her, Ariana smiled and winked. His face reddened and he turned away.

What on earth was that about?

Ariana eyes slid around the room like a knife cutting through butter. When she got to me, she smirked, every bit as nasty as she'd been in the lunch room. Instead of cowering under her gaze, I smiled back and waved. If she wanted to hate me, I'd give her a reason.

It wasn't worth letting someone get to me that early in the show. I survived Dominic the Douche and his secret wife; I wouldn't let this bitch get the best of me. Kill 'em with kindness, like Mom always said.

The producers opened the front doors and herded us into the living room. A gray sectional couch sat against one wall, surrounded by beanbags scattered around the carpet. What looked like a human-sized cat tree took up most of the middle of the enormous living area. A green plushy material covered several levels of seating. I couldn't help but run one hand over it as I followed everyone to one side of the room. When my hand sank into the fabric, I knew I'd found my spot.

A short Asian woman with asymmetrical black and red hair entered the room, wearing a headset. She carried a clipboard in one hand and large metal hoops in the other. I eyed those silver rings curiously.

"Hi, everyone! My name is Leanna, and I'm your liaison to the producers. I'm here to help ensure that all my little Fishies, that is, you guys"—she gestured at us—"are comfortable here in our Fishbowl.

"First, put on your wireless mikes. You won't remove these until you win or are eliminated. They're water resistant, so you take them into the shower and pool." She handed each of us a metal ring that looked like a necklace.

Once everyone wore their microphones, she continued. "Now, I'm going to pull you up to introduce yourselves. Give me a couple of sentences with your name, your age, where you're from and what you do. Easy." She motioned to the nearest contestant, a tiny girl with copper-colored curls and a smattering of freckles.

Her eyes danced as she spoke. "Hi, guys! My name's Carrie, but my friends all call me Birdie because I love to tweet!"

By "tweet," I assumed she meant she sang. However, I'd soon learn she only spoke in sentences of one hundred forty characters or less, sometimes with hashtags. I wondered if she'd trained herself to do that, or if it was the natural result of having most of her interactions on Twitter for the past few years.

The redhead continued. "I'm twenty-five years old and a #writer from #Nashville."

A tall, good-looking guy with black hair, brown eyes, and light brown skin strode to the middle of the room. He held himself with confidence, not arrogance, and spoke with frank directness that reminded me of a politician. I half-expected him to start shaking hands and kissing babies—

not that we had anyone under about twenty in the house. His introduction revealed a slight Indian accent. "Hello. My name is Raj. I'm twenty-three, and I work in advertising."

A pretty, muscular blonde with wide brown eyes and big dimples jumped to her feet. She flashed a perfect beauty queen smile at the camera, waving jazz hands. "Hey, there! My name's Rachel, I'm a twenty-two-year-old waitress from Sioux City, Iowa, and I led my school to back-to-back cheerleading championships my junior and senior years. Go Bulldogs!"

Leanna beckoned to the next contestant, an All-American quarterback look-alike with his sun-kissed blond hair, blue eyes, and perfect, golden tan. He reminded me of the guy from *Friday Night Lights*. Until he opened his mouth. "Yo, yo, 'sup! My name's Joshua, but my friends call me J-dawg!"

J-dawg? No way would I manage to call him that with a straight face. I'd wind up looking like some airhead who giggled over every other word just because he'd chosen a ridiculous name.

He threw his hands around in—was that a gang sign? Would we have to spend our lives avoiding dark alleys if Joshua lost? Who was this guy? "You losers might as well go home now, because the J-dawg is here and everyone else needs to clear! I am the man, and I'm gonna make you all scram!"

Did he always talk in rhyme or had he practiced that ridiculous opening? And why did he talk like a gangster? He looked like the epitome of a corn-fed Iowa boy. A Norman Rockwell painting practically hung in the air behind him. He and Rachel could've stepped out of a toothpaste commercial.

"Hello, darlings!" The guy who looked like Rodrigo Santoro stood in front of us. Although the resemblance wasn't as strong in person, his black hair and quick smile were easy on the eyes. Too bad he'd yet to glance at the female contestants. "My name is Ed, and I'm twenty-five years old. I'm a comedian born in Brazil, raised near Boston, and I am awesome. You'll see."

Justin introduced himself as a twenty-five-year-old law student from Miami about to start his third year. Law school might actually become interesting if I sat next to him. I shook the thought out of my head. Not only had Ariana staked her claim, but I didn't join the show for love. I needed loads of cash, not to moon over some guy like a teenager.

In addition to being a beautiful woman who wanted to jump Justin's bones, Ariana oozed charm. "Hello, America! I'm Ariana and I'm twenty-one. Don't let these boobs fool you—I'm a member of Mimza. I'll prove that brains plus beauty is a lethal combination."

Mimza? What was that? A few feet away, Birdie chuckled. When I caught her eye, she sidled toward me.

"She means #Mensa," Birdie whispered.

"The high-IQ society?" My tone matched hers.

"Yeah. Which means she probably isn't a member, because most of them know how to pronounce it. #Dumb."

The woman from the bathroom, Skye, introduced herself while we were talking. I didn't hear what she said. Next up was Mike, a short, muscular black man who introduced himself in song. I recognized his voice from the bus.

"I am Mike, from Pasadena! I'm twenty-six years old. I sing and write songs." He held that last note an impressively long time, ending with a sweeping bow.

Maria from Texas introduced herself as a teacher. She carried herself regally and spoke precisely. Along with her flawless brown skin, tumbling black curls, full lips, and beauty mark, her carriage made me wonder if she used to be a pageant queen. Good thing this contest wasn't about looks.

I missed the next contestant, unfortunately, while practicing my opening under my breath. I'd have to catch up with him later.

Finally, it was my turn. I bounced to the front of the room, hoping to convey confidence. "Hi, everyone! My name is Jen, and I'm an unemployed, homeless marketing assistant from Seattle! I recently broke up with my boyfriend because, for an entire year, he forgot to mention his wife! Oh, and I'm so broke I considered running away with the Peace Corps. Send me your pity votes!"

Okay, I didn't say that. The key to winning this competition probably didn't include showing all of my vulnerability in my first eleven seconds on camera.

"Hi, everyone! I'm Jen! I'm twenty-four. I'm a marketing assistant in Seattle, and I absolutely love puzzles, mazes, trivia, and races. I'm so excited to be here!"

Much better. Leanna flashed me a thumbs-up, and I beamed as I rejoined the group. I'd successfully survived my first "live" television moment.

My remaining doubts vanished. This was going to be fun.

After the introductions, Leanna walked to the front of the room, clipboard in hand. "Okay, my little Fish! I've got some information for you, and then I'll take you on a tour.

"The most important thing you need to know is that these walls are made of *glass*. That makes them hard to see. Do *not* walk into them. It won't feel good. You already signed a waiver promising not to sue if you hurt yourself."

That elicited some nervous titters as we examined each other. Great. I would go home maimed, in addition to being broke, unemployed, single, and homeless. Every girl's dream. Maybe if I got lucky, I could also get an STI.

Oblivious to the direction my thoughts took, Leanna continued. "If you guys need anything—toilet paper, a special brand of mac and cheese, whatever—a member of the production team will get it for you. The only things we won't bring you are gum, electronics, and weapons. Oh, and illegal drugs."

No ecstasy or assault weapons, check. At least the producers had a sense of humor.

"Now, I'm going to go over the rules real quick. Listen closely, because I don't like repeating myself. Your host will be in after our tour, but she's mostly going to smile and look pretty. She won't hang around to chat."

We had a host? I hadn't thought about that. I'd watched *The Bachelor* and *The Bachelorette* just enough to develop an unreasonable infatuation with Chris Harrison.

Just as I started to get excited, I realized that Leanna said our host was a "she." And Chris worked for a different network. Damn.

Guess I'll have to win and be invited to lots of fancy reality show parties so I can meet him. Do they have reality show parties?

"Get to know your production team. We are your friends. Unless you piss us off. Then, we tell the editors to make you look bad."

She laughed, and so did everyone else, but she wasn't kidding. I suspected that, if Leanna got pissed, she could tell the producers to hire a look-alike to run around screaming and banging her head on the walls wearing nothing but a peanut butter bikini. And of course, we'd already agreed to let them.

Note to self: do not piss off Leanna.

She was still talking. "Okay! On Wednesday, the viewers will vote on mini-activities. Participation *is* optional, but you may benefit if you play along. Your main challenges are on Thursdays. The winner—or the captain of the winning team—is immune and guaranteed another week in the Fishbowl. Two people will be nominated for elimination.

"After the Sunday night show, the viewers pick a third contestant to be up for elimination. We'll give you the results Monday morning. You vote Tuesday morning. Meanwhile, the viewers grant immunity to one of the three people up for elimination.

"Voting is through the show's website or text message. There's a mobile site and an app. There are many ways to vote. I have personally tested all of them. The results are announced Tuesday night, and the eliminated player leaves immediately. Questions about the rules?"

No one spoke. Mike and Ariana exchanged a confused look, but we all just stared at Leanna in silence.

"Great! Phew! That's a lot of information. Okay, let's go take a look around."

It really was a Fishbowl. All the outside walls were glass, made possible because the property stood in the middle of a huge ranch, with no other buildings in sight. A wall lining the property and a huge setback ensured privacy. The interior walls were also made of clear glass—there was no hiding. We trooped behind Leanna to the top floor.

"Up here is the girls' bunk."

The massive room held three twin beds on each side and closet doors on either side of the entrance. The closets were also glass, so no hiding there, although the racks of clothes could provide some concealment once we unpacked for anyone who preferred to change away from prying eyes.

The beds perched atop drawers, which ensured we each had some space for our clothes. Even if some people (*cough* Rachel and Ariana *cough*) brought approximately eleven suitcases each. A nightstand stood beside each bed, and a couple of extra dressers leaned against the far wall.

The entire room shone. Sheer blue and green curtains billowed around each bed, giving us the illusion of privacy. The swirling blue and green pattern on the bedding matched. Throw pillows and lamps shaped into starfish and seashells decorated the room. I might have thought the "fish" theme would appear overdone, but it came together nicely. Or maybe, as someone recently homeless, my excitement stemmed from having a guaranteed place to sleep for at least a few days.

"Don't get too excited, boys. The floor *is* made of glass, but it's completely impossible to see through it. No peeking up the girls' skirts." Sure enough, an opaque blue-green glass made up the floor. Several rugs tossed around the room further obscured any efforts to peek up from below.

Leanna said, "If you want to try, though, we might get some funny footage for our viewers, so knock yourselves out. But not literally."

While our guide spoke, Rachel played with her fingernails. The guy whose name I missed stared out the window. Birdie might have been praying or meditating; if she weren't standing, I'd have thought she fell asleep. No one was paying attention but me.

We headed down the glass stairs to the second floor. Justin motioned for me to go ahead of him. I started in front of the crowd, but hung back when J-dawg and Ariana started to elbow each other out of the way. We'd have plenty of time to fight for the cameras attention after the tour.

"On this floor, we have the boys' dorm to the right." A quick glance showed me a room similar to ours, except with darker blues and greens and steel bed frames. Instead of dressers, a pirate's chest stood at the foot of each bed.

"There's also a smaller living area ahead of us. The School Room is beyond the living area. That's what other shows call the Confession Booth. You'll periodically be called to talk directly to the viewers about what's happening. The walls are glass, but they're thick. We've got heavy curtains on the inside. No one can see or hear you when you're in there, unless you go in together."

The idea of becoming close enough with someone to share the confessional brought a smile to my face. Looking around, I wondered again who my confidants would be. Maria gave me a friendly smile. And Ariana's instant dislike gave us something in common.

"This way, please." Leanna led us into the largest bathroom I'd ever seen.

Thankfully, the glass around the toilet was tinted a green so dark no light penetrated it.

Green and blue glass fragments twinkled from the countertops. The shower stalls were mostly clear glass, but the doors contained a large area of darkly tinted glass, from about one foot off the ground to well over my head. No one could watch me shower. The glass floor was made up of tiny multicolored
pebbles, replicating the bottom of a fishbowl.

Leanna continued to gesture around the room. "Now, listen up, because this is important." She paused to ensure everyone watched her. After she cleared her throat a couple of times, we did.

"Here, you have a dual shower stall. There is also a private shower in the back corner. There are no cameras in the showers themselves, but the cameras'll catch you going in and out. You've got a hook inside for your towel or a robe. That camera in the corner covers the entire room, which means it will record anything above or below the tinted glass. Keep that in mind, especially if you're not going in there alone. There will be no anonymous shower sex. I'd prefer you not have non-anonymous shower sex, either, since I'm the one who'll have to come break things up, but that's a whole 'nother ball of wax.

"The toilet is to your left. There is a camera in there, too, but you're just going to have to trust we won't turn it on unless we have to. We need it so people can't hide in there, crying, kissing, doing drugs you snuck in with your bags, or whatever. Don't worry—we don't want to watch people in the bathroom, either, and the footage isn't going to turn up on YouTube."

Leanna led us out of the bathroom into a big hallway and gestured to two closed doors. "These are your changing rooms. We don't have regular cameras in there. However, if you're in there more than sixty seconds, the lights go off, the door slams shut, and you're stuck. At that point, infrared cameras turn on. You don't want that. Change quickly."

I wondered how long it would take before my fellow contestants started sneaking into those booths to make out. The most likely suspects were the Homecoming Queen and King. They'd been making eyes at each other since the producers took off our blindfolds. Now, neither appeared to be listening as Leanna explained that, if anyone got locked into a booth, we'd have to call production to open the doors.

"You could find yourself waiting a while, because we might not be thrilled at the idea of rescuing you, especially in the middle of the night or on a weekend. Got it?"

"Hey." Justin nudged me gently.

I hadn't realized he stood nearby. My arm warmed where he'd touched it. He had such a friendly smile I couldn't help returning it. "Hey."

"Five bucks says those two lock themselves in together within a week." He gestured at Rachel and Joshua, still grinning at each other like teenagers who snuck out of Bible camp for the first time.

"I give it three days."

He chuckled. "You're on!"

We shook, and his dimples flashed. Even if his crooked nose prevented him from being conventionally good-looking, Justin was still attractive. Oh, he could be downright dangerous.

Dangerously fun. I tossed my hair before following the rest of the group down the stairs. Maybe a little flirting would be okay, after all.

Our tour ended on the ground floor. "Down here, you've got the main living area, the kitchen, and a games room. There's a pool table and dartboard in there. That room is converted into the voting booth on Tuesday mornings. There's a small laundry room behind the kitchen. Yes, you do your own laundry and, yes, there are cameras in there, too. Any questions?"

As she scanned the room, I met Leanna's gaze and shrugged. Even if there had been anything else I wanted to know, I wasn't ready to call more attention to myself. I'd figure it all out.

"One last thing: Outside you will find the pool, the hot tub, and the grounds. Most of you will spend a lot of time there, taking advantage of our beautiful Southern California weather. For the most part, you are free to roam the grounds. If you want exercise, it's about a third of a mile to make a complete circle.

"Any blocked areas are off-limits. We'll build most of your challenges in the back, so don't go poking around areas we've closed. You won't like the way we edit you if you try. The entire property is fenced in, so there's no escape."

She probably didn't mean that as ominously as it sounded. Beside me, Maria shuddered.

"Welcome to *The Fishbowl*, everyone!" Leanna smiled and waved, then left. The energy in the room dropped about three levels.

The twelve of us glanced at each other, alone for the first time.

Chapter 7

Scenes from the School Room, Week 1:

Skye: *Dude, no one told me I'd have to share a bedroom with five other women.*

Joshua: *Whaddup, bitchez? Check this out! This is gonna be AWESOME! I'm gonna be the most EPIC VILLAIN in REALITY SHOW HISTORY. It's gonna rock! You'll love this and that's no mystery! America, please vote to save me. Let the villain stay to make this show not gay! Thanks, bros! Thanks, hoes!*

Ariana: *Hi, America! Can I tell you a secret? I don't want the others to know, but my little girl is really sick. That's why I'm here. I need to win the money for her treatment to save her life. Please vote for me so I can help her!*

Maria: *Okay, y'all, what is going on with that Joshua? He's so rude! Why is he walking around calling us all fat 'n'ugly? Does he want us to send him home? And Ariana? I hate to be un-Christian, but dear Lord, she is so stupid, it hurts to try to have a chat, y'all.*

The girls went upstairs to unpack. I hurried to claim some space on the bathroom counter before it exploded with makeup and hair care products.

Standing in front of the sink, Skye examined an invisible pimple in the mirror. She'd changed her hair since our first meeting. Now short brown locks with pink tips stood gelled into rows of various-length spikes. She wore heavy black biker boots laced up to her knees, a short plaid skirt with a chain belt, and torn fishnets. She also wore a stud in her nose and a ring in her right eyebrow. Suddenly, I felt boring.

After I put my clothes away in the trunk next to my bed, Birdie, Skye, and I decided to check out the swimming pool. We'd heard the boys splashing outside while we unpacked, and it sounded like fun. I changed quickly into my most flattering new suit, a navy two-piece padded to give me some nice curves without being porny. The three of us headed downstairs while the other women figured out where to store all their extra clothes. Score one for my limited budget requiring me to pack light.

To get outside, we had to walk through the kitchen. Leanna had gestured toward it during her tour but hadn't taken the time to bring us into the room. When I got my first glimpse, I stopped so fast Skye nearly walked into me.

"Dude, watch where you're going." She brushed against me and continued outside.

"Sorry," I murmured absently.

Skye muttered something else as she walked away. It didn't sound polite.

Stainless steel appliances shone against the far wall, from the enormous refrigerator to the double ovens to the dual sinks. The gleaming countertops were made of glass etched into waves, as were the cabinets and the large table set off to the side. A matching glass island sat in the center of the room, next to a row of bar stools. The stools and chairs, thankfully, didn't appear to be made of glass. The tops of the bar stools were shaped like fish, though.

"Jennifer? Hello? You okay?" Birdie waved one hand in front of my face.

"I'm sorry," I said. "It's just so beautiful. If they'd asked me to design my dream kitchen, this would be it. Well, I mean, it's my dream kitchen for eating in after I order takeout. I love it!"

"I'm not denying it's nice." She tugged my left hand. "But let's check out the #pool!"

She headed through the open door. I followed, squinting into the bright sunlight. Suddenly, a mountain stepped in front of me, blocking the path.

"Oh, I'm sorry!" I stopped short and looked up at the person I had nearly walked into. Then looked up some more. And a little more. The brick wall before me was only averagely good-looking, but those—wow. I'd ever met anyone with muscles that big. His forearm had to be as big as my head.

Note to self: do not make this guy angry.

Walking into him would've felt about as good as colliding with one of those glass walls.

"You're. . ." I'd missed his introduction earlier. "Abraham, right?"

"Abram." He smiled and held out his right hand. "I'm a contractor from Salt Lake City. And you're Jennifer."

"My friends call me Jen." His hand swallowed mine in a firm, warm grip. He met my eyes as he spoke. "Sorry I nearly walked into you."

"Don't be. I didn't see you coming, and I stepped right into your path. It's entirely my fault."

"Oooh, Jen, it's sooooooo nice to meet you!" An unnaturally deep voice came from beyond the patio doors. Joshua stood near the pool, staring at us. "Oh, Abram." He continued, now in a terrible falsetto. "I'm so excited to meet you, too! You're so big and strong. Let's get married and have a thousand babies!" Kissing noises followed.

The rest of us stared at him with a mixture of disgust and horror. Only the cheerleader—Rachel, I think—giggled.

"That's so bizarre," Ed commented. "Here I thought they only cast adults for this show. Guess a tall child managed to sneak in."

"What are you, peanut butter and jealous?" Joshua sneered. "Maybe you wanted Abram to yourself?"

Why was he so nasty?

"Nope. I prefer my men a little less butch. And a lot more gay. But, congratulations! You've managed to establish yourself as a complete jerk-wad, and we've only been in the house about five minutes. It's a new reality show record. Way to make enemies immediately."

"Well, aren't you funny?" Joshua glared at him. "Want me to leave your new beard alone? *Sí, sí, gringo!* Let's go get a taco, eh?"

Instead of looking at Joshua, Ed directed his comment to me. "Do you think he knows that Brazil and Mexico are two different countries?"

Joshua's face turned purple.

I shrugged. "I wouldn't put money on it."

If possible, Joshua looked even angrier. He'd laid the bait, but no one bit. When he opened his mouth, I expected him to breathe fire. Abram's words cut him off.

"No offense," he told me, "but I think my wife would be powerfully angry if I had a thousand babies with you. I'll have to pass."

"That's a relief," I laughed. "I only wanted to have eight hundred ninety-two babies. A full thousand would be a real handful."

At that moment, Rachel stepped through the glass doors on to the patio, carrying a tall, frosted glass in each hand. "Joshua! There you are! I've been looking for you everywhere! You look thirsty. I brought some iced tea to help cool you off." She handed him a glass and pulled him away from the rest of us.

The conflict momentarily defused, I examined the pool where I planned to spend large amounts of time over the next few weeks: a typical large, kidney-bean shaped pool stretched across the backyard, almost seven feet deep in the far end and closer to three or four feet deep near the steps. Sadly, the pool did not include a diving board. Connected to the shallow end via a low wall was a large, round hot tub.

On this warm June day, the pool called to me. Several of the others were already there. I jumped up, touched my toes, then dove into the deep end, away from everyone else. Mentally, I congratulated myself on not splashing when I broke the surface.

With a gasp, I broke the surface. "That's cold!"

"Of course it's cold," Skye said from her position floating in a tube. "You think they'd heat the pool?" She snorted and turned away from me.

"Just a bit of a shock," I said. "It's such a warm day, I hadn't thought about the water temperature."

I wrinkled my nose at her back, wondering if she treated everyone like that or if I'd somehow rubbed her the wrong way.

"Nice dive," Raj said.

"Thanks," I said. "I dove a bit in school." *For seven years of high school and college.*

After swimming to the nearest empty raft, I pulled myself out of the water. As I shifted into a comfortable position, I caught Rachel looking at me. She tilted her head at Joshua, then Ed, and winked. I smiled and winked back.

* * *

"So, do any of y'all have kids?" Maria posed the question at a group gathered in the living room after our first dinner. "I've got a two-year-old boy. He's staying with his daddy for the summer."

From my perch at the top of the giant green couch tower, I surveyed the room, trying to figure out who was missing. Ed and Raj lounged on two of the lower levels of this massive green thing. I still wasn't sure exactly what it was, but it cradled my back and gave me room to stretch out my legs. Some kind of sofa installation art or something.

Skye, Maria, and Abram sprawled on the sectional, and Justin sat nearby on a large green and brown shaggy rug, idly twisting the strands with his fingers. Joshua wasn't there, and neither was Mike. They never returned after being called into the School Room. Rachel was confessing now; the producers were giving us each a turn to introduce ourselves. I waited nervously to be called.

Skye made a rude noise as she shook her head emphatically. "No, thank you! I want to be able to enjoy my life. I have nieces and nephews, and they're great, but my favorite part of hanging out with them is handing them back over to their parents at the end of the night. Kids aren't for me."

No one knew what to say to that. After a moment, Abram raised his hand. "I do. My wife and I have four boys."

Really? He was so young!

Even though it was rude to ask, I leaned forward. "How old are you?"

"Twenty-four. We got married right after high school. Our oldest is five. We also have three-year-old twins and a baby. I'm hoping to win money for their college educations."

Ariana spoke up. "I have a seven-year-old daughter. I trusted the wrong person when I was younger, and he took advantage of me." She paused for dramatic effect, wiped her eyes, and continued. "It wasn't something I wanted to happen. But she's wonderful, and I'm blessed to have her."

Maria patted her hand. "How awful. I'm sorry that happened. You're so brave to share it with everyone."

As everyone murmured in agreement, Ariana waved one hand. "It's fine. I'm over it."

Did anyone else get skid marks from that one-eighty? I wanted to ask, but didn't.

Her abrupt attitude shift made it seem like she'd practiced the speech but hadn't anticipated our reactions to it. I remembered my earlier conversation with Birdie. Maybe Ariana was pandering to the viewers already.

An awkward silence fell. No one else seemed to know what to say. Finally, Justin spoke. "What about you, Jen? Any kids?"

I shook my head. "None yet. I'm too young. Maybe someday, when I meet Mr. Right."

Ariana rolled her eyes. "You don't think you need to meet 'Mr. Right,' do you? You know how babies are made?"

What was the appropriate response when one adult asks another if she understands sex? *"Yeah, I've had the birds and the bees talk. Thanks."* For a long moment, I just gaped at her.

Thankfully, Rachel entered, breaking the tension. "You're up, Jen. They want to see you in the School Room."

"Thanks. I'll be back." I eased myself to the ground and headed for the stairs, narrowly avoiding the edge of a glass wall.

I'd seen enough reality shows to know the rooms reserved for talking to the cameras were pretty small. Still, when I got my first glimpse of the School Room, I checked behind the door to see if something more lay on the other side. It wasn't a room so much as a broom closet, about a foot wide and not much deeper.

Leanna had said we could bring someone else in here with us to talk to the cameras, but I didn't think it would be physically possible to put more than one person in the room at a time unless we gave each other lap dances while interviewing. My traitorous mind went again to Justin, and again I shook the thought away.

Thick red curtains covered the walls. I'd expected to find someone to talk to, but only a folding chair facing one wall awaited me. A large mirror covered the top half of the wall. A camera presumably lurked behind it. Speakers hung in the ceiling next to an overhead camera. I wondered why they skipped the ocean theme in this room only.

Once I settled into the chair, a voice came out of those speakers. "Hi, Jennifer."

I addressed the ceiling. "Hello? Please, call me Jen."

"Don't look up. Talk to the screen."

It felt odd to talk to myself in the mirror, knowing others listened. "Okay, sorry. What should I say?"

From my limited experience watching reality shows, the contestants went into the interview room and said whatever was on their minds. That wasn't true. The producers directed the conversation carefully. They asked pointed questions about the house, the other contestants, and my first day. It wasn't until the end that they asked if I had anything else to add or if I wanted to share anything with the viewers.

"Hi, America! Thanks for watching. I hope you like what you see! I can't wait to let you all see what I have to offer over the next few weeks. We're going to have a great time. This could be the beginning of a beautiful friendship."

* * *

Wham!

The next morning, something hard slammed into my left shoulder. Ow. A glass wall jumped right out in front of me. That was going to leave a bruise. That's what I got for stumbling into the bathroom before I woke up.

Another bang and a yell sounded from the vicinity of the boys' room. At least I wouldn't be the only one covered in bruises. Getting used to living in a house made of glass took time.

After only one day in the Fishbowl, I already missed modern technology. I must've reached for my phone fifty times during the first day, wanting to check my e-mail, look something up, or post to Instagram—only to find my fingertips skimming empty pockets. I couldn't remember the last time I didn't have all the world's knowledge at my fingertips. Poor Birdie suffered from Twitter withdrawal. She'd kept wiggling her fingers when she spoke, as if typing.

Now, I rubbed the dull ache in my shoulder, considering the wall that leapt out at me. The idea of living in a glass house was pretty cool. But it would be better if we could see the walls somehow and avoid them.

My thoughts raced during my quick shower in the solo stall. Why was the water so cold? Steam rose off the other shower as someone moved around inside. The dark legs poking out the bottom belonged to Mike.

Was it not possible to use both showers at once? That's some pretty poor plumbing for a house a dozen people shared.

Hmm. . .this shower is tucked away; it's more private. The other is right in front of the cameras—and it holds two. Would the producers direct all the hot water to that shower?

Why wouldn't they? They'd set us up to bounce off invisible walls all summer.

This train of thought continued while I dressed and blow-dried my hair. I rummaged through my makeup bag when an idea hit me: What if I marked all the walls? Bright red lipstick would be visible from a couple of feet away.

Twenty minutes after I finished my makeup, every wall on the second and third floor bore a red "X" in the upper right-hand corner. With the lipstick in my pocket, I skipped down the stairs to get some coffee and mark the remaining walls. Maybe there was a way to avoid bruises, after all.

Later that night, I won my bet. Birdie, Justin, and Ariana sat around the edge of the pool, feet trailing in the water, sipping drinks and chatting. Some of the other Fish lazed around on rafts. Abram and Mike had gone inside to play pool. Everyone else had scattered.

All of a sudden, a faint shriek filled the air, followed by muffled banging. The sounds originated from the second floor.

Those of us surrounding the pool rose to see what happened. Skye, lying on her raft, grunted and rolled over, unconcerned. After a shared glance with Justin, the two of us walked toward the changing rooms. Birdie went to check the first floor, but Ariana followed us upstairs.

As I walked up the stairs, the muffled shouts became more clear. "Hello? Who turned out the lights? Let us out!"

Joshua's voice. The shrieking sounded suspiciously like Rachel.

Our hunch turned out to be correct. When I set foot on the second floor landing, the shouts clearly stemmed from the area where I'd changed into my swimsuit earlier. I walked down the hall to see light spilling through the open door of one of the changing rooms. Darkness peeked out the bottom of the other closed door. Justin reached to open it, but nothing happened when he turned the knob.

Ariana's face turned white. "They weren't kidding about the doors locking? I'll go find someone."

She darted down the stairs. No need to hurry. America would find this pretty hilarious, and the cameras captured everything. The producers wouldn't be in a rush to drop everything and come unlock the door at what had to be after midnight.

I could practically hear the commercial.

This week on The Fishbowl: *Danger lurks around every corner! Who can you trust? And who will be trapped in the dark?* (With sounds of Rachel screaming, of course.) *Find out Sunday on* The Fishbowl*!*

Maybe I'd been watching too much TV.

"Joshua! Can you hear me?" Justin pressed his head against the door. "It's Justin. Tell Rachel to be quiet for a second."

Mercifully, the high-pitched squeals beyond the door stopped.

"We're trying to get you guys out, but the door's locked. Ariana went for help. Just hang out and stay calm. Can you do that?"

The door muffled Rachel's response, but Joshua's voice came through clear enough. "We'll try. Thanks, man."

The other contestants disbanded—probably to talk about Rachel and Joshua.

As Justin moved away from the changing room door, I held out my hand. "Five dollars, please!"

He grinned. "You won, fair and square. I even tried to water down their drinks to buy a few days."

"You didn't! That's cheating!" Mock-horror filled my voice.

"Okay, I didn't, but I thought about it. Sadly, though, I don't have five bucks on me. They took our wallets when we got here, remember? I'll have to owe you."

"I charge interest. You have to pay me $5.03 when this is all over."

He gasped. "How ever will I manage that? I am but a poor law school student!"

"Tough luck, buddy. You should've thought about that before making the bet."

Justin tilted his head and caught my eyes. "You know, Ariana invited me in there earlier."

My heart plummeted into my stomach. The irrational emotion I tamped down felt oddly like jealousy.

What was wrong with me? Why did I care?

I kept my tone neutral. "Oh, really?"

"I told her no. Said I couldn't handle being the first one to get locked in."

That elicited a chuckle. Suddenly, the noises coming from behind the door became louder. Rachel moaned. I blushed and lowered my voice.

"Do they know they're on national television? This isn't being filmed for public access. Or, you know, Animal Planet."

Justin leaned closer and matched his tone to mine. "They probably think no one will know what they're doing, since the door's closed."

I buried my face in my hands, shaking my head while rubbing my temples.

Justin gestured at the door. "I can't listen to this. It's not right, and some of the noises are freaking me out. Is she part rabbit?"

As he turned to walk away, a twinkle in his eye made me wonder if maybe the threat of being locked in wasn't the only reason he'd rejected Ariana's offer. The warmth spreading through me made me wonder if this summer had room for love, after all.

Chapter 8

More Scenes from the School Room, Week 1

Justin: *Well, the first week has been interesting. I didn't expect anyone to be so offensive from Day 1. My strategy? Right now, I'm just sitting back and watching. Might as well let the drama bombs get themselves sent home first.*

Ed: *So, why are all the walls made of glass? Is the entire series going to be nothing but us bouncing off them, week after week? I'm about ready to start a running tally. Wall: 17, Fish: 0. Maybe we should have a pool to guess who can get through each week with the least bruises.*

Raj: *This whole experience is seriously unreal, man. But it's cool.*

Birdie: *Can I get a keyboard? Am I allowed to tweet my interviews? What? No? Oh, this whole thing is #killingme #Notgonnamakeit.*

Rachel: *I met Joshua during the audition, and he was so different. Sweet and funny. I pulled him aside to talk. Really? People thought we were having sex? On national television? My parents raised me better than that. We were just funning with you.*

Wham!

Ow.

On Thursday morning, I glared at the object that attacked my right shoulder as I exited the girls' bedroom: A glass wall. Where did that come from? What happened to my Xs?

"They cleaned them all off." Skye stood behind me, smirking.

"What?"

"Last night, the PAs came in and cleaned the walls. They removed your Xs."

"Awesome. So they want us walking into walls?"

She shrugged and walked toward the stairs. "They want good TV. Maybe they think accidents are funny. If you can't take it, go home."

Wham!

I suppressed a laugh as a dull thud sounded at the bottom of the stairs, followed by a muffled curse. Skye had been so cool and unconcerned about the walls she'd walked right into one.

She acted so above the rest of us, I didn't understand why she applied for the show in the first place. I appreciated the reminder that she was a mere mortal like the rest of us.

Later that morning, the producers gathered everyone into the living room. We clustered on the couches and waited to see why they'd called us. After a moment, a door opened in the corner of the room. When they revealed who stood on the other side, I gasped and sat up straighter. No one had disclosed our host's identity. It was Bella Martinez!

Bella Martinez had starred in a hit TV show in the late 1990s about a group of teenagers in a band. Think if Hannah Montana grew up and sang with others. I loved it so much I dressed as Bella's character for Halloween one year. My brother, Adam, dressed as the drummer. Of course, we'd been watching the show in syndication about ten years after it aired, so no one got our costume. We didn't care. It was fun.

Yes, I was a geeky fangirl. Bella Martinez stood in front of me, and I couldn't take my eyes off her.

Bella must have been in her late forties, but she looked about twenty-five. Even up close, I couldn't find a single wrinkle. Her breasts were perkier than mine. A white sundress set off her brown skin perfectly. Four-inch, glittery gold heels twinkled at her feet. When she reached the front of the room, she flashed a beautiful, million-dollar smile.

"Hello, everyone, and welcome to *The Fishbowl*! How are you?"

We cheered excitedly. They'd told us to always act enthusiastic for the cameras, but I didn't have to fake bouncing up and down and clapping: I sat ten feet from a woman I'd idolized as a child.

"I'm Bella Martinez. I'll be your host for the next ten weeks. We're all going to get to know each other intimately. To start, I'm going to go over some of the rules."

Some of the other contestants wore deep, serious looks. I realized that they were trying to look like they paid attention, in case the cameras focused on them. Joshua's scowl made him look like he needed to find a toilet ASAP, and Rachel's wrinkled brow suggested she hadn't understood a word Leanna said. Those two were a match made in heaven.

Not wanting to get caught daydreaming, I dragged my gaze back to Bella as she continued. She basically reiterated what Leanna had told us on the first day, to get it on tape for the viewers. She did mention one thing Leanna hadn't covered.

"Since this week's challenge is completed in teams, each losing team will nominate one person for elimination. Are there any questions about the rules?"

Skye raised her hand. "Do I really have to share a bathroom with these beauty queens all summer? I can't get anywhere near the mirror!"

"As the summer progresses and people are eliminated, that shouldn't be an issue."

"Can we vote for who leaves based on how much space they're taking up?"

"You can cast your vote for any reason, within the choices you're given." Skye opened her mouth again, but Bella cut her off. "Anyone else?"

Ariana stood, forcing everyone to notice how her hot-pink minidress traced every inch of her body. If it were any tighter, I'd be able to count her ribs from across the room. Could she even wear underwear in that?

"Who's going to cook and clean for us?"

"I would direct that question to Leanna."

Joshua smirked. "What's up with the pampered princess over there? 'Will the producers give me someone to do my makeup and hair?'"

Bella ignored him. "No more questions? Great!" Rachel clapped a hand over Joshua's mouth and hissed in his ear. "Then it's time to talk about your first challenge! Are you ready?"

We cheered enthusiastically. Rule #1: whenever asked if you are ready, respond with lots of arm shaking, cheering, and head nodding. Wait, that's Rule #2. Rule #1 was "Don't piss off Leanna."

"Okay! You may have noticed on the way in that there is a maze on the property!"

Really? How had I missed it?

"You'll enter the maze in teams of four at five-minute intervals. The team getting through the maze in the least amount of time wins. The captain of that team gets immunity for this week. It's not just any maze. At many of the intersections, you will see a clue telling you which way to go. If you choose correctly, you continue to the next turning point. If you choose incorrectly, well, we might have left a few surprises for you." Bella smiled mysteriously and met everyone's eyes in turn to gauge our reactions.

We each arranged our faces in a manner we hoped looked appropriately intrigued. I pursed my lips slightly and tilted my head to the left, wondering if I should also widen my eyes a bit.

"For the first challenge, we will choose your teams randomly. You'll pick captains among yourselves." She shook a small golden Fishbowl, and paper rustled. She pulled slips out, one at a time, and read the names aloud. "The first team is: Maria, Birdie, Ed, and Raj!"

My head swiveled around the room as she read each name, trying to gauge the strength of each team and remind myself of everyone's names.

"The second team is: Abram, Rachel, Mike, and Skye!"

I smiled at Justin when I realized we'd be on the same team. Our hostess drew all of his attention; he didn't seem to notice me. Bella continued to pull names. The realization of who else hadn't been assigned to a team yet dampened my premature excitement.

"Joshua—and, last, but certainly not least—Ariana! Everyone find your teammates!"

I gave each member of my new team a high five, a smile plastered on my face.

Joshua piped up. "Let's make this happen! I call Cap'n!"

Justin directed his question to the rest of us. "Is that cool?"

"Dude, I called dibs!"

I shrugged. It wasn't worth an argument. Besides, I'd seen enough TV to know the losing captain usually went home early in the game. Instead of debating, I changed the subject. "I'm so excited about this challenge! I always wanted to explore a real live hedge maze!"

"Well," Justin said, "it's probably not a real *live* hedge maze. Unless they planned this show twenty years ago, we're more likely about to walk into a real hedge maze made of Astroturf."

"Good point. Close enough. I've never been in a real Astroturf hedge maze, either."

Joshua started to say something, but a call from Bella interrupted him.

"Okay, everyone! Are you ready? Let's go to the maze!"

Our team drew the second position. The maze stretched about twenty feet wide and so long I couldn't see the end. Hedges (whether real or fake) towered above my head. Now, I'm not that tall, but Abram is, and the hedges dwarfed him, too.

Five minutes after the challenge started, the producers gave us the signal to enter. I felt like Harry Potter competing in the Tri-Wizard Tournament. If I'd been with Brandon instead of three strangers (on national television), we'd have broken off branches and started waving them around, throwing out Latin words.

Fresh evergreen scent filled the air. Fresh enough that it must come from a can. The maze smelled exactly like my tiny fake Christmas tree, which was weird because the hedges didn't look like Christmas trees. And either the producers trapped birds inside the hedges, or they'd pumped in canned bird noises. A little cheesy, but I didn't care.

Joshua and Ariana charged ahead into the maze and made their decisions at the first turns before I got to the signs. Luckily, the first couple of clues were fairly easy. I paused long enough to verify their choices before following. Justin trailed a few steps behind me.

I caught up to Joshua and Ariana at the third sign, located in a corner of the maze, and asked them to wait a minute for Justin. Ariana read the sign aloud:

IF YOU NEED THREE KNOCKS ON HEAVEN'S DOOR, GO LEFT.
IF YOU KNOCK TWICE, GO RIGHT.

I turned to the left, but Joshua pulled me back.

"What are you doing?" he demanded.

"The answer to the clue is 'knock-knock-knockin' on heaven's door.' I'm going left."

"What are you talking about?" He scratched his head. "It's 'knock, knock,' not 'knock, knock, knock.' We go right."

"What?"

"Duh! Don't you know anything? I thought you were supposed to be so smart. It's 'Knock, knock! Who's there?' Not 'knock, knock, KNOCK.' Any idiot knows that."

Okay! At least his confusion made sense, if not why he was being a jerk about it.

"It's a song, Joshua." I sang a few bars of the chorus, before breaking off, unsure if their dirty looks stemmed from my atrocious singing voice or the song itself. "It's an old Guns n' Roses song from the early '90s."

"Actually, it's a Bob Dylan song," Justin said. "It came out in the '70s. GNR did a remake. So did another band, a couple of years ago."

Joshua continued to argue that we didn't understand knock-knock jokes. Just as I wondered if perhaps I'd need to sing the entire song—which wouldn't go well for anyone—Justin came around the corner to the right. Mud covered his once-white sneakers and the lower half of his legs. Dots of mud splattered his arms. A smear ran across his cheek.

"Hey, guys. I went right. Giant mud puddle. Jen's right. We don't want to go that way."

Finally, Joshua shut up. I flashed Justin a grateful smile as Joshua shoved past me and charged down the left-hand path. I let him go. Justin smiled back, and butterflies fluttered in my belly.

Ariana grabbed Justin's hand. "Ohmigod, Justin! That's so great! I love the way you took charge. You're so smart. You saved us a ton of time those two would've wasted with their arguing."

As she continued to gush at his fabulous maze-walking abilities—what had he done that wouldn't have happened if we'd followed Joshua?—I walked down the path, deeper into the maze. Just because we'd had a nice conversation at the audition didn't mean I had any claim on Justin. Or that I wanted one. I needed to keep my eye on the prize.

I had no job, nowhere to live, and no money. An on-television fling wasn't an immediate necessity.

At the next fork, I found Joshua, moving his lips while he read the next clue. Peering around his shoulder, I pitched my voice so Justin and Ariana would hear me.

HOW MANY LICKS DOES IT TAKE TO GET TO THE TOOTSIE ROLL CENTER OF A TOOTSIE POP?

IF THE ANSWER IS THREE, GO STRAIGHT.

IF THE ANSWER IS 5,247, TURN RIGHT.

I hoped Joshua knew this commercial, or we might be about to have another pointless argument. As I finished reading, Justin and Ariana caught up.

"The world will never know," Justin deadpanned.

"One, two, three! CRUNCH." I laughed. "Let's go straight."

The other two stared at us like we'd sprouted extra heads. "What the heck are you dorks talking about?" Joshua asked.

"It's from a super old commercial," Justin explained. "It was apparently a big hit, because MythBusters did an episode about it a couple of years ago."

"It still airs," I said. "It's one of the longest-running commercials ever."

"Is it on Prime or Netflix?" Joshua asked. "Only losers still watch regular TV."

Ariana stepped in between us. "C'mon, guys, we're wasting time. Let's go."

After a few similar discussions, we exited the maze. A white ribbon broke as Joshua, still at the front of the pack, burst out on to the lawn. A bell sounded. Once all four of us stood on the outside, a couple of production assistants moved us away from the exit and handed us small paper cups. I stood and sipped my water while waiting for the others.

Three electronic boards showed each team's progress. We'd gotten through in forty-two minutes, thirty-two seconds. Surprisingly, the team before us hadn't come out yet. The third team was still in there, but we didn't know where. I hadn't seen or heard anyone else in the maze.

Ariana looked at the timers and huffed. "Forty-two minutes! If we lose because Jen kept arguing with Joshua—"

Thankfully, screaming and splashing inside the maze swallowed whatever else she wanted to say. Apparently, one of the other teams found one of the surprises.

"Well, sounds like we'll have a better time than them," I said.

"And we beat the team that went in before us," Justin added. "Calm down. There's nothing we can do now."

"By the way," I added, looking pointedly at Justin's mud-spattered clothing, "thanks for taking one for the team."

"No problem." He smiled at me. My traitorous stomach flip-flopped. I wasn't here to fall in love, or hook-up, or whatever. Justin was competition, and you weren't supposed to get hot and bothered whenever the competition was around. At this rate, if we wound up in the final two, I'd be sunk.

Ariana sniffed loudly. "If we win, it will be because Justin saved the day! That was sooooo manly, the way you took charge when those two decided to act like children—"

I walked out of earshot before I gave in to the urge to kick her. I seethed, not believing that Ariana was telling everyone it was my fault that (a) Joshua didn't know a really old song and (b) acted like an ass because I did. Besides, if anything slowed us down, it was her strolling along at the back of the group, monopolizing Justin's attention.

At that moment, the first team emerged from the maze. Something covered all four of them. Was it paint? Blue and green splotches streaked

Raj's face and hair. Yellow and red spatters decorated Maria's black hair. Birdie's T-shirt shirt now looked tie-dyed. Ed must've been walking in the front of the pack: all four colors obliterated his rainbow T-shirt and streaked the front of his black shorts.

The third team's timer showed fifty minutes, twenty-seven seconds. No matter when they finished, we'd beaten them. My team won!

When Team Three emerged more than ten minutes later, Bella gave the official results. As our team captain, Joshua received immunity from elimination. For a split second, I wished our team had lost. The more he talked, the more I suspected the others would've voted to send him home, too. Instead, Bella asked each team who was most responsible for their loss.

"Raj." Maria spoke up instantly. "I hate to be the first to call someone out, but I told y'all he went the wrong way, and now I've got paint in my hair."

Birdie and Ed nodded.

"Raj? Do you have something to say for yourself?" Bella asked.

He shrugged and ran one hand through his short black hair. "I wish I did, but I messed up. I went the wrong way, and that's why we lost. All I can say is, 'Please, America, don't let me go home for one dumb mistake.'"

"Okay," Bella said. "Thank you for your honesty. What about Team Two? Abram, who would you nominate for elimination?"

He shuffled his feet, examining his shoes. "I think everyone did their best. I wouldn't single anyone out."

Rachel snorted. "For cryin' out loud. Skye argued every clue and got us lost. If I had my druthers, she'd be the one—"

Skye stepped toward Bella, cutting Rachel off. "Whatever. Bella, she didn't make the slightest effort to answer any of the questions. Maybe I was wrong, but at least I'm not some blond bimbo who lets others do all the work. I vote for Rachel."

Rachel clenched her fists. "I may be blond, but I'm not a bimbo! I did 4H for ten years and earned the most badges in my county! Just because you're jealous—"

"Ladies, please." Abram spoke quietly, but he had such a presence that everyone turned to look at him. "Why don't we hear what Mike has to say?"

Mike's head had been swiveling back and forth between the two. He leaned forward, consuming every word. When Abram said his name, he threw his shoulders back and rubbed his bald head. He looked disappointed that Rachel and Skye weren't going to roll on the ground, pulling each other's hair.

Watch out for him, I warned myself. *He could be trouble.*

"Yes, Mike, what do you think?" Bella asked.

"Skye," he said finally. "She says Rachel didn't help, but she never had the chance. Skye read each clue and charged off before anyone could say anything."

"You're just saying that because I wouldn't have sex with you!" Skye accused.

"That's a flat-out lie!"

"Okay, okay, everyone," Bella said. "You each get one vote. Raise your hand if you think Rachel should be up for elimination."

Both of Skye's hands shot into the air.

"It's one vote per person, Skye." Sunlight glinting off the metal in Skye's face somehow made her glare seem more menacing. "And who votes for Skye?"

Rachel and Mike had their hands up almost before she finished speaking. Abram's hand moved only a hair slower. Three to one.

Raj and Skye faced elimination. For the moment, I was safe.

* * *

One thing I never knew about reality television was how filthy everything could be. When twelve people lived in a two-bedroom house, things got dirty. Messes were made. Dishes piled up everywhere, both in the kitchen and out. Some of the other women wore so much makeup that, after a couple of days, it caked every towel in the house. Washing helped a little, but the cloths would never be white again.

On Saturday, Birdie and I begged the producers for bleach. When it arrived, she informed everyone that, if they needed her, she'd be in the laundry room. I collected as many towels as I could carry before joining her.

Upon opening the laundry room door, a wall of steam hit me. Fog obscured the glass walls. Even after stepping into the room, I didn't see Birdie anywhere.

After I called her name, she revealed herself by standing up in the far left corner. "Here," she said sheepishly.

"How did you do that? There's no place to hide, right?"

"There are cameras." She pointed at three black devices on the ceiling that covered the entire room. "But here, no one can see you from the door. I'm hiding from the other contestants, not the viewers. Hi, America!"

Curious, I went to stand in the corner. Although we were behind the kitchen, the backs of the appliances stood against the connecting wall.

One of the dryers stood between us and the door. Ariana and Mike had been in the kitchen when I walked through, but neither of them was visible from my vantage point.

"It's good no one does laundry. If the others knew they'd find privacy, they'd be here making out faster than I can say, 'raging libido.'"

I laughed. "Well, I won't tell anyone. Especially if you don't mind if I sneak in here once in a while when I need some peace myself."

Birdie shook my hand. "Deal."

Together, we finished and folded the towels. "You really don't think anyone else will ever do laundry?"

"I'm not sure some of them know how to do laundry," Birdie said, rolling her eyes. "Abram's wife does all his, and Ariana lives with her rich daddy in his penthouse on the Upper West Side."

"Oh, really?" My ears perked up.

"Yeah, you were in the School Room when she told us. Her dad is some big shot, so she and her daughter live with him." She paused as if mentally composing a separate tweet. "She works a couple of days a week as a massage therapist and mostly mooches off him."

Ariana didn't mention being an actress.

If she didn't want us to know, that information could come in handy later. I filed it away. "Massage, huh? I guess that explains her chiseled arms. What else did she say?"

"She tried to convince us again she's some kind of super genius. Claimed to get an art history degree in two years."

"Do you doubt her?"

"Honestly, I don't care. I'm more interested in how she plays the game than what she knows or doesn't know."

The rest of the weekend passed uneventfully. On Monday morning, Bella brought the results of the first viewer vote: Maria had been nominated for elimination. No one exhibited surprise, not even Maria. She mostly sat on a chair on the back patio, tanning, while the rest of us got to know each other. She hung back from conversations, listening instead of engaging.

A week after entering the house, I knew nothing about her other than what she said in her introduction: Her name was Maria, she taught third grade, and she lived in Texas. She also didn't seem to be a threat. Which meant it might be in my best interests to keep her around. Maybe I should vote to send home someone with more personality.

If only Joshua didn't have immunity. He had loads of personality.

Before the vote on Tuesday, the production team took over the games room and covered the glass walls with sheets. When they finished, they called us in one at a time to vote.

The room had been transformed. A shimmering blue and green cloth covered the pool table. Three fishbowls sat on the cloth, each with a picture of Skye, Raj, or Maria on the front. A set of shelves with different colored containers designed to look like fish food hung on the far wall. My name printed on a green bottle told me which to choose.

The speakers in the corners crackled, and one of the production assistants spoke. None of them other than Leanna had introduced themselves, but it sounded like the one I thought of as "Tall." He towered above everyone except Abram.

"Jennifer, take the fish food with your name on it, and 'feed' the bowl with the picture of the person you want to be eliminated."

Okay. As usual, I directed my response at the ceiling. "Got it. Thanks."

I grabbed the green fish food and held it over the bowl with Skye's picture. It must've been taken at the audition: she glared at me from under green and purple spikes, not the brown and pink Mohawk she currently sported. I preferred the original look.

Pretty much everyone agreed her team's loss had been Skye's fault. The container tipped, and I tapped the side. Green glitter drifted into the bowl.

Crackle. "A little more, Jen. Make sure we can see it."

"Oops. Sorry." I shook my wrist, dumping green glitter into the bowl with a thud.

Am I still too nice for TV, Skye?

Later that night, Bella brought us the results: Skye had the most votes. The viewers hadn't saved her. Everyone gathered to say good-bye, pretending to be sad to see her go as those of us remaining breathed a collective sigh of relief. One competitor down, ten to go.

I'd officially survived my first week.

Chapter 9

<u>Jennifer in the School Room, Week 2:</u>

I'm so grateful to have made it through the first week on The Fishbowl. *I had fun during the first challenge, and I can't wait to see what else they have in store for us!*

Sure, Joshua's a jerk. I can't figure him out. Is he just a belligerent imbecile? Or is he playing the part he thinks America wants him to play? And if so, what does that say about what he thinks of the American people? Honestly, it's almost like we're all acting out Romeo and Juliet, *and he's playing Puck from* A Midsummer Night's Dream. *So bizarre.*

Yes, Ariana is obnoxious. I think she's got a thing for Justin. She sees me as a threat. That's ridiculous. I'm not here to hook up. I'm here to win $250,000. If she wants to waste her time on a non-existent rivalry for a guy, that's fine with me. I'm focused on winning challenges.

They said we'd be getting our first mini-challenge today. I'm not sure how it will be different from the main challenges, but here's hoping for puzzles.

Wednesday morning the producers blared a car alarm through every speaker in the house. Fury and confusion flowed as everyone scrambled for their clothes, occasionally smacking into the random wall in the rush of activity. Three or four thuds sounded, followed by exclamations.

Everyone except me, that is. Always an early riser, I sat in the backyard doing Pilates in the early morning sunlight, gathering my thoughts. Luckily, I managed to witness the chaos without being part of it, because I'd already grown tired of slamming into glass walls. I kept reminding myself to slow down and pay attention to my surroundings. Otherwise, they could air an entire episode of me walking into giant sheets of glass.

Okay, that might be funny.

As each person reached the foot of the stairs, one of the production assistants wearing earmuffs pointed toward the living room. When the blaring stopped, I took it as a cue to head inside. Leanna waited in front of the couch with her headset and clipboard.

"Okay, everyone. This week, the challenge is going to require preparation, so you need to start today. This isn't a mini-challenge. You must participate in order to get the information you need to complete your challenge tomorrow.

"For this one, it's every man for himself. There are no teams this week. We're testing how well you listen to each other and retain information. Early in the audition process, you each answered a series of questions. We recorded your responses. For the rest of the day, your job is to talk to the other contestants and find out what answers they gave."

Easy enough. I'd always been a good note-taker.

"We've removed all writing implements from the house. You'll have to remember what the other players tell you."

Okay, no notes. Check. Still, this shouldn't be too tough. Some of the others looked a bit worried, but I could handle this.

"Tomorrow, you'll use the things you learn today." She paused and gazed around the room meaningfully. "You may not refuse to talk to your fellow contestants. You don't have to interview other contestants, but you must answer any question you are asked. Anyone who doesn't do the interviews will suffer serious consequences. So—let's pair up and start talking!"

Ten minutes later, I sat across from Joshua while he pondered the answer to my first question.

"Sparkle Puss."

I tilted my head and rubbed my chin. "You named your first pet Sparkle Puss?"

Joshua didn't reply. Mentally, I shrugged. Maybe he had sisters or something. Okay, next question. "Where did you go to school?"

"The Goldberg Academy of Privileged Assholes."

I showed him my teeth in what couldn't really be described as a smile.

"You know, I really believe that. You were probably at the top of your class. What's your favorite color?"

"Rainbow glitter." He crossed his arms and leaned back in his chair, crossing his ankles in front of him.

At that point, I dropped all pretense of being polite. He was totally messing with me. This jerk wanted me get all the questions wrong so I'd be eliminated.

"Your favorite color," I said, "is rainbow glitter?"

"Yup. That's right." His arrogant smile, the tilt of his head, even the way he sat back and crossed his legs dared me to defy him. My hand itched to slap that smirk off his face.

"That's what you wrote on your interview sheet during the auditions?"

"Absolutely! You don't believe me? Whatever. Haters gotta hate."

The list of questions crinkled as my hand reflexively closed into a fist. I focused on not throwing the pages at him and forced myself to take deep breaths before responding.

"No, it's just interesting that since every inch of your body screams 'homophobic redneck farm boy' and your entire personality screams 'homophobic jackass gangster' your favorite color would look like a gay pride flag. Is there something you want to tell me?" I leaned forward, patted his knee, and lowered my voice. "Don't worry, I won't tell Rachel. She'd be crushed. But you should think about coming out on your own. Being gay is nothing to be ashamed of. Some of my closest friends are gay."

As I spoke, Joshua's face turned almost purple. He struggled between his desire to make me lose the challenge and his irrational fear of being labeled gay in front of all of America (most of whom would care more that he's a dick than about who he sleeps with).

Finally, he gritted his teeth. "Yellow. My favorite color is yellow. Hello!"

"Excellent," I chirped, all sweetness and smiles. "Glad to hear it. Now, what's your favorite food?"

The rest of the interviews were fairly straightforward. The questions themselves weren't that revealing. Ed cracked me up with some of his responses, but he was genuine. No one else radiated Joshua's level of hostility.

My easiest interview by far was with Justin. We sat outside next to the pool, chatting and sipping iced tea until the sun went down. It was only when the others wandered outside that I remembered I still needed to talk to Maria and Raj.

No one told any deep, dark secrets. There wasn't any way of knowing whether the information was true—the producers would only see whether it matched.

Everyone could be lying or playing a role.

* * *

The next morning we gathered again in the living room to learn about the full challenge. Once we settled into our usual places, Bella sailed through the front door in a gauzy blue sundress and silvery sandals, trailing the scent of baby powder in her wake. She reminded me of a commercial for feminine wash.

"Good morning, Fishies!"

"Good morning, Bella!"

"Are you ready to hear about your challenge?"

We responded with a resounding "Yes!"

"That's great! You spent yesterday getting to know your fellow contestants. Now, we're going to see what you remember. One at a time, you will be taken to a board with twenty questions about the other contestants. The answers are printed on a stack of cards.

"Read each question on the board, find the card with the correct answer, then climb up the ladder to hang the card next to the matching question. You may only carry one card at a time; however, once the cards are on the board, you can move them around without climbing down.

"When you've got it, race to the buzzer. If the answers are correct, the board will light up. If they're wrong, go back and try again. Whoever finishes in the least amount of time is the winner and is guaranteed to remain in the Fishbowl for another week. The two contestants who take the longest will be up for elimination, along with a third contestant that the viewers choose."

They got shots of us nodding and agreeing, and Bella left. They didn't want any of us getting too friendly with her. She probably sat in her chauffeured town car playing on her phone until the challenges ended.

The producers came in and out every ten minutes or so, taking people one at a time down to the site they'd constructed. I wondered what they were doing with everyone who finished—no one came back to the house.

I stretched in the back of the room while mentally reviewing the information the others gave me. Rachel and Joshua whispered in one corner. Ariana lay on the couch, apparently napping. Mike strummed the air as his lips moved silently. Too bad they wouldn't let him sing.

When my turn came, I sized up the area. A sheet covered a giant board. A ladder ran up the left side. A large bin a few feet away held a bunch of square cards. Those must be the answers.

Running back and forth would take up the most time. The best strategy was getting all the answers on the board and then rearranging them. That way, I'd get to read everything at once instead of spending half my time flipping through cards.

The sheet dropped, revealing a list of white questions on the black board, and a green light flashed. I darted to the bin and grabbed the first answer card. Without even looking at the questions, I ran to the board and climbed to the top of the ladder. I placed the card next to the highest question, jumped to the ground, then ran back for another card.

By the fourth or fifth trip, my breath came in pants. Once I'd finished hanging about half the cards, I ran out of steam. The good news was that all of the highest spots on the board were full. I didn't have as far to climb. I allowed myself to pause and read the next card while walking back to the board.

"Mexican."

That was Raj's favorite food. He'd commented that everyone expected him to prefer Indian. He asked if Maria had been required to list tacos or flan. (Incidentally, she liked chimichangas. Yum!) No, Indian was Ariana's favorite. I took an extra second to find "Raj's favorite food," which was thankfully located near the bottom of the board. I hung it up and lowered myself carefully.

The short respite was enough. Knowing I'd gotten one answer correct gave me a burst of energy. In a flash, I got the rest of the cards on the board. Then, I read and swapped them. Justin liked blue; Mike's favorite music was rock (which he played and sang). Being a good listener was finally paying off.

I wasn't surprised when the remaining two questions were about Joshua. Those were the ones I couldn't answer. No card read "rainbow glitter," or any of the other nonsense responses he gave me. Obviously, his favorite food must be pizza, since "skiing" didn't make sense. I placed the last two cards, jumped the ground, and ran to the buzzer. When I got there, I mustered every ounce of strength left to smack it as hard as I could.

The board lit up. I'd gotten them all right. Yippee!

I sank to the ground, exhausted. A moment later, two members of the production team led me to where the other Fish waited.

"How'd you do?" Joshua asked. His tone was casual, but he must've been dying to know whether his sabotage paid off.

"You know, I forgot to look at the timer! Oops." I smiled sweetly, wondering what other tricks he had up his sleeve.

Of course I lied. I finished in four minutes, fifty-seven seconds.

Tall told me on the way to the waiting area that they didn't expect anyone to break five minutes, which sent a rush of excitement through me.

I smiled gratefully when Justin appeared and handed me a cup of water. "Thank you!"

He sat next to me, and Joshua wandered away. "I told him it took me thirty-seven minutes. Jerk. None of the answers he gave were on any of the cards."

"Me, too! He said his favorite color was rainbow glitter."

"What? That's *my* favorite color!" Justin gasped in mock horror. "I can't believe he stole my answer!"

I couldn't believe how easy it was to sit and talk to this guy. Cute, smart, and charming? There had to be a catch, right? Like maybe he secretly had eleven ex-wives buried in his basement. Or maybe he couldn't enjoy sex unless bearded midgets in neon orange tutus tickled him.

We chatted as the other contestants trickled into the room. By the time Ariana horned in, we were deep in conversation.

"I've always wanted to see the Louvre," Justin said.

"What's that?" She plopped down between us, forcing me to scoot off to one side to avoid an actress in my lap. "Some kind of horror movie? The Ooze?"

Justin's eyebrows knit together. "The Louvre? In Paris?" At her vacant look, he said, "It's the most famous art museum in the world."

"Oh! Of course!" Ariana laughed a shade too loudly. She learned forward, giving us an eyeful of her perfect cleavage. Something pinged in the back of my mind.

"I thought you said you had an art history degree?"

Justin tilted his head at her. "That's right. You've never heard of the Louvre?"

"Obviously, I've heard of the Loouve," Ariana trilled. "Like I said, I thought you said The Ooze. I love the Loouve. I've been there a million times."

Then why don't you know how to pronounce it?

"I'd love to see it. I've only ever been to the Met, during my high school's senior trip," I said instead. "Ariana, what's your favorite piece there?"

She snorted. "You think you're so smart. You can't fool me. The Mets are a baseball team."

Justin gaped at her. "The Met is a huge museum. The Metropolitan Museum of Art? Don't you live in New York City? It's in Central Park."

She opened her mouth, then closed it. Twice. The wheels turned inside her head, but she'd been caught. No way anyone with an art history degree had never heard of these places. Especially since she lived in New York. It's not like I mentioned some tiny Seattle art gallery hidden in a back alley behind the Pizza Hut.

Finally, she lifted her chin and sniffed. "I'm sorry, guys. I'd love to stay and chat, but Jen, you need a shower. I'm going to sit somewhere less pungent." She rose and glided away to sit with Mike. He beamed up at her as she settled beside him, her breasts almost grazing his nose.

With Mike distracted by her attributes, Ariana shot Justin a wounded look. For a moment, shame filled me. "I guess I wasn't very nice to her. But I didn't think anyone would lie about something so irrelevant as a college major."

"Me, neither. Why would anyone care?"

"Who knows?"

Justin leaned toward me and gave an exaggerated sniff. "Anyway, for what it's worth, I think you smell fine for someone who just ran a marathon."

I laughed. "Thanks! You, too."

Later that night, they gathered us to announce the official results from the challenge. I plopped on the couch between Ed and Birdie, trying not to appear anxious when Bella entered.

"In this envelope, I have the results. However, before I get to that, there's something we need to discuss."

Curious, I looked around the room. Justin caught my eye and tilted his head slightly toward Joshua. In his shoes, I'd have been sweating, but "J-dawg" wore the same smug, arrogant look as usual.

Bella dropped her smile and continued. "The purpose of this challenge was for you to get together, talk, learn about the others in the Fishbowl, and see who remembered what. As such, there was an implicit requirement that you'd provide honest answers to the questions."

I clapped my hands over my mouth to suppress a grin. We all knew Joshua had cheated! "J-dawg, the answers you gave your fellow contestants did not match the information you provided to the producers. You also fed different answers to each contestant, creating confusion. As a result, you have been disqualified. You are automatically up for elimination. I'm sorry."

A silence fell across the room. I wanted to cheer, but knew it would be unsportsmanlike. Instead, I arranged my face into an expression showing appropriate concern and shock.

Birdie nudged me. "Relax. You look like you have diarrhea."

I settled for wrapping my arms around my knees and hiding my smile against my legs.

"As for the rest of you, I'm sure you want to know your scores. Everyone stand. When I call your name, you may sit." She paused while we arranged ourselves. "Birdie, Rachel, Raj, Ariana, Justin. If I have called your name—congratulations! Your scores were not the worst."

Wait a minute. I was one of the worst? I thought I did really well.

"Abram and Jennifer, you completed the challenge in the least amount of time. One of you is the winner and is guaranteed another week in the Fishbowl."

This time, I allowed the corners of my mouth to stretch upward.

"Mike and Maria, one of you had the worst time and is therefore up for elimination."

After another dramatic pause, she continued. "Congratulations, Abram! You had the fastest time! Well done!"

My smile faltered, but picturing the way Justin looked at me earlier brought it back.

"Jennifer, you were only three seconds behind him. Excellent job! You may be seated."

Second place! Not bad.

Abram's height gave him an undeniable advantage. I didn't begrudge him the victory, although I was disappointed.

"Well done, man." I offered him a high five.

"You, too!"

"This was a tight race." Bella went on, dragging the results out for the sake of drama. "The total difference between first and last place was less than five minutes. Maria, Mike, only 1.8 seconds separated you. That's very close."

Maria bit her lip and smoothed her silky curls. Mike rubbed his head, looking from Bella to Maria and back.

"Mike, I'm sorry, but your score was the lowest. You are up for elimination."

Maria shook his hand and sat, trying not to look relieved.

"The episode airs on Sunday night. On Monday morning, we will let you know who else the viewers have nominated for elimination. Have a nice weekend, everyone." She waved and flashed another smile, then sashayed out of the room.

"Hey, Jen," Joshua said. "Sorry you didn't win because men are more athletic than women."

Behind me, Birdie let out a sound of outrage, but I forced myself not to react. That was, after all, what he wanted. After only a few days, his ridiculous insults were more tiring than upsetting. I opened my mouth to respond, but Ed beat me to it.

"Hey, Joshua, I'd love to say I'm sorry your lying ass got caught cheating and you're up for elimination, but I'm not. This Fishbowl will be a better place once you're gone."

Muscles bulged under Ed's tight T-shirt as he crossed his arms. If Joshua noticed, he didn't react.

"Oh, so now Jennifer needs you to protect her? Jen, are you hiding behind the gay guy? That's pathetic."

I'd heard enough. "I don't need anyone to protect me. Your opinion means nothing, so no response is required. If that's the best you've got, you should give up. When you talk, all I feel is hot wind rushing past my face."

"Like this?" Joshua leaned closer and exhaled heavily. His breath reeked of beer.

Ed lunged across the couch, but Justin and Ariana caught him. I stepped backward, trying to stay out of Joshua's reach.

Rachel stepped in, forcing him away from me. "Let's go, Joshua. You're drunk, and you're not making any friends."

"I don't need to make friends with these fat, ugly losers!" Joshua spat at us.

Rachel walked forward, making him take another step back. She grabbed one arm and turned him so their backs were to the rest of us.

"You need them to not vote you out if you want to win. Come on. I'll get you something to eat." She pulled him toward the kitchen. Raj went to help.

As they dragged him through the door, Joshua yelled over his shoulder. "I don't need their votes! America will save me, totes! Watch me, yo! Everyone loves the villain! When the votes are in, I'll be here, chillin'! J-dawg forever, bitches!"

Silence fell over the room as Rachel shut the kitchen door. Justin and Ariana let go of Ed, who dropped on to the empty couch, his head in his hands. He took deep breaths, exhaling slowly.

Mike fiddled with a guitar pick, walking it back and forth across his knuckles. "Here I thought I'd have to persuade you guys to let me stay, but now I'd like to thank Joshua for doing the heavy lifting. Who's up for some pool?"

Everyone laughed as Abram and Ed followed Mike out of the room. I stayed on the couch and silently counted the votes on my fingers: Justin, Ed, Birdie, Mike, Abram, Raj, and Maria were all voting for Joshua. Plus me. I didn't know about Ariana, but it didn't matter. Joshua would have at least eight out of eleven votes.

The viewers probably wouldn't vote to save him, unless they adored badly manufactured drama. There was an excellent chance we wouldn't have to put up with Joshua much longer.

* * *

The viewers voted to put Maria up for elimination again, but we'd reached a consensus long before Bella gave the results. Joshua was leaving, as long as the viewers didn't save him.

After dinner, most of the Fish gathered in the living room after dinner to wait for Bella and the results. Rachel and Joshua joined us last. She patted her blond hair nervously and adjusted a bra strap as they entered. His T-shirt was inside out.

"Thank you for joining me, everyone!" Bella smiled as she held up the envelope. "I hold in my hand the results from the second elimination. Are you ready?"

"YES!" Ed, Maria, and Birdie responded in unison. They exchanged a look and burst out laughing. I giggled. Joshua glared at them. Rachel stared at the floor.

Once they composed themselves, Bella opened the envelope. I wondered if she knew the results ahead of time and pulled the same blank piece of paper out of the envelope every week for dramatic effect.

"I'm very sorry, J-dawg, but your fellow contestants have spoken. You have been eliminated. Please pack your things. You will be leaving *The Fishbowl* immediately."

Maria started clapping before Bella even finished the first sentence.

The only one who acted genuinely surprised was Joshua. He must've thought America would like his shtick. His jaw dropped and his eyes bulged as he jumped to his feet, spread his arms, and threw his head back.

"What?" he roared. "No more J-dawg! I got robbed!"

Joshua grabbed one of the green cushions off the floor and threw it at the couch. Birdie dove out of the way, but Abram reached one long arm out and caught it easily. He stood and crossed his arms over the pillow, towering over Joshua. Ed, several inches shorter but well built, stood next to Abram.

Bella made a hand motion at the doorway, and two members of the staff inched toward the living room entrance. Probably in case Joshua needed to be escorted out.

No one else said anything. If he hoped to provoke another fight, he wasn't going to get his wish.

"'Sup, America? You couldn't save the J-dawg? What if I do this?"

He dropped to the ground, grabbed his legs, and spun in a circle. Then he laid flat and began humping the ground. Oh, dear Lord. He was break dancing.

"I'm sorry, Joshua, but you need to go now. You've—"

Joshua spun up on to his head and began to rotate in circles. It would've been cool if it wasn't such a bizarre reaction to being eliminated. Maybe he'd have stayed longer if he'd spent more time doing tricks and less time being a jerk.

Finally, the security staff persuaded Joshua to leave the room. Rachel followed.

"You guys," Bella admonished us. "You're required to go stand in the hall and say good-bye. You don't have to pretend you're sorry to see him go."

Abram moved toward the doorway first. "I guess we owe it to Joshua not to be sore winners."

To me, it was less about being a sore winner and more about never wanting to see that jerk again. Still, Abram was right. Reluctantly, I followed. The others crowded behind me as we waited to say good-bye.

"Oh, yeah? Well, I'm glad to leave all you snoozers!" Joshua thundered down the stairs, dropping his suitcase at the bottom.

When he continued to rant and rave, Tall and a couple other members of the production team hovered outside the open front door.

"I don't want to hang out with you losers! You haven't seen the last of me, bitchezzzzzz!" He made no effort to move toward the front door.

Two production assistants came into the house and grabbed Joshua's shoulders. As they wrestled him out the door, he continued to yell, "You'll regret eliminating the J-dawg! I'm going to haunt your dreams! I—"

Mercifully, the door slammed shut, cutting him off. Ed moved forward and picked up the suitcase lying forgotten in the hallway. When he opened the door, Joshua's shouts filtered into the room, although the words were unintelligible.

Ed tossed the suitcase out the door. "Good-bye! Be sure not to write!"

As he slammed the door a second time, the entire hallway heaved a sigh of relief.

"And GOOD RIDDANCE!"

Chapter 10

Jennifer in The School Room, Week 3:

I'm so glad Joshua is gone. No, I will NOT miss him! He was so rude. That can't be his normal personality. He must've been putting on an act. Still, he was no fun to be around.

That night, when he was in my face? I was a little freaked out. Sure, I'd like to think Joshua isn't the sort of guy who would hit a woman unprovoked, but he'd been drinking, and I thought Ed might punch him to defend my honor. Not that my honor needs defending, and not that I care what Joshua thinks.

Oh, right, Ed. Joshua's a lot bigger than he is. I'm glad Rachel stepped in. For some reason, that jerk listens to her.

Another thing no one ever told me about reality television: there are times when being on the show could be excruciatingly dull. The day after Joshua's departure, it rained all day. We were confined to the house and bored out of our minds. Living in Seattle, I'm no stranger to rain, but I didn't plan to spend my summer in Los Angeles getting drenched in thunderstorms.

At home, a rainy day meant surfing the Internet, watching TV, cleaning my apartment, doing laundry, baking cookies, or redecorating. One Saturday, I'd painted a bunch of different-sized crystal plates I found at Goodwill and hung them on the walls. No one believed my artwork cost less than ten dollars.

That wasn't possible inside the Fishbowl. When it rained here, ten people sat in a room talking about cabin fever. Not exactly riveting television. We played charades for a while, but it didn't take long to run out of ideas.

Finally, Ariana asked the producers for a sketch pad and some charcoal. One at a time, we sat for portraits. After we'd established that she didn't know famous art museums, I was surprised to see that the results showed talent, if they weren't one hundred percent accurate.

Justin's cute, but he didn't look like Ryan Gosling. And why did she make my chin so huge?

I pushed the thought aside and asked the producers for ingredients to make cookies.Baking occupied me for a couple of hours. Unfortunately, the cookies disappeared so fast, I realized two things. First, I didn't want to spend the rest of my summer baking constantly for other people. Second, if I did, we would all gain ridiculous amounts of weight. We needed more options.Maria and Rachel painted each other's toenails in the second-floor sitting room while Birdie gave herself a manicure.

"This is the third time I've done my nails this week," she informed me. "Look. I learned tiger stripes!" She raised her hands against the backdrop of her red hair and growled.

Raj, Ed, Abram, and Justin played darts. The last time I played darts, I somehow threw one straight up in the air. The plastic end hit me in the head. In my defense, it was college and I'd been drinking, but I didn't need to try again on national television. Mike and Ariana were nowhere to be found. Mike seemed okay, but I wasn't in a hurry to find Ariana.

I watched the game for a while, then asked the producers for board games or a deck of cards. They refused. Desperate for an activity other than climbing the walls or eating, I asked for construction paper, markers, and scissors. When I got them, I sat at the table and made a deck of playing cards. I spent the entire afternoon teaching Ed how to play Casino, an old card game I used to play with my grandmother, while Birdie watched.

After dinner, Justin approached me. "Did Grandma teach you any other card games?"

"Just Spite & Malice. It's fun, but we need two decks. And I'm not positive I remember all the rules."

He left the room. A few minutes later, he returned with the leftover art supplies. This time, he helped me make the cards. When we realized I didn't remember enough of the rules to teach anyone else how to play, we invited Rachel and Ed to join us in a Speed tournament. An hour later, Justin and I played for five (imaginary) dollars a game until moonlight bathed the kitchen.

"I hope you win the grand prize, Justin, because at this rate, you're going to owe me hundreds of dollars before we get out of here."

He glanced at our scrap of paper. "Ahem. At the moment, I owe you exactly ten dollars."

"What about our bet? And the interest?"

"Excuse me. I owe you ten dollars, three cents. You've only won one more game. Final match? Double or nothing?"

I yawned and stretched. I liked hanging out with him, but we had a challenge in the morning. "Some other time. I need to get my beauty sleep if I'm going to compete against all you athletic-types tomorrow."

Rain beat against the roof when I crawled into bed, exhausted but happy.

When I awoke, early morning sunlight streamed through the glass. I sighed with relief. I wouldn't have been able to stand another entire day locked inside, even with my homemade deck of cards and all the junk food I wanted. Too bad I couldn't bake a Venti non-fat caramel macchiato with extra foam.

I found Ed on the landing. We found cereal on the kitchen counter with a note from the producers, encouraging us to eat quickly. As I debated whether to wake the others, alarms sounded. A moment later, footsteps pounded down the stairs.

After breakfast, Leanna gathered us into the living room. "Okay! For our next challenge, we're going to take a field trip."

A person could only walk in circles around the backyard for so long. Everyone cheered.

"Make sure you're wearing athletic clothes with socks that cover your ankles. Ladies, you'll want sports bras. Meet me back here in five minutes."

A frenzy of activity followed.

Wham!

Ow. That was a wall. Again. Stupid invisible glass walls. I rushed through my routine. Ariana and Rachel grumbled at not having enough time to do their makeup, but Ariana always rolled out of bed looking perfect. She offered thinly veiled requests for compliments disguised as a problem. Ariana, Queen of the Humblebrag.

Three and a half minutes later, I stood in the entry hall, ready to go.

Half an hour later, we reached our destination. Removing the blindfold they'd made us wear, I squinted into the sunlight.

Birdie's voice told me where we were. "Awesome! I love #JumpQuest! We're going #trampolining!"

Jump Quest? Sure enough, we stood in front of a trampoline place. Our challenge was jumping? Weird.

Tall and the production assistant I'd come to think of as "Curly Beard" herded us inside the building and handed out special high-topped shoes. Then, they directed us to a large trampoline, divided into squares. Bella waited there in pristine workout clothes.

"You're going to play dodgeball, with a twist. When a ball hits you, I'll ask a trivia question. If you get it right, you stay. If you throw a ball and someone catches it, again, we'll ask a trivia question. Whoever gives the correct answer first stays in," she said. "Each ball is a different color. The color of the ball determines what kind of question I ask you. For example, purple is music, blue is geography, etc."

Ew. I almost as good at music trivia as I was at singing.

Please, God, if you could just help all the purple balls swerve around me, I promise to always help little old ladies crossing the street.

"Yell your answers, because you can't wear your microphones for this challenge."

Tall collected our microphones. After three weeks, I felt naked without it.

"Also, you may have noticed you're on a trampoline. One person per square, please. The dividing lines are not bouncy—don't jump on them. It is possible to bounce off the walls, but be careful!

"We'll play three games. The person who lasts the longest through all three games is immune this week. The two players with the least amount of playing time will be up for elimination. Ready?"

Bella held up the golden fishbowl and drew names. I wound up on a team with Birdie, Mike, Raj, and Maria. We lined up on one side of the court, facing Justin, Rachel, Ariana, Ed, and Abram—all the athletic people. Awesome.

Blowing a whistle, Bella threw out three balls. With a flurry of activity, the game began.

Usually, I'm not bad at dodgeball. I'm in pretty good shape, and I can dodge well enough. The problem is, I can't throw. Someone always catches it.

Note to self: only throw ball at Ariana.

I could probably answer questions faster than she could.

For the first game, I hid toward the back of the court. I wanted to let the people in front eliminate some of the players on the other team for me. Unfortunately, Justin threw a ball that sailed past the boys and collided with my shoulder almost immediately.

Breet! That must have been the fastest the teenaged referee ever blew her whistle.

"Jennifer!" Bella called me from the sidelines. "Finish this quote, 'Quoth the raven, _______.'"

Oh! I knew that. I shouted, "Nevermore," and scooped up the ball.

I waited until Ariana faced away from me, then aimed, trying not to bounce all over the place. Once I had her in my sights, I let the ball fly. Oops. The foam ball weighed almost nothing; my throw missed Ariana by several feet. Worse, I'm not sure the ball even made it across the centerline. How embarrassing. I ducked as another ball whizzed over my head.

Breet! Ariana was out. Someone else got her.

Whap! Oops. Maybe I should've been paying attention to the game instead of the "Mimza" member.

"Jennifer! What is the capital of Burundi!"

"Umm." No idea. My only thought involved a line from a comedian's skit my mom watched when I was a child.

"Five seconds!"

I had nothing. "Eddie Izzard?"

Behind me, someone laughed. Bella smiled at me. "I'm sorry, Jennifer, but that is not correct."

"I didn't think so."

*C'mon! How many people know that? I mean, other than. . .*I wracked my brain. *Burundi-ans? The people of Burundi? What are they called?*

On the sidelines, Ariana sat smirking. Not wanting to talk to her, I picked a spot several feet away, but she didn't take the hint. She rose to her feet and approached, then cocked one hip and leaned against the wall beside me. For a second, I was right back in Dom's bedroom, looking at his wife. A wave of dizziness made me almost miss her words.

"Guess Justin doesn't like you as much as you thought."

Lost in the memory of the most humiliating night of my life, I must've misheard her. "What?"

"He aimed that first ball at you. I saw him." She tossed her hair and patted my shoulder condescendingly. "It's okay, Jen. Really, you might have had a shot with Justin if I weren't here. He does seem to like you well enough."

Why did they take our microphones?

I fumed for a split second, until I realized I could also speak my mind without being caught. Justin wasn't Dominic, and Ariana had no claim on him. I didn't have to give up without a fight this time. A glance around verified that no one else stood nearby.

"You know what I like about you, Ariana?" I pitched my voice so she could hear me over the music without having to get any closer to her.

"What?"

"Nothing. I can't wait until we send you home. You are a nasty, horrible person."

Ariana sniffled. "How could you say such a horrible thing to me? You're so mean!" She dropped to the ground and sobbed into her knees.

What the. . .? Oh no.

Everyone stared at us. The room had gone silent when the producers paused the music. Bella stood poised to ask someone a trivia question, but everyone heard me.

My face flamed. The whistle blew, and the music resumed. Ed joined us on the sidelines. He started to say something, but I shook my head and inched farther down the wall. Tears of humiliation stung my eyes.

What was I thinking? I knew she was an actress. She was putting on a show for the viewers. Of course.

I cheered for my team mechanically, not focusing on the game. Why had Justin aimed for me? Did he want to send me home?

The second game went much better. By hanging in the back and ducking frequently, I made it to the end. But in the third game, a ball again hit me early on. I didn't see who threw it, but I suspected a busty brunette with a bad attitude.

After the final game, we lined up to hear the results. Ariana had the shortest amount of time overall. I came in second-to-last. Abram won two games and came in second in the third, so he won immunity again.

"Way to go, Abe!" Rachel high-fived him so enthusiastically she bounced backward across the trampoline and fell on her butt against the far wall. She sat, hard, and burst out laughing. Raj and Ed helped her to her feet as we all hid grins.

The other results didn't matter. Me versus Ariana. Could I beat her in a popularity contest? Sure, in the challenges, I could outwit her, but this was different. I had to convince the other contestants they'd rather have me around than the sultry, leggy siren.

I wished everyone hadn't heard me yell at Ariana. She was too good at playing the victim. Briefly, I considered bribing the other contestants with more cookies.

A terrible thought struck me: Who would Justin vote for? He definitely threw the ball at me in the first game. People usually aimed for the players they wanted to get out. Just like I did.

When the results were revealed, would I find out he'd chosen the woman he wanted in the house, and I wasn't her?

* * *

For the next few days, I couldn't sit still. My legs jiggled any time I sat. In the kitchen, I tapped my fingers on the counter so loudly Ed sent me to run laps around the yard. Even in the hot tub, I played with my hair.

Birdie and Ed were on my side, but I couldn't figure out how to count the votes until we knew who I was up against. At the moment, I only knew of three votes against Ariana. She would undoubtedly vote against me. I worried Justin might, too. I couldn't read him.

As much as I liked spending time with him, I couldn't be sure he felt the same way. Maybe he only hung around me to make Ariana jealous. Or maybe he wanted to set up a love triangle for the viewers. This was, after all, first and foremost a game. TV viewers liked drama, especially love stories.

On Monday morning, we learned the viewers nominated Raj for elimination.

That didn't make much sense to me, but I hadn't been paying attention to him during the game.

I followed Birdie and Ed into the kitchen. "Raj, really? Didn't he win the first game?"

Birdie started a pot of coffee, and Ed began to chop vegetables. "He got hit with a ball in the first game and the refs didn't notice. He stayed in the game. Rachel called him a #cheater."

"Ohhhh, wow. I can see why America might not like that. Especially after Joshua. Is this house full of cheaters?"

Ed shrugged, pulling eggs out of the fridge. "It's dodgeball. It's practically a rule to pretend not to have been hit if you think you can get away with it. The ball glanced off his foot. It's possible he didn't feel it, especially on the trampoline."

The faint hope that had been building within me vanished. "So you don't think he cheated?"

"No, not really." Ed tested the pan, then cracked an egg into it. A sizzle sounded as a delicious aroma filled the air. "But don't worry, Jen. I'm still voting for Ariana. She hates me because I'm immune to feminine wiles."

Birdie brought a stack of mugs to the counter. "We might be better off talking everyone into voting for Raj. Sorry, Jen, but Ariana is #playingthegame well."

"She really is. Look at how she set you up. No one heard her goad you, but we all got an earful of you calling her a horrible person." Ed grinned, and my face flushed. "It was amazing. I'm thinking about making it my ringtone when I leave. Someone has to post the video on YouTube."

"It's not my fault! She's a professional actress." Briefly, I filled them in one what I learned before the show started. "My best friend and I watched her movies. Her acting's definitely improved."

"That explains a lot. She's good at manipulating the audience."

"Don't forget the way she plays the victim whenever possible," Birdie chimed in. "'Abram ate the last cookie! They're all such bullies! Wah!'"

"So what do I do? Tell everyone she's a professional?"

Ed said, "It might not make a difference. Actress or not, she's here to play the game, and she's doing well. Raj is a loner. It might be easier to get people to vote for him. Deal with one week at a time."

I sighed. He was right. I didn't want to go home yet, and I didn't like being up for elimination. But if America wanted Raj to go home, maybe I could use that to my advantage.

"Well, you won't have to convince me." Rachel stood in the entrance to the kitchen, wearing a light green cover-up that made her tanned skin glow. Her blond hair lay in twin braids down her back. I'd felt about six years old when I wore the same look, but it worked for her.

"Sorry, I smelled coffee. Not eavesdropping." She walked around the kitchen and pulled a stack of plates from a cupboard. "My vote goes to Raj. I definitely hit him. I bet Abe's with me."

After breakfast, Ariana permanently attached herself to Justin, so there was no way to ask about his vote. Every time I turned around, she was bringing him a drink, lounging next to him on a raft, or watching him like a hawk.

Even if I hadn't been developing a huge crush on him, it irked me. I had to keep reminding myself that I wasn't here for love. After what happened with Dominic, I might never be ready to trust someone again. And this situation didn't exactly breed trust and honesty.

If only Justin weren't quite so cute. Charming. Funny. Or if that lock of blond hair wasn't always falling adorably across his forehead. Or if his lips weren't so soft and kissable.

I shook myself mentally. That kind of thinking got me nowhere.

Instead I tallied the votes in my head: Birdie, Ed, and I were voting for Ariana. Rachel and Abram were voting for Raj. Maria would probably vote for Ariana. They had a weird, unspoken grudge match like the ones that sprung up between the prettiest girls in high school (who always became "best frenemies"). Raj was pissed he couldn't vote for Rachel, since she accused him of cheating.

So, Ariana had three or four votes, Raj and I each had at least two, and Mike refused to tell anyone what he thought. I would've respected him for it if I hadn't had been so terrified that my time in the Fishbowl might be coming to an end. If I were eliminated this early in the game, I had no idea what I'd do when I got home.

Chapter 11

Scenes from the School Room, Week 3:

Maria: *The capital of Burundi is Bujumbura. Why?*

Ariana: *The others are all so mean to me. Jennifer uses big words I don't know to make me look dumb. Why do they make fun of me? It's not fair. I can't help if I'm not smart. It was so embarrassing when she yelled at me! She's a big bully. And I thought Justin and I had a real connection, but he ignores me when she's around. I want Jen to go, ASAP.*

Raj: *I honestly didn't feel a ball hit my foot at any point during that game. There was no whistle. But I don't think Rachel would lie about it. There was a lot going on, I could've missed it.*

Birdie: *Thanks for adding the trivia to the dodgeball game so those of us who aren't super athletic had a chance. #Brainsnotbrawn*

The pending elimination haunted me, making sleep impossible. I tossed and turned until Maria slipped something under my pillow. A tiny, hard oval.

It felt like a pill, but that didn't narrow it down much. Could be anything from Lortab to birth control to Viagra. I wondered if Maria would try to poison me.

Probably not, but I should know what I held before I considered taking it.

Since my restlessness bothered at least one person, I inched toward the door. Clouds blocked the moonlight filtering through the glass. One hand against the wall, I felt my way to the ground floor.

My eyes adjusted enough in the dim light to navigate into the kitchen. I wondered what time it was, but no clocks hung in the Fishbowl. We told time based on our stomachs and the sun. If the producers wanted us to be somewhere, they blasted alarms. Heck, I only kind of guessed what day it was.

A silent, empty kitchen greeted me. I flipped on the lights and examined the pill Maria slipped under my pillow. Xanax? I laughed. Thoughts of the elimination kept me awake, but I didn't need anti-anxiety pills. With a shrug, I dropped it into the sink. Then, I grabbed a beer from the fridge and went outside. Maybe it would calm me enough to sleep.

The clouds shifted, allowing the moon to illuminate my path to a chair by the pool. No reason to turn on the outdoor lights. I leaned back, put my feet up, and sipped my beer, wondering if this was how I'd spend my last night in the Fishbowl. Not a bad way to pass some time, even if I didn't know where I'd go once I left. To Brandon's couch, probably.

When the patio door behind me slid open, I jumped about a foot.

"It's okay. It's just me. I thought you might want to see a friendly face."

The moon sat high in the sky. As Justin walked toward me, I wondered if I'd fallen asleep and started dreaming, like in the airport. Could I pinch myself without him noticing?

"Hey," I said. "What are you doing up?"

"Couldn't sleep. Then I heard someone walking around, so I came to investigate. I'm glad it's you." He sat sideways on the chair next to mine, facing me.

My heart beat faster.

Calm down, Jen. He hit you with the first ball, and this isn't third grade. Boys aren't mean to girls they like. Not the kind of boys I want to date, anyway.

"You okay?"

I didn't want to like this guy, especially when it was clear Ariana was into him—and there was some weird tension between them—but I couldn't help it. My pulse sped up every time he looked at me. Not that I could tell him that.

"I hate to say it, but I'm a little freaked out about the elimination tomorrow. I thought a beer would help me relax." I took a sip and fanned my face, wondering if it was the beer making me warmer.

"Well, you know, it's a good thing I'm here. You shouldn't drink alone."

"But you're not drinking."

Justin leaned forward and took the bottle from my hand. He took a long swallow, then handed it back. "Now I am."

"Excellent." I turned the bottle to sip from where his lips had touched the rim. Juvenile, yes. I didn't care.

"So, I really wanted to talk to you. Without everyone else around."

"Really?" I struggled to keep my tone casual.

"In that first game—"

"Ah, yes. You tried to get me eliminated."

"No, I didn't."

"You thought you were throwing at someone else?" Now I'd gone from "casual" to "petulant," but it beat showing my infatuation.

"No! I mean, not exactly." He ran one hand through his hair and took a deep breath. "This is all wrong. Yes, I threw the ball at you."

"I saw that. Or rather felt it. Right here." I showed him a spot on my elbow. Since he'd helped put me up for elimination, I wasn't feeling gracious.

"Can you let me explain?"

His frustrated tone took the wind out of my sails. I had no right to give him crap for playing the game. "I'm sorry. Continue."

"I had the blue ball—literature. Ariana was aiming for you with the purple ball. I knew if I hit you first, she'd throw at someone else. You were one of the only people who brought a book to the audition, and you've admitted not being into current music. I figured you'd have a better chance with a lit question. I know it's stupid, but I wanted to help."

I couldn't believe he'd even noticed the book poking out of my bag at the audition, much less that he'd remembered it.

"What you did was make me wonder if we're friends."

"Yeah, I see that now. I screwed up. I'm sorry."

I dragged on my beer and didn't answer. Could I believe him?

He moved to the edge of my chair and squeezed my hand. "Please forgive me. I don't want you to leave. I want to be friends."

Justin met my eyes squarely, without a hint of evasion. The blackness of his pupils swallowed his gorgeous green eyes. His hand warmed mine. When I realized how close our faces were, I blushed. Nervously, I wiped my palms on my shorts. Did he feel the same connection I did, or was this all part of the game?

"I want to believe you, but I don't know."

"Jen, I'm so sorry if I played any part in you being up for elimination. If you leave now, I'll never forgive myself."

He touched my chin with two fingers, bringing my gaze up to meet his. Damn those green eyes. I searched them for answers, wishing I knew whether he was putting on an act for the audience. Even with the lights off, the cameras stationed in the yard would capture us. The producers filmed everything, day and night. Everyone in America would know if we kissed. For a moment, I struggled to remember why that was bad.

"I guess it's not your fault, since I got the question right," I said begrudgingly, shifting slightly backward.

"If that is the best I can get, I'll take it. But I'm going to work on complete forgiveness. I'll pay you double interest on our bet—six cents."

"Well, then," I laughed. "Maybe I'll have to reconsider once I get my money. I'd hate to have to send Birdie to break your kneecaps."

The image of five-foot-tall Birdie coming after Justin with a baseball bat cracked him up. I laughed, too, crossing my legs and settling more comfortably in the lounger. My knee practically touched Justin's leg. He didn't move.

We sat quietly for a few minutes. I wondered if he heard my heart pounding. Even not wanting to get caught kissing on national television with a near-stranger, I found something about Justin irresistible. Possibly his smile. Or his dimples. His brains. The ease of talking to him. His personality. The fact that he was practically perfect for me in every way.

That line of thinking wasn't helping. I needed to change the subject before I started calling him Mary Poppins.

"It's a beautiful night." I gestured at the sky.

"Yes, it is," Justin said, his eyes never leaving my face. Did he lean forward slightly? Only inches separated our lips.

The warmth definitely wasn't the beer. I licked my lips nervously and leaned in, closing the gap. If he moved the tiniest bit. . .

"So—"

Floodlights blazed across the yard. We both jumped and sat upright. Spots danced before my eyes. When my vision finally cleared, I wished it hadn't.

The patio door now stood open. Ariana posed in the doorway, wearing only what appeared to be a washcloth. She sauntered toward us.

"Hey, guys. I'm sooooo sorry to intrude. Hope I'm not interrupting. I didn't know anyone was out here. It's such a beautiful night, and I wasn't tired, so I wanted to go for a quick dip. I expected to be alone."

She gazed at Justin from beneath lowered lashes. The tip of her tongue moistened her lower lip.

When I changed for bed, I'd been thinking about the elimination, not seduction. With dismay, I compared my blue-piped gray tank top and shorts to Ariana's lack of clothing. Until about five seconds ago, I'd thought these were super cute summer pajamas.

Ariana turned her back to us and adjusted her towel. She tossed her silky black hair over one shoulder. "This is so embarrassing, you guys. I wasn't expecting anyone else to be up, so I didn't stop to put on a swimsuit. I figured they wouldn't run the cameras late at night. The cool water feels so delicious on my naked body. Don't you love it?" She stared at Justin, like I wasn't there.

I couldn't believe her nerve. I would never in a thousand years interrupt two people about to kiss—probably—by ripping my clothes off and inviting them to ogle me. Because I'm not pure evil.

A million nasty responses filled my brain, but I couldn't let her get the best of me again. Instead, I said, "I'm going to bed. Good night, Justin."

Ariana shook out her hair and moved to open her towel, but I'd seen enough. I rotated on one heel and walked toward the house. Justin moved to follow me.

"Oh, shoot!"

We both stopped to see what the problem was. Mentally, I cursed myself for not ignoring her.

"My microphone's tangled in my hair. Justin, could you help me, please?"

Lucky she didn't ask me. I would've cheerfully strangled with her with the damn thing.

"Sure, no problem," he said.

As Justin moved toward her, I stalked into the house.

By the time I got to my bed, tears of anger and frustration stung my eyes. I wiped them away, not wanting to give Ariana the satisfaction of making me cry. It didn't matter that she couldn't see me.

After a few minutes, I lost the battle. Silent tears flowed down my cheeks. No matter how much I told myself I didn't care about Justin, that I didn't need or want a summer fling right now, my heart overruled my brain.

Miserably, I closed the curtains around my bed, pulled the sheet over my head, and hugged a starfish pillow to my chest. I forced myself to breathe deeply.

A memory flashed before my eyes. Some show, a couple of years ago. Strangers living together in a big house. Early on, two of them got drunk and hooked up. The guy regretted it. The girl spent the rest of the show making moony eyes at him. I'd been so embarrassed for her I'd spent half the season watching while peeking out from under a throw pillow.

Maybe, even though I hated her, Ariana had saved me the humiliation of making out with someone I barely knew on camera. Maybe I should thank her.

Maybe.

* * *

My half-hearted attempt to cheer myself up evaporated overnight. I woke in a foul mood. In the bed beside me, Ariana snored lightly. I resisted the urge to check to see if she'd done her makeup before going to sleep.

Maybe I could stick her hand in warm water, like in camp.

Instead, I showered and dressed and went down to the kitchen. Ed and Birdie were already up, making breakfast. For once I didn't help. When they greeted me, I waved my hand and grunted. I poured coffee, then flopped on to a stool and scowled at my mug.

"Okay, seriously, what's wrong?" Ed whined. "You can't be this upset about the vote, because you know you're not going home."

"Honestly, if going home means getting away from that horrible cow, I'm starting to think it's okay."

In a whisper with one eye on the doorway, I filled them in on what happened during the night. When I got to the end, Birdie gasped and dropped the spatula. It took her a moment to recover enough to speak.

"No way!" she exclaimed. "No way he fell for her act. You know he was right behind you on the stairs."

"Yeah, really, Jen, you should have waited. You might have gotten to talk to the guy, and you wouldn't have to wonder."

I sighed heavily. "Why? We're not dating, he doesn't owe me anything, and I don't want to seem crazed with jealousy."

"But you are," Ed pointed out as he flipped the pancakes. "Wouldn't it at least be nice to know if your jealousy is unfounded? And, for what it's worth, I think it is. He seems to like you."

"You think so?" I hated the whine in my voice. "Ugh. This is so stupid! What am I doing? I'm here to win prizes, not pant after some guy! I'm not sixteen anymore! I'm going to send that bitch home, and then I'm going to win $250,000!"

"That's the spirit!" Ed cheered as he placed a plate of pancakes in front of me.

I smothered the stack in maple syrup and dug in. Whatever happened during the day, I'd need my strength.

"Uh, Jen? Those were for everyone."

Oops.

Guiltily, I pushed the stack toward the middle of the table. "Any chance the cameras missed that?"

The voting began after breakfast. When I entered the booth, I didn't hesitate. I snatched my container of fish food off the shelf and dumped every last piece of green glitter into the bowl with Ariana's picture on the front. Too bad the producers counted the colors in each bowl and not the volume. Still, I found it satisfying to violently shake glitter into the bowl decorated with her smug, smiling face.

Even after I emptied the container, I shook it again for good measure. And again. Then I dropped the plastic jar into the bowl before leaving the room.

Waiting for the results was sheer torture.

I wanted to talk to Justin, but Ariana made sure that never happened. She followed him around like they were handcuffed together. I couldn't figure out why he let her, since he stiffened whenever she spoke. Surely, if he didn't enjoy the attention, he'd tell her to leave him alone. Was he talking to her for the show? Or to me? Or both? Maybe the whole thing was an act.

The night before, I could've sworn he felt something. I was sure he'd been about to kiss me before we were interrupted, but maybe I'd transferred my feelings on to him.

Since I couldn't get a second alone with Justin, I distracted myself. I did Pilates with Rachel, but I was too tense to get into it. After about ten minutes, she got frustrated.

"Seriously, Jen, you need to settle down. You're killing the mood. Either calm down or go do something else."

"Sorry, Rach."

"You're upset about the elimination. I get it. Really, I do. But you can't sit here, all bouncy and jittery. Every time I try to plank, you distract me."

I stood, brushing dirt and grass off the back of my gray yoga pants. "You're right. Sorry."

Rolling up my mat, I returned it to the house. Instead of staying inside with the others, I ran laps around the property.

After I burned some nervous energy, I found Ed by the pool. "Need to practice your comedy routine?"

"Moi? Of course not. I'm naturally hilarious." He glanced around the backyard. "Well, okay, there may be a few new jokes I could try. . ."

Ed cracked me up doing impressions of everyone in the house and talking about reality shows. At one point, I thought Justin watched us from his spot on a raft floating in the pool. Or, I told myself he looked at me instead of sleeping behind his dark glasses. But when Ed improvised Red Sox fans on the subway after a loss to the Yankees, Justin cracked a smile. I knew it.

Before I could beckon to him, the producers called me into the School Room to talk about the possibility of being eliminated. They had me film my reactions to every possible outcome, leaving me both confused and tired. I'm not a great actress—I hoped the responses didn't come across as fake as they felt. Who knew that saying, "I'm really grateful to have made it this far" over and over could be so draining?

Finally, finally, finally, Bella appeared. "Good evening, my little Fish! Are you ready to find out who's going and who's staying?"

"YES!" Perhaps I answered too emphatically.

"Okay! But before I get to that, we have a surprise!"

I wanted to scream and shake her until the results came out. Somehow, I managed to restrain myself. Possibly because Ed stood with his hands on my shoulders, applying gentle pressure. I bit my lower lip.

"For the first time, our viewers have voted to save the eliminated player!"

Fuuuuuuuuuuuuck. I'd forgotten they could do that. My eyes widened as I surveyed the other contestants, who also looked shell-shocked. Who did they save?

Hope fluttered in my stomach. That hope quickly died.

"Congratulations, Ariana!"

Oh, no. The viewers liked her? How? Why?

"That means, tonight," Bella continued, "either Jennifer or Raj will be leaving *The Fishbowl* forever."

Had the producers instructed her to speak as slowly as humanly possible to drag out the pain?

"Jennifer."

I gulped as Bella caught my eyes. It felt like she led me to the gallows.

"You had the second lowest score in the challenge."

She addressed Raj. "You did well in the dodgeball game, but America put you up for elimination, anyway. I'm sorry, Raj, but you had the second highest number of votes from your fellow Fish. You have been eliminated and must leave *The Fishbowl* immediately."

My shoulders sagged with relief. I couldn't believe my good luck. Hopefully, the cameras caught the very real look of relief on my face. The viewers needed to understand how badly I wanted to be here.

As we gathered around Raj to say good-bye, something touched my elbow. Someone said my name quietly. When I turned, Justin motioned away from the rest of the group. Was he going to tell me he didn't want me to stay? Was that a guilty look on his face?

"I wanted to let you know I didn't stay out there last night. With her, I mean. I pulled her hair free, and I bolted. I wanted to catch you downstairs, but you'd gone to bed."

At the thought of him wanting to spend time with me, my traitorous heart lifted. "Thank you."

Still, I couldn't forget that he spent the entire week with Ariana and not a second with me until after everyone else slept. That he stayed to help her the night before. That I'd seen them whispering together a few times, even if he frowned and fidgeted. That he only wanted to talk to me when no one else was around.

With that in mind, I turned away from him. "I need to say good-bye to Raj."

Behind me, Justin mumbled something. To my hopeful ear, it sounded like, "I voted for Ariana."

His tone was low. I couldn't trust that my heart wasn't distorting his words into what I wanted to hear. I didn't turn around.

Chapter 12

Jennifer in The School Room, Week 4:

Being up for elimination freaked me out. I really want to be here.

Finding out my fellow contestants didn't want me eliminated was a huge relief, but they're not the only ones who matter. I need to appeal to America, too. That's tough, because I don't know what the viewers want or how to give it to them. I wish there were some way for the people watching to send me a clue.

I couldn't believe America voted to save Ariana. Maybe they didn't like Raj? He's nice enough, but he kept to himself a lot. That may not be great TV. Meanwhile, Ariana is a total drama bomb. Maybe the viewers like the love triangle?

Pst! Viewers, do you know what's better than a love triangle? A love line. Two people in a relationship are better than three. Wouldn't it be way more awesome if Justin picked me, and no one had to wonder? How can we make that happen?

Early Wednesday morning, the now-familiar alarm called us to the living room. Bleary-eyed, we trudged down the stairs.

Wham!

A muffled yell sounded from the boys' room. Apparently, Ed hadn't put in his contacts yet. There were many glass wall accidents early in the morning, late at night, or when we'd been drinking.

Settling myself on the couch, I watched everyone else stumble in. Did Ariana sleep in full makeup? Had she done her hair before going to bed? She looked like a fashion model—and I knew she was in bed before the alarm. Curiouser and curiouser.

While I studied my enemy, Leanna joined us. "Okay, everyone! Today, we have a mini-challenge! Anyone who successfully completes it will get an advantage in this week's main challenge."

"What's the advantage?" Mike wanted to know.

She smiled mysteriously. "Well, see, we're not going to tell you until after you do it. But it's something you're likely to want."

The front door opened, and a line of assistants walked through with baskets full of produce, headed toward the kitchen.

Leanna continued. "For the rest of the day, you may only eat fruits and veggies. Water is allowed. Sorry, guys, but beer is not considered a vegetable. We'll leave the other foods, but if you give in to temptation, you lose."

I raised my hand. "Leanna, are condiments or dip okay? Like, can we put butter on our veggies?"

"Yes, you can. Olive oil and spices can be used to cook. Salad dressing is allowed. Smoothies are fine, as long as fruit is the primary ingredient. But no meat, beans, bread, etc.

"This is an individual challenge. If you all succeed, you all get the benefit tomorrow and enter the challenge on a level playing field." With a wave, Leanna left. "Enjoy your breakfast, everyone!"

Crap. I forgot to ask if coffee's a vegetable. Coffee grows on a plant, right?

Birdie grabbed my hand and gently tugged me off the couch. "C'mon. Let's go see what we have for this bizarre #diet."

Half-awake, I followed her into the kitchen to unload the baskets. A wide variety of fruits and vegetables awaited us. We wouldn't starve.

Behind me, Ariana crowed about how easy this challenge would be for her. "Before I entered this house, I was completely vegan for fifteen years. It's very easy to avoid meat and animal products if you have self-control. I won't have any problem."

"Ignore her," Birdie advised me. "She's lying."

"How do you know?"

Justin, entering the room, overheard us. "When you don't eat meat for a long time, your body loses the ability to process it. We've been eating eggs, bacon, turkey, hamburger—the works—since we got here. If she hadn't eaten any animal products for years, she'd spend half her time locked in the bathroom."

"How do you know that?"

"My sister was a vegetarian in high school and college. Reintroducing meat into her diet took a long time—and it hurt."

Sweet juice ran down my chin on to the counter as I grabbed a tomato and bit into it like an apple. Ignoring it, I took another bite. "Does she still lose if we tell her cheese is a vegetable? You grow cheese plants in The Sims."

They both laughed, but I wasn't sure I was joking. I couldn't run back into the room five minutes later and accuse her of lying about something she hadn't even said to me. At best I'd look petty, but more likely mentally ill.

First she lied about being a genius, then a vegan. Would America ever see through Ariana's stories? How much longer would we have to put up with her shit before someone called her out? Who did she have to be up against before she got eliminated?

* * *

"Good morning, Fish!"

The next day, Bella gathered us into the living room to prepare us for the Week Four challenge. I was still pissed the viewers saved Ariana. I also couldn't forgive Justin for choosing to spend time with her when we both faced elimination. Especially since Ariana used every opportunity to remind me, constantly giving me knowing looks or making snide comments no one else noticed.

"Most of you did a great job on the midweek challenge." She drew the next word out until it was twice its usual length. "Unfortunately, Maria, I'm sorry, but peanut butter sandwiches are not a vegetable. Neither, Ariana, is bacon, even if you eat it while hiding in the changing room."

I sat up straighter.

"Everyone else, well done!" Bella said, "For this week's elimination challenge, you'll work in teams of three. Maria and Ariana, if your respective teams don't win, you will automatically be up for elimination."

My ears perked up. Automatically?

Can I throw the challenge if I wind up on her team? Without the viewers noticing?

"We'll give each team a disposable camera," Bella said. "You'll get a series of clues directing you to take specific pictures. Careful—these aren't digital cameras. You won't be able to erase pictures taken by mistake. The first team to turn in their camera with the correct pictures wins!"

I smiled to find myself paired with Ed and Rachel. Ed and I grew closer every day. Rachel was far more tolerable now that she wasn't batting her eyes at Joshua. I liked her about fifteen times better since "J-dawg" left.

"Since this is a puzzle challenge, Jen, you should be team captain," Ed said.

A smile spread across my face. He wanted to get me immunity if our team won so I couldn't go up against Ariana two weeks in a row. The gesture filled me with warm fuzzies.

"I agree," Rachel said. "You're one of the smartest people in the house."

"Thanks, guys. I'll try not to let you down."

Leanna walked around, handing out packets holding a set of clues, pencils, and a disposable camera. "Listen up! You can solve clues in any order. You must solve every puzzle to win. If you run out of pencils, I'll have more for you here. If you run out of film, that's unfortunate, because there's no more. Ready? Go!"

"Jen, this one is all you," Rachel said, passing me the paper and a pencil. "Let's find a table where you can work it out."

I read as we headed into the kitchen to find a table. A word search hid the first clue among twenty words hidden in a grid. The remaining letters spelled out the clue.

"I'm on it. This shouldn't take long. You guys look at the other clues."

"This one looks like a cryptogram," Ed said, reading one of the other pages. He took a pencil from Rachel and sat. "I'm all over it."

Once we split up the work, it didn't take long to figure out each of the clues. There was a squicky moment where we worried one clue was directing us to take a picture of Ariana's pink thong, but thankfully, Rachel found her mistake before things got awkward. Instead, we snapped a shot of Abram's green shoe.

After we took the last photograph of the dragon statue in the front yard, Ed and I raced back to the house triumphantly. Rachel skipped beside us, waving the camera over her head.

When we got to the living room, our smiles faded. Maria, Justin, and Mike got there before us. Bella lounged on the couch as Leanna used a portable printer to print out their photos. Mike paced, wiping sweat off his brow. I wondered how long they'd been standing there.

A wave of disappointment hit me. I'd been so sure we won. To hide my feelings, I gazed through the window at the pool. After a moment, Ed tapped my arm.

"Don't give up yet," he whispered. "Listen."

Behind us, Leanna spoke to the other team. "Sorry, guys, but that's wrong."

My ears perked up. I started to turn, but Ed put gentle pressure on my right elbow. "Wait. . ."

Behind me, Bella spoke. It sounded like she'd moved off the couch. "Maria, Mike, Justin, I'm sorry. The winning team is the first one back with all of the right photographs. One of your photographs is incorrect. If either of the other teams turns in the correct six photographs, that team wins."

Muffled cursing traveled from the other side of the room. It sounded like Mike.

"These shoes are killing me," Bella said. "I'm going out to the car until everyone's done. We can shoot all the results at once. I need a smoke."

"But—" The sound of the front door closing cut off Leanna's protest. "Ohhhkayy. Team Three! Stop pretending you weren't listening and come over so I can check your pictures."

I held my breath while Leanna printed each shot. When the picture of the shoe printed, Mike kicked the couch, and Maria groaned. Justin swallowed and rubbed the back of his neck, but said nothing.

". . . Five, and six! That's it! Congratulations, guys!"

We won. As Team Captain, I won immunity!

I hugged Ed and Rachel. We jumped up and down in a circle and cheered, just as the third team entered the room with their results. The scowl on Ariana's face made victory even sweeter.

* * *

Before dinner, I met Ed and Birdie for a quiet celebration. Our hushed cheers brought Justin into the room—or maybe he saw Ed gyrating with his hands over his head and wanted to make sure he wasn't choking.

I poured a glass of wine and grabbed a barstool. "So, Maria versus Ariana, huh? The two pretty girls face off? That should be interesting."

Justin glanced at me. "They're not the only pretty girls here." I blushed. "It's good she didn't do the mini-challenge. It would probably be my ass on the line if she had."

"Why?" Birdie stirred something on the stove. The familiar aroma of cumin drifting from the pot made my mouth water.

"We turned in one of the wrong pictures, and it was my fault. I thought we needed a picture of Rachel's yellow sweatshirt. No one double checked my work."

"I can beat that," Birdie told him. "Ariana wasted half our film taking duck face #selfies. We'd have voted against her no matter what."

"You're kidding!" I couldn't believe she would do something so stupid when she was automatically up for elimination if her team lost.

"Nope. Wish I were. If you were still wondering if she lied about being a genius, stop."

"That's awesome! Here I wanted to ask if you threw the challenge to get her eliminated."

Birdie laughed. "No need. She screwed up all by herself."

This was the best possible outcome: I was safe for another week, and my greatest enemy in the house might be eliminated. Also, Justin thought I was pretty. What a great day.

Chapter 13

Scenes from the School Room, Week 4:

Ariana: *What? They gave us a camera! How was I supposed to know it wasn't digital? What is this, 1992? This is just another example of how everyone else is out to get me.*

Ed: *I'm glad I was teamed up with Jen and Rachel. They're amazing. They made the challenge fun.*

Justin: *Everyone in this house has a different strategy. I don't know what Ariana's is, but she tells these transparent lies, and it's starting to bug me. No, you're not a member of Mensa. You didn't study art history. You're not vegan. What else is she lying about? Besides, every time I try to take two seconds to talk to Jen, Ariana is in the way. So, yeah, I'm ready for her to go.*

Abram: *Yes, we knew these aren't digital cameras. Look, it says disposable on the side.*

On Monday morning, my euphoria at being immune from elimination evaporated. The bells summoned us into the living room, and Bella came in to announce the results of the vote.

"As you know," she began, "Ariana and Maria were named team captains because they did not complete last week's mini-challenge."

Stop telling us what we know, Bella. Get to what we don't know. Who is it?

"Jennifer, you were the captain of the winning team, and as such, you are immune from elimination."

Knowing the cameras would be on me, I smiled and nodded.

"How does it feel?"

"It feels awesome. I'm very proud of my team. We worked well together."

Ed and Rachel murmured their agreement.

"Well, then," Bella continued, "you'll be happy to know that the rest of your team is safe this week. Neither of them were nominated for elimination." She wasn't talking to me anymore, but I flashed smiles at both of them.

So. . .Who is it?

"The viewers have voted," Bella announced. She must have taken lessons at increasing drama. These long pauses killed me.

"I'm very sorry, Justin, but you are up for elimination this week." Not caring that she'd just dropped a bomb, Bella waltzed out of the house.

My heart sank. I poked my head over the side of the tower to where Justin sat, mouth open.

He gave me a sheepish look and shrugged. "Nothing I can do about it. I made a mistake, and we lost. Or maybe America hates lawyers-in-training."

"Well, there is that. You should've told everyone you're a plumber or a fireman. That might have made a difference." My faltering smile failed to hide my concern that he might be leaving.

"Good point," Justin agreed, climbing down. "I'm off to the School Room, so I'll let everyone know I lied about that law school thing."

About ten minutes later, I migrated into the kitchen to help Birdie with lunch. She stuck a glass of Merlot in my hand. It was early to be drinking, but I took it. Taking a deep breath, I swirled the red liquid. Immediately, I calmed. That must've been the effect of the floral bouquet, not the alcohol.

"Drink. Calm. It's okay. Justin's not going anywhere. #Wineisgood."

"It doesn't matter," I grumbled. "Have you seen the way Ariana is all over him?"

"I've seen the way he talks to her just enough to be polite and seeks you out instead. Don't give up yet."

Birdie picked up a knife and started chopping. As usual, she relaxed immediately. Maybe she just needed something to do with her hands now that she'd been detached from her screens.

"Look, Ariana fucked up that challenge. She is single-handedly responsible for our loss." Birdie snorted. "Selfies with freaking #duckface, no less. She looked ridiculous."

"Okay, well, you and I will vote for Ariana. Sounds like Abram will vote for her, too. Ariana will vote for Maria, because she doesn't want Justin to go home before she can figure out how to seduce him."

"Abram will vote for Ariana. He's too nice to say, but he's furious with her. #DontpissoffaMormon."

That made me laugh. At that moment, Ed walked in, shaking his head.

"Ariana just showed me the pictures she took during the scavenger hunt. I guess she sweet-talked one of the producers to get them. Did your team get different clues than we did? 'First clue: take a picture of the most self-centered person you know. Second clue: make the stupidest-looking face you can. Third clue: plank somewhere silly.'"

I glanced at the doorway, wondering who else was out there. Keeping my voice low, I covered my microphone with one hand. "Does that mean you're voting to send her home?"

Immediately, the speakers crackled. "Jen? We can't hear you."

That's the whole point.

Ed smiled at me. "Don't worry about the mics and the cameras. It's not like the viewers can tell the other players what we're talking about. And I doubt the producers would." He tilted his head toward the ceiling. "Right guys?"

The speakers in the ceiling remained silent.

"Besides," Birdie chimed in. "Everyone is having the same conversation somewhere."

"Okay, fine." I repositioned the microphone. "Ed, who are you voting for?"

"Good question. What's your strategy? Do you vote for the person who messed up the most, or do you vote for the strongest competitor? Justin made a mistake, but Ariana's was worse. If we're here to win, do I want to be in the finals against the hot liar or the athletic lawyer? Justin's smart, guys."

Ed paced back and forth, keeping an eye on whoever sat out by the pool and casting frequent glances at the visible areas of the living room. "Or do I want to win against a school teacher who has yet to show us her personality? The other guys are likely to vote for Justin. If I want to keep him around, then I have to decide the best way to do that. Maria's a sleeper. She could bust out at any time and do something so awesome it blows the rest of us out of the water. Do I want to see that?"

He washed his hands and went to help Birdie at the counter.

"And who is America more likely to save? We already know the viewers like Ariana. Do they like Justin more? Apparently not, since they put him up for elimination. It could have been about the challenge, but it also could have been personal. There's no way to know. Do I want to risk wasting a vote on Ariana, when I think it's a vote for Justin? Or do I vote for Maria, knowing it's unlikely America would save her based on what she's shown us so far? A vote for Ariana will likely get Justin eliminated. A vote for Maria probably won't."

His answer impressed me. He made some points I hadn't considered. Maria was nice enough, but she hadn't bonded with anyone in the house. She'd gotten along with Raj, but he was gone. She drifted from one group to the next. She didn't participate much in group discussions. She hadn't shown much personality to anyone, including, I guessed, the viewers.

If everyone voted for Maria, America wouldn't save her, unless the producers gave her an amazing edit. I didn't see it. She flew too far under the radar. On the other hand, if we split the vote into Ariana and Justin, we'd guarantee one of them would go—probably Justin. It might be better for my head, not to mention my heart, if he left now, but I couldn't stand the thought of seeing him go.

"But Ariana is a terrible human being!" I whined.

"To be fair, she's not as bad as Joshua. I'd take another week of her over him any day."

"That's because she's not trying to seduce your almost-not-quite-should-be boyfriend," I grumbled.

"I'd like to see her try!" Ed said. "I get that you hate her. She's obnoxious. She's a liar, and not a good one. She tells stupid lies that insult our intelligence. But she's also got a fan base."

Who watched the show? College guys who would to save Ariana so they could keep ogling her every week? Bored housewives and tween girls who were as infatuated with Justin as me? Did America vote for Justin because they were tired of the love triangle?

Would the producers rig the vote and eliminate Maria, to see if they could squeeze more drama out of the three of us? Would they do that?

Of course they would. I'd quickly learned that the "reality" show business was a lot less about reality than about entertainment, manipulation, and ratings. After all, in reality, I seldom had to share a shower with a stranger to get hot water. Or eat only what random people chose for me. I also spent very little of my time at home in Seattle trying to decide who to remove from my life permanently.

Maybe I should have spent more time thinking about removing people like Dominic.

"And don't forget," Birdie chimed in, "America saved Ariana last week. Would they turn on her so fast?"

Unfortunately, this point hit on the most important fact available to us. For some reason, the fans liked Ariana—or, at least, they'd wanted to keep watching her. Probably because she was beautiful and caused lots of drama. Did they like her more than Maria? Why had they voted to put Justin up for elimination?

If my thoughts whirled any faster, I might fall over.

"Thanks, guys. You've given me something to think about." I tilted my head and downed the wine in one gulp. "If anyone needs me, I'll be in the hot tub until lunch."

The afternoon dragged as I agonized over whether the satisfaction of voting for Ariana outweighed the risk of backfiring and sending Justin home. On top of that, my inability to get any time alone with Justin made me want to bang my head against the wall. I'd hoped for a chance to talk, just in case, but Ariana followed him everywhere.

After lunch, I found her sitting in the small sitting room outside the School Room while Justin gave an interview. She pretended to be doing her nails, but she couldn't fool me.

I barely refrained from asking if she followed him into the bathroom, too.

If he left, I'd have to say good-bye in front of everyone after the results were announced.

An hour before the vote, Rachel found me jogging laps around the backyard. I was huffing and puffing away, face burning, hair stringy and sticking to my face, when Rachel pulled up beside me looking as if she'd stepped off the pages of a Lululemon catalog.

Sometimes, I had to remind myself not to hate her. But, after spending the first two weeks of the show supporting Joshua and apologizing for him, she'd redeemed herself remarkably. I liked her more every day.

Rachel fell into step beside me. Since she'd never joined me on a run before, I figured she had an ulterior motive. "What's up, Rach?"

"Okay, look. Birdie and Abram are voting for Ariana. They're pissed she blew the challenge and, honestly, she deserves to go home. Mike is voting for Justin, because he's a bigger threat. Maria is voting for Justin, because America might save Ariana again. Justin won't say, but he's not voting for himself. Ariana and Ed are voting for Maria. If you and I both vote for her, she's leaving. No one thinks the viewers will save her, least of all Maria."

I have no idea how she managed to get all that out while jogging. I felt like keeling over at my nice, steady pace. Rachel'd raced halfway across the property, and she wasn't even breathing hard.

"But we both vote for Ariana, she'll have four votes, Justin will have two, and Maria will probably have three, depending on what Justin does. That means Maria goes anyway, but we're stuck with smug Ariana for another week. If we don't agree, everyone could wind up with three votes. Then what?"

Who gave speeches while exercising? I stared at her until my foot caught on a rock. Instead of risking injury, I slowed to a walk.

"What happens if there's a tie?"

"Who knows? They probably make it up. Whatever boosts ratings."

"What if we're wrong? What if America saves Maria?"

"Unless Justin votes for Ariana, they'll tie. And then, again, it's anyone's guess what happens. Voting for Maria is practically a guaranteed extra week with Justin. Ariana's probably not going home either way, so there's a low risk."

"Why are you telling me this?"

"Because I want to beat the strongest competitors, and Maria isn't one of them. In the end, I'd rather be standing next to either Ariana or Justin when they declare me the winner."

I'd seriously underestimated her. This wasn't the blond bimbo she played during the first weeks of the competition. She was smart, calculating—and right.

"Okay," I held out my hand. "You're right. It's a deal. I'll vote for Maria. I'll convince Birdie."

We jogged back to the house. I appreciated that, although Rachel could have easily left me in the dust without breaking a sweat, she kept pace with me all the way across the yard.

Tuesday morning, I picked up my green glitter and surveyed the three fishbowls on the table. I wasn't sure whether I was on board with the whole "fiercest competitor" thing—because, I mean, a win was a win was a win, right?

That $250,000 would spend the same whether I beat Justin or Maria or Fluffy, the pit bull living on the next property.

The numbers worked out, though. In life, trusting the math had rarely let me down. Finally, I sprinkled my "fish food" into Maria's bowl. The others were right.

I peeked in the bowls, looking for other glitter, but the crackling of the speakers made me stand upright.

"Arm's length sprinkling only," a disembodied voice warned me.

Damn. I'd thought I was so sly, pretending to trip and catch myself on the edge of the table. Good thing I never wanted to be an actor.

But, more and more, I wanted to be a reality show winner.

At the end of the day, Rachel's plan worked. Maria got the most votes and was eliminated. We looked appropriately sad for the cameras, but no one expressed any surprise. My sad face didn't have to be faked: being stuck with Ariana for another week caused great disappointment.

We lined up to say good-bye to Maria, who accepted her elimination with grace. She stood in the hall, laughing and joking with Ed.

I hugged her. "I want to let you know I'm sorry to see you go."

"'Cause you were hoping for Ariana?"

"Well, sure. But it would've been nice to get to know you."

"It's all right. I know it's part of the strategy. No hard feelings. I'm glad to have made it this far." To the rest of the group, she said, "Later, y'all! Happy swimming!"

With a wave and a smile, she walked out the front door. Four down, seven to go.

Chapter 14

Jennifer in The School Room, Week 5:

You know, when I signed up for this show, I wanted an adventure. But I had no idea how much fun it would be. Trampoline trivia dodgeball? Awesome! And we rocked the scavenger hunt. I like how the challenges combine mental and physical abilities, so people like Abram and Ariana can't pound the rest of us.

Well, yeah, if it were only about winning, it would be better for me if the challenges were only mental. But the physical aspect is fun. I'm doing well, and I'm excited to see what happens next.

I'm sorry to see Maria go. She was quiet, and maybe not the most exciting person in the house, but she's also reasonably neat and pleasant. In the long run, she would've been easier to beat than Ariana—clearly, since she's gone and Ariana isn't—and I like the idea of sending the stronger players home as early in the game as possible. Of course, I suppose the fact that it's hard to send them home is what makes them strong players.

Wait, that's stupid. Don't tell anyone I said that. Can we reshoot?

On Wednesday morning, the alarm roused everyone when the sun peeked over the horizon. I hadn't managed to put on my workout clothes yet. That meant, unfortunately, I was going downstairs to be televised in my Seattle Mariners boxer shorts and a thin V-neck T-shirt. I supposed it could have been worse, though. Ariana wore some sort of practically see-through lacy teddy.

Having seen her movies, I knew she had no problem being filmed naked. In fact, she'd probably donned that outfit for the purpose of feigning dismay that she was "caught" on camera (with perfect hair and makeup). I had a decent figure, but what I wouldn't give for her self-confidence.

As I headed for the stairs, Ed grumbled on the landing below me. "I hate when they call us before I get coffee. It's so hard to smile and look pretty for the cameras this early."

When I got to the living room, I climbed past Ed on my way up the couch tower and planted a kiss on his cheek before settling on to the top level. "Never fear, Sleeping Beauty. I'll make you coffee when we're done."

He smiled and patted my knee. "You're a true friend. Don't forget the cream and sugar."

Leaning his head against the side of the couch, he promptly went back to sleep. I envied people who could do that.

A moment after we were all settled, Leanna entered. "Your hostess is sleeping," she said with a yawn. "We'll dub her in later, looking fresh and beautiful. I don't have to look fresh or beautiful, so you're stuck with me for now.

"This morning, we have a challenge for you all. Anyone who successfully completes the task will receive a benefit at tomorrow's elimination challenge." She paused for effect. "If you fail, you may find the consequences a bit blindsiding."

That didn't sound good. I nudged Ed to make sure he was awake.

Leanna held up two plastic fishbowls and shook them. Something inside rustled.

"In this bowl," she said, shaking the bowl in her right hand, "I have the names of all of the female contestants. In this bowl"—shaking the other—"I have the names of all of the male contestants. I'm going to pair you up."

She gestured over her shoulder. "The bag behind me contains several scarves. You and your partner will be tied together for the rest of the day. Figure out how to do things. If either of you unties the scarf, for any reason before tomorrow morning, *both* of you forfeit the benefit of the midweek challenge.

"For tonight *only*, the girls may sleep in the boys' dorm and vice versa. I recommend adjacent beds, though, since sharing a twin may not be all that comfortable. Any questions?"

Birdie raised one hand hesitantly. "#Shower? #Bathroom? #Changing?"

Leanna smiled. "You have five minutes to get dressed once I announce the pairs. I recommend clothes that go on and off easily. The larger shower holds two. You can both fit in the School Room if you squeeze. As for the other stuff, be creative. If you don't close the doors all the way, you'll manage."

Huh. How interesting.

I mentally reviewed my wardrobe. My swimsuit tied at the top and neck, so I could put that on to shower. And then, I had a stretchy tank dress. If I pulled one strap over my head and around my shoulders, I could shimmy in and out of it. Maybe. This could work.

Leanna set the boxes on the coffee table. Then, she pulled slips out of the bowls. "Okay, let's see who's up first! Ariana—"

Not Justin, notJustin, notJustinnotJustinnotJustinnotJustin, I prayed fervently.

"—and Ed! Congratulations! Come get your scarves!" A noise on the level below me sounded suspiciously like Ed swearing under his breath.

Ariana wandered up to grab a scarf, and Leanna continued pulling names. "Next, we have Birdie and Mike."

They glanced at each other and shrugged. Birdie already sat on the floor, so she leaned forward half-heartedly to get a pink scarf, which she draped around her neck. Leanna kept pulling names.

"Rachel and Abram! And that means the final pair is Jen and Justin. Come on up, guys."

My pulse quickened at her words. I was about to spend twenty-four hours literally tied to the guy who made my heart go pitter-pat and my brain go, "What?"

As soon as Leanna released us, I ran upstairs and put on my halter swimsuit. One of the production assistants bound me to Justin, who wore only swim trunks. I refused to let my eyes follow the trail of blond hair bellow his belly button. If I was already checking him out, how would I ever make it through the whole day?

In the shower, Justin barely looked at me. We were alone, together, surrounded by sexy steam and soap bubbles, in one of the only places cameras wouldn't record us, and it felt as erotic as showering with my brother. Disappointment flared within me. He really must be pretending interest for the audience.

While I regained control of my emotions, I blow-dried my hair, trying to avoid blasting hot air in Justin's face. When that fun ended, he stood outside the girls' closet while I discovered I could not, in fact, put on my stretchiest tank top while tied to someone else. With a sigh, I shimmied the shirt down my legs and threw it in a heap on the floor. Justin allowed me to pull him into the room so I could rummage through the hangars. He stared at the back corner, although my bra and panties covered as much as my swimsuit.

Not interested in me in the slightest. I knew it.

Several minutes later, I pulled out something I'd forgotten I owned. "Wait a minute. What's this?"

A stretchy, soft emerald green wraparound dress. The straps wound around my torso to tie around my neck. I'd bought the dress on my shopping trip the day before leaving for the show. Until that moment, I'd forgotten about it, but it worked.

"Can you get into that?" He sounded doubtful.

"Sure I can—there's nothing to step into or pull over my head. I just need help."

Justin averted his eyes while trying to follow my directions. I twisted and contorted myself into the dress. My skin tingled wherever his fingers brushed against me. Silently, I cursed myself.

"You okay?" he asked, tying the top in a bow. "I know it's not exactly perfect."

Better he think the problem was the clothing. "It's close enough."

The dress wasn't wrapped properly, but it covered what I wanted hidden and fit loosely enough to be comfortable, even when nothing else about this situation was.

Justin had no shirt he could pull over his head without the use of both arms, so a few minutes later, we went into the kitchen to make coffee. It took a couple of tries, and he poured water all over the counter, but we managed. We'd just flipped the switch and sat at the table when someone shrieked, pulling our attention to the doorway.

Birdie stormed into the room, Mike trailing behind her with one arm outstretched. Wet hair streamed down her back. She wore only a bandeau top and a skirt.

"God! You're such a pig! What is wrong with you? #Creep."

Once he caught up, Mike leisurely walked to the table, pulling Birdie along behind him. He smirked but didn't answer.

Abram entered the room a footstep behind them, dragging poor Rachel behind him. "Is there a problem?"

"No," Mike said.

"Yes," Birdie said.

Abram pulled himself to his full height of six-feet-about-a-zillion inches, then leaned forward and crossed his arms as best he could. He was so quiet and such a nice guy, I sometimes forgot he was freaking huge. He could snap Mike in half without breaking a sweat. He narrowed his brown eyes to slits and set his mouth in a hard line. He didn't speak, he growled.

"Birdie?"

"That #cretin grabbed my ass when I was trying to blow dry my hair. Now it's going to be all frizzy."

"She bent over right in front of me!" Mike protested.

"That's how you dry long hair!" Birdie yelled.

My mouth dropped. I couldn't believe he'd put his hands on Birdie without permission. And he wasn't contrite. The bastard grinned, showing his teeth. Beside me, Justin gasped softly.

"You know if I untie this thing, you lose, too, right? #Jackass."

"Touch her again," Abram growled at Mike, "and Birdie will spend the rest of the day dragging your detached arm behind her. I don't care if I get sent home. You will not touch an unwilling woman while I'm around."

"Or me," Justin added.

Rachel and I exchanged a look. "Or me," we said.

Mike flinched. "Look, man, I didn't mean anything by it. She was there, her ass was right next to my hand. I thought it would be funny. I didn't think everyone would freak out."

Abram did not break eye contact. "Apologize to her."

Still looking at Abe, Mike insincerely muttered, "I'm sorry, Birdie."

"Don't let it happen again," she said.

"I won't." He finally looked at her.

"I'm glad we understand each other." Abram crossed his arms, still giving Mike a hard look.

For a long moment, Mike glared up at him. Then, he took a step backward. "C'mon, Birdie. Let's go."

He strode angrily out of the room with Birdie trailing behind.

Later that afternoon, Abram and I sat on the side of the pool, swinging our feet in the water. Rachel and Justin floated nearby on rafts, their tethers stretching back toward us. Their feat impressed me, but it wasn't a task I felt prepared to tackle. I was fine, sitting in the shade and watching.

I lowered my voice. "Abram, that was decent, what you did for Birdie earlier."

He blushed and examined the ground. "I didn't do anything. I have six sisters. If I stood back and let him maul her, even as a joke, they would all take turns removing my fingers when I got home." He smiled, clearly trying to lighten the mood. "And then I'd have to spend my entire $250,000 on replacements."

"Well, then, that would certainly make this a summer not well-spent. How would you do construction with no fingers?" My eyes met Rachel's over Abram's shoulder. She mimed pulling Abram into the water, and I nodded. Silently, she held up three fingers.

"Exactly!"

One. "You better practice your synchronized swimming, then. Come on!" *Two.*

"Wha—?"

Three! Whatever Abram had been about to say was cut off. I grabbed his free hand and pushed off the side of the pool, slipping into the water. At the same moment Rachel, yanked on her scarf. He lurched forward, then caught his balance slipped out of my grasp, grabbing the side of the pool with one hand. With the other, he pulled back, sending Rachel topping into the pool. She found herself bobbing on the top of the water, suspended by a scarf. On the other raft, Justin rocked back and forth with laughter.

"You realize I'm bigger and stronger than you and could leave you treading water all day?" Abram said to Rachel.

Huh. Perhaps we hadn't thought things through. She pouted up at him. "You wouldn't really do that to a damsel in distress, would you?"

"To a damsel who *caused* her own distress?"

Out of the corner of my eye, I spotted Ed and Ariana, both in swimsuits, sneaking through the foliage behind us. Ed raised one finger to his lips and shook his head slightly. I smiled.

Rachel spotted them at the same moment I did. "So, Abe, *are* you going to leave me hanging all day?"

Before he answered, Ed and Ariana jumped out from the bushes. Rachel lunged away, pulling on the scarf a second time. They pushed Abram from behind. Unfortunately for them, he was ready. With his free arm, Abram reached up, locking his long fingers around Ed's wrist.

Ed, and by extension Ariana, both tumbled into the pool with him. I laughed. Everyone splashed around me, thoroughly soaking not only me and Rachel, but also Justin, still on his raft. Then Ariana shrieked about getting her hair wet, which only made everyone laugh harder.

* * *

Later that night after changing into our jammies, Justin and I set up a sleeping area in the boys' dorm, primarily to spare the hassle of navigating an extra set of narrow stairs. We were shoving two twin beds together when a flurry of movement across the room caught my eye.

Mike and Birdie stood next to two twin beds pushed together near the far wall. Birdie had a stack of pillows and cushions on the floor in front of her. She'd taken all the cushions off the sofa in the small living room and was constructing a wall between the beds. Mike watched with a bemused expression on his face, not helping.

"Hey, Birdie?" I called. "What on earth are you doing?"

"I'm creating a bootie barrier. I don't want that jerk to let any of his parts stray across the beds into me. Not even by 'accident.'"

Mike made a face. "Dude, seriously, I'm sorry about earlier. I don't want to touch you. I promise. You're not my type at all. I like 'em taller and hotter."

"If it's all the same to you," Birdie replied loftily, "I'm not taking any chances."

I clamped my lips together, but a soft giggle escaped at the look on Justin's face.

"Hey, Jen, do you think we need a bootie barrier?" he whispered.

God no. We need no cameras, an hour alone, and a good Chianti to loosen us both up. Except that was never going to happen.

"I'm good," I said, testing the pillows in search of the softest ones.

Across the room, Birdie grumbled on her side of the "booty barrier." For her sake, I hoped we wouldn't have to spend much more time with our partners.

Chapter 15

Scenes from the School Room, Week 5:

Birdie and Mike: *"I have nothing to say while this Neanderthal is around. #Pervert."*

"Neanderthal? Is that a racist comment?"

"Ummmm, no."

Rachel and Abram: *"Cool challenge. I won't need a stepladder all day."*

"It's cool. I've got four kids. I'm used to short people hanging on me all the time."

Ariana and Ed: *"Wait. Mike did what? I can't believe him!"*

"I knew Ariana was strong, but she's stronger than I am. If anyone's looking for me, I'll be pretty much doing whatever she wants."

As soon as I woke up the next morning, I untied the scarf. Justin didn't stir. I rubbed my wrist for a moment to get the blood flowing. Briefly, I considered asking if he wanted to join me for breakfast, but he looked so peaceful I couldn't stand the thought of waking him. Besides, I needed to process our day.

I showered, dressed, and ate a bowl of cereal in blissful solitude, enjoying the ability to move both of my arms any way I wanted. While I sipped my coffee, the other contestants drifted into the kitchen one at a time.

A few minutes after everyone finished breakfast, the speakers in the corners blared music. That was our signal. Time to get fired up. I danced my way up the stairs to get ready. When the music stopped, we gathered in the living room dressed in workout clothes, ready for the elimination challenge.

Bella greeted us. "Yesterday, you and your partner spent the day learning how to work together. Most of you did well. Good thing you practiced, because today, you're going to need teamwork."

She paused, giving us the chance to look around. "For this week's elimination challenge, there are four stations. You'll learn what you need to do when you get there. You will be judged on each task and ranked at the end. Both members of the losing team will be eligible for elimination.

"Oh, and one more thing. The entire challenge will be completed as a three-legged race. If at any time, one of you unties yourself from your partner, you will automatically be up for elimination."

What if everyone does it? Is everyone up for elimination?

Somehow, asking seemed like a bad idea. I didn't want to give the producers any ideas.

From my position on the couch, I examined Justin. Any hopes he'd be excited at spending another day tied to me were dashed by the sight of him talking to Ariana quietly. For the hundredth time, I cursed myself for being a lovesick fool. Our "connection" was a ratings gag. Nothing more.

Bella clapped her hands. "Okay! Everyone get to your first station, and we'll get you all tied up."

Ed winked as we walked toward the backyard. "All tied up, huh? I like the sound of that."

"Be careful what you wish for., Rachel retorted from behind me. "I was the Sioux City Junior Miss Hog-tying Champion in 2003."

"Really? That's fascinating. Will you teach me how to do a sheet bend?" Rachel giggled.

I missed her reply as one of the production assistants directed us down a path on the right side of the property, opposite the maze.

When we got to the first station, I spotted two tables about the size of card tables, set about a football field apart. A small wooden crate sat on top of each table.

Once my right leg was securely tied to Justin's left, Curly Beard explained the task. "Okay, you start here. At the first table, each of you picks up an egg and a spoon. Then, you turn around and carry your eggs in the spoons to the box at the other end. If *either* of you drops an egg, you both go back. If you lose the other egg, too bad. You'll be ranked based on how many eggs you get into the box in under ten minutes."

Justin smiled. "That doesn't sound too difficult."

I nodded. I'd done this at summer camp at Lake Washington. Fifteen years ago. When we got the signal to go, Justin started for the box—and I promptly fell on my face.

"Oops! Sorry!" He picked me up.

I focused on brushing myself off so he wouldn't see my blush. "It's fine. Let's try going slower, okay?"

"Sure. I forgot your legs are shorter than mine."

I stuck my tongue out at him. "Right. Let's go."

We started walking again. I fell on my face again. This was harder than it looked.

Finally, on the third try, we made it to the first box. We each picked up a spoon and placed an egg. We turned and—

Splat! Justin's egg smashed to the ground. We started again. This time, we made it four steps.

After a couple of minutes, we managed to work out a system. Finally, we got the first pair of eggs into the box. Mine broke as I slid it into the crate. I wondered if it would count, but it was too late to worry about it. We turned and raced back to the starting point. We fell. We stood and walked quickly to the starting point. That worked much better. A couple of minutes later, we had two more eggs in the box.

When we finished the third pass, I glanced at the clock. Only two minutes left. Things weren't looking so good. I sighed as we turned to head back to the table containing the eggs one last time.

"Hold on a sec.," Justin said. I stopped. "They said we have to go back and forth together, right?" I nodded. "Did they say we *both* have to walk?"

I gave him a confused look. "What do you mean?"

"I can carry you a lot faster than this, even with our legs tied together. Quick. Don't move."

Without waiting for me to agree, he bent and turned, wrapping one arm around my waist. When he stood, my legs came off the ground. There was enough slack in the ties for my right leg to slide up, leaving the scarf tied around my ankle. We were still tied together, but he could move.

Our faces were only inches apart. His pupils dilated. I knew he felt something! With just the slightest movement on my part, we'd kiss.

"You okay?"

"Better than okay." I smiled down at him, silently begging him to close the gap. More than anything, I wanted that scarf to disappear so I could wrap my legs around his waist, bury my hands in his hair, and sink into him.

The air hummed with electricity.

"Great," he said. "Let's go."

Oh, right. We still had a challenge to complete. I hope he didn't feel my heart thumping against his shoulder.

Justin started to move. Surprised at his strength and speed, I grabbed his shoulders and held on for dear life. Then, he jogged with me back to the first table. He set me down, we grabbed two more eggs, and he carried me back to the first box in time to deposit our last two eggs as the buzzer sounded.

Curly Beard motioned us to the sidelines and dug through our box. He tossed out a shell and kept poking.

After a moment, he raised his head. "Seven!"

Without any idea what the others would score, we couldn't know if that number was any good. Still, we high-fived and cheered as if it were the best result in the world. If we beat the others, they'd use the footage. If we lost, they'd show us looking silly.

The second challenge took place on another large field, this one with a row of targets set up at each end. A table in the middle held bows and arrows with everyone's assigned color. White lines divided the field into sections.

I suddenly wished I'd spent more time playing darts in the games room. Not that I had any idea if darts skills translated to archery prowess. A product-ion assistant I didn't recognize approached and explained the challenge.

"Okay, see those targets?" He pointed as he spoke. "Girls' targets are to the right. Boys' targets are to the left."

He continued, "Your targets are the second ones from the front of the field. Jen, you get green arrows, and Justin, yours are blue. You'll walk to the table and pick up one bow and one arrow only. Then, you walk to the line and fire. One arrow at a time. Alternate targets.

"You have six chances to hit the target three times. We'll score the first three arrows of each color to hit. You get zero points for hitting the wrong target. You get zero points for using the wrong color arrow. Your scores will be added together. You've got eight minutes."

"By the way," he added with a smile and a wink, "each contestant must keep at least one foot on the ground at all times."

Damn. No more sexy times, apparently.

"When the light turns green, you're off."

I put my left arm around Justin's waist and adjusted his arm on my shoulder. When the light changed, we were ready. By now, we tottered along well enough.

"Do you want to shoot first?" I asked as we hobbled toward the table.

"Nope. Ladies first. You grab the bow; I'll find an arrow."

The arrows lay scattered all over the table. As I reached for the bow, my trembling hand sent a stack tumbling to the ground. I swore under my breath.

"Don't worry about it," Justin said. "We'll dig through them later. Look, here's a green one."

Back and forth we went, moving steadily if not with any grace or speed. My first arrow missed the target by about a foot.

"Aim lower next time," Justin suggested.

"Thanks for the tip." I laughed as we walked toward the table to pick up another arrow. "Here I thought the arrow soaring over the target meant I should shoot to the left."

He made a face but didn't respond.

The first blue arrow sailed into the middle of the bull's-eye. "Nice shot!"

Justin smiled. "I played on the archery team in high school. Taught archery to middle school kids."

Wow. My hot lawyer had a sensitive side. I apologized for laughing at his advice earlier.

"Here. Let me show you."

He moved closer, adjusting the bow in my hands. My body wanted to sag against his muscular frame, but I forced myself to focus on the task at hand. When his hand brushed mine, I inhaled sharply. Justin's eyes met mine questioningly.

"Sorry. That tickled," I said.

He looked skeptical, but the clock ticked down behind us. He helped me set the bow against the string and explained what to do. As long as I blocked out the shivers that went through me when his voice caressed my ear, I'd be fine.

How could this much chemistry be an act? Was it all in my head? Did he truly not feel the same things I did?

With Justin's help, my second shot still missed the target, but it was much closer. His second shot landed about a millimeter from the first. When his second arrow thudded into the target, I let out a breath. Maybe his skill would make up for my lack thereof.

Finally, my third green arrow hit the second ring of the target. It wasn't perfect, but at least my score wouldn't be zero. Justin's third arrow somehow landed between the first two, although I couldn't see how.

"Take your time, aim steadily, take a deep breath, and let it fly. We have plenty of time to do this. There's no need to rush. You can do it."

The ticking clock behind me suggested otherwise, but Justin's words calmed me. Even if it were all for show, knowing he believed in me helped. Not having his arms around me for this third shot allowed me to focus. I breathed in deeply, focused on the target, and set the arrow. I dragged the bowstring back to my right ear. Then, I exhaled and released the string. It worked!

The arrow still wasn't anywhere near the bull's-eye, but it was on the target, and closer than the last one. My fifth shot flew wide and to the right. I took a deep breath to focus my final shot. I pulled the bowstring back, sighted on the middle of the target, and let the arrow fly as I exhaled. My final green arrow flew through the air and landed on the edge of the bull's-eye.

I did it!

* * *

When we approached the third station, angry voices drifted across the field toward us. Birdie and Mike. If this week was about cooperation, one of them might be going home. It was selfish, but I hoped it would be Mike. Birdie and I grew closer every day. Plus, she didn't grab people's asses without permission.

Justin and I rounded a corner, and a burst of laughter escaped me when we got to our third station.

On one of the outside walls of the maze, someone had hung a giant picture of a donkey without a tail.

"Oh, that's awesome!" I said. "It's Pin the Tail on the Donkey!"

"Ready?" The production assistant I thought of as Overalls asked. We nodded. "Okay!" She slipped a blindfold over Justin's eyes, then mine. "Can you see anything?"

I craned my neck, but got only the barest suggestion of light. No grass, no sky, nothing. I couldn't see at all, but I smelled Justin's deodorant, the detergent we all used. Beneath that, I caught a whiff of the unique scent of him. I swallowed hard. This challenge was going to kill me.

"Jen? All good?" Overalls asked.

"I can't see a thing."

"Great. I'm going to spin you around now. One, two, three." While she spoke, someone grabbed my hand and pulled me in a circle. I couldn't be sure they only spun us three times.

What I did know was that, at the moment we were released, I tripped over one of Justin's feet. We went down. We stood. And went down again. Our limbs tangled, parts of him touching parts of me in a way that took my breath away. Not being able to see him only made the sensations stronger.

"You okay?" Justin asked.

"Yeah, I'm sorry. Let's get up. Do you have the tail?"

"Yup. No idea where the maze is, though, or the poster."

We struggled to our feet. "Hold on a sec." I licked one finger and held it up. I have never understood what that was supposed to do. Not surprisingly, it told me nothing. I lifted my face to the sun's warmth.

"Any ideas?" Justin asked. "We have to move before they push us."

"The sun is on the left side of my face," I told him. "The maze is on the south side of the property, I think. And it's late morning. So, left should be east, which means if we go that way. . ."

"Are you pointing?"

Right. He couldn't see me. "Oops. Sorry. Let's try walking straight. Put your arms out and let me know when you feel the maze."

We walked forward tentatively. After about a dozen steps, Justin stopped. "I've got it. Good call."

One more small step, and I touched paper. My hand moved left on to the scratchy wall of the maze. "Here's the edge."

"Great! Where does the tail go?"

"Not a clue!" I stated with certainty.

"Well, I appreciate your enthusiasm. Hold on. The tail was just above my eye level. You're at the edge of the poster, so. . .let's. . .try. . .THERE!" Paper crackled, and something pulled me backward.

We stumbled back a few more steps, me almost hoping we'd fall down again. When Justin stopped, I removed my blindfold.

"Well, we got the tail on the paper." I laughed.

The tail hung in the white area of the poster, about ten inches above the drawing and four or five inches to the left. Nowhere near the donkey.

Justin removed his blindfold as well and shrugged. "Whatever. It's the best I've ever done at this game. There's still one more challenge."

"True, and we're doing pretty well so far."

As we waited for the final station, Justin and I sat in the grass. "What are the odds being dizzy will help in the last exercise?"

I pretended to think about it. "Hmm. Slightly less than the odds of getting cast on a reality show in the first place."

"In that case, we're golden."

Between falling down repeatedly, the laughter, the dizziness, and the presence of the PAs, our sexual chemistry faded into the background.

"Tell me about yourself. You're going to law school?"

"Yeah, in Miami. I grew up there, and my sister still lives nearby."

"Your parents?"

"Happily married for thirty years and still going strong. I hope to be that lucky."

"Me, too." During college, more than one purported psychology major suggested my spotty dating resume came from "daddy issues." It made me hesitate to say more, knowing America watched and weighed my every word. "So you've lived in Florida your whole life?"

"Nah. I went to New Orleans for college, but my mom got sick, so I moved back after graduation."

"I'm sorry to hear that. Is she okay?"

"Yeah. She beat cancer. Twice, actually. Once when I was a little kid."

"That's wonderful. Good for her."

"Fuck cancer," he said.

He looked so sad for a minute, I wanted to lean forward and put my arms around him. Instead, I squeezed his hand, rubbing it with my thumb. My skin tingled from the touch. Our eyes met, and my breath caught in my throat at the longing I saw. Or maybe it was only my own need, reflected back at me.

I'd wanted to kiss him so badly earlier, and I could've sworn he felt the same. But he hadn't made a move. He was here to win, and he was smart. He knew how to play the game. How could I know I wasn't part of that? Was he hyper-focused on the tasks in front of us, or completely uninterested?

I'd been so sure of Dominic's feelings. From the day we met, I never doubted his loyalty, his desire for me. And then I'd found out he wasn't loyal at all, that desire didn't equal love, and that the whole thing was a lie. Maybe one day I could trust again, but here? When we were all living an illusion? Hoping any of this meant anything felt naive at best.

I should just woman up, strap on some ovaries, and ask Justin how he felt. The show handed me the perfect opportunity by giving us this alone time, and I might not get another one. I dropped the grass I'd been absent-mindedly twisting with my free hand. "Hey, Justin?"

"Yeah?"

Before I could figure out exactly what to say, one of the PAs caught my eye and pointed around the wall separating us from the task. I forced a smile, hoping my voice didn't reveal my disappointment at the interruption. "It's time to go."

The final station contained a three-foot cube sitting in the middle of a giant platform. That was odd. Were we solving a giant Rubik's cube? That didn't have any colors on it? Okay, maybe not.

The PA pointed at the giant cube. "Each side of this cube has a different puzzle on it, based on one of your fellow competitors. The pieces are in that pile over there. You're allowed to carry up to one piece at a time each." He gestured at two teetering stacks of cardboard about ten yards away.

"There's a puzzle on each side of the cube, including the top and bottom. Your score is based on how long it takes you to put all the pieces together."

As he explained, I bounced on my toes, clapping. I loved figuring things out! None of the other stations had been the type of thing I excelled at, but this looked easier than the "Polar Bear in a Snowstorm" puzzle my brother gave me for a college graduation present.

"It's not enough to make the pieces fit. The puzzle has to make sense. When you're done, hit the button." He gestured to a large red button on the opposite side of the cube from the pieces. "If everything is right, it'll turn green, and a bell will chime. If it's wrong, go back and find your mistakes. Stand over here. When the light turns green, you're on!"

A moment later, we headed to the cube. Slowly but surely, the puzzles took shape. One side included a yellow bird; another depicted tools and a Bible. We did all four sides first, then turned the cube to tackle the top and bottom. When I placed a piece with a woman on a stage next to the Brooklyn Bridge, I wondered what my puzzle looked like.

What did I represent to the other contestants? How did the producers see me? Was I just a big Space Needle or was there something more? A stack of hospital bills? An unemployment check?

Finally, we placed the last piece and hobbled as quickly as possible toward the button. I hit it with all my strength.

Nothing happened.

We waited. Justin pushed the button. Still, nothing happened.

"One of the pieces must be wrong," he said. "C'mon!"

The side facing us showed Birdie's puzzle, which looked fine. They'd even colored the Twitter logo yellow to create a bird dominating the centerpiece. We moved on to Ed's puzzle on the next side. Again, everything fit: the New England Patriots logo and a microphone.

Something about that jumped out at me.

"Justin? What does Mike's puzzle look like? Is there a microphone?"

"Didn't we give Ed the microphone because he's a comedian?"

"We did, but maybe it's not right. Mike sings, remember?"

Carefully, Justin shifted the cube until he saw the other side. "Right. Mike has a guitar. . .and a coffee cup. He likes coffee, right? Doesn't everyone?"

"Yeah. Is it Starbucks or a California-based chain?"

"Nope, it's Dunkin' Donuts."

The line from the commercials ran senselessly through my head. *America runs on Dunkin.* After a moment, I snapped my fingers. "That's it! Dunkin' Donuts is big in the Northeast. Let's switch these two pieces."

We made the change and raced back to the finish line. Well, we staggered awkwardly at the maximum speed possible. This time, when Justin punched the button, bells rang and a green light flashed. I whooped and bounced on my toes.

We did it!

Chapter 16

More scenes from the School Room, Week 5:

Rachel: *So if both members of the losing team are up for elimination, does that mean both members of the winning team are immune? Abram and I killed it.*

Birdie: *For the love of God, just tell me I never have to spend another second of my life tied to Mike. Lie if you have to. #ICantEven.*

Ed: *None of my friends are going to believe I spent the last two days tied to a hot female masseuse. Nice scarves, though. Very sturdy. By the way, I'm taking them home with me. That's cool, right?*

Justin: *Interesting challenges. What's next? Duck, Duck, Goose? Spin the Bottle? Seven Minutes in Heaven?*

After the challenge, the PAs took us one-by-one into the School Room. I hurried in hopes of catching Justin alone, still wanting to talk to him about what I'd felt during the challenge when he'd put his arms around me. When his breath sent tingles down my spine as he explained the basics of archery. When we tumbled to the ground together. I had to know if this was real or just some figment of my imagination.

On my way downstairs, I stopped to freshen up and check my makeup. Voices echoed while I stood at the sink.

No, not in my head. One of them sounded like Ariana. If I ever started to imagine voices, I certainly hoped they wouldn't sound like Ariana. Anyone else would be preferable. Maybe Kim Kardashian or that guy who played the parrot in Aladdin.

Curiously, I stood to find the source of that noise. The voices came from above me. Aha! Someone had left the window open in the tiny restroom. Ariana spoke to someone on the porch underneath the room.

That porch was. Oh, um, well. We weren't really supposed to talk about it. But, it was the designated smoking area. That patio was the only place in the entire estate without cameras, because the network wasn't allowed to show us smoking on TV. When Joshua was in the house, Maria hung out there purely to get away from him.

I'd never noticed before, but apparently, the porch was also situated to allow a person using the toilet to overhear every word spoken on it, at least if you opened the window.

How did I miss that earlier?

Snatches of conversation drifted into my ears.

". . .love me. . ."

Who is she talking to?

I needed to hear this better. Maybe if I stood directly under the window.

". . .so gullible. . ."

Who is she talking about?

Argh!

I stretched on to my tiptoes, but got little more for my efforts.

". . .viewers eating. . .hand. . .so easy. . ."

Ohmigod! Ariana is out there, telling someone how she is manipulating the viewers and lying to them and I. Can't. HEAR. Her.

I raised my foot, prepared to stomp the ground in frustration. When I realized she might hear me, my foot stopped an inch above the floor. Instead, I braced it against the glass wall. My rubber shoe slipped on the smooth surface. Couldn't climb up that way. I lowered the lid of the toilet and climbed on to it instead. The window was still about a foot over my head. The words became only a little clearer.

". . .don't have. . . daughter . . ."

I examined the window. A tiny rectangle sat a few inches from the ceiling, about six inches wide and two or three inches high. Sticking my head through it would be impossible. Instead, I braced my hands on the edges and placed one foot on the toilet tank.

Another voice, lower, drifted through the window. "So you weren't raped when you were fourteen?"

"Jennifer? What are you doing?"

The voice came from the ceiling. Naturally, the producers would choose this moment to check the camera in the toilet.

Tinkling laughter—the kind that makes you want to strangle the person making it—reached my ears. For a second, her voice got louder. "That's ridiculous. I seduced my father's driver. Poor guy never had a chance."

"Shh! Are you getting this?" I hissed. "She's lying to the viewers to get them to vote for her!"

The lower voice rumbled again. Because the producers distracted me, I missed most of his response. ". . .love triangle?. . ."

"You need to get down before you hurt yourself," the voice said.

"Give me a minute!"

I gripped the window ledge with both hands and hauled myself on to the tank. With one foot wedged against the far wall of the tiny chamber for support, I pressed my face against the window. Not surprisingly, I couldn't see anything. Dark mesh covered the porch on all sides, including the roof.

I held my microphone necklace toward the window and shoved my ear into the opening. Finally, I heard complete sentences. The producers better be picking this up.

"Don't be silly," Ariana purred. "You're the one I want." Wait a minute. Was she out there with Justin?

"I'm just playing up the Justin thing for the ratings. America loves drama."

"Oh, yeah?"

He sounded skeptical. Now that I'd squished my head between the ceiling and the window, the voice had a familiar low, musical quality.

"Why not play up the in-house romance between us? The viewers love that shit. And you have to admit, we are smokin' hot together. We'd steam up TVs all over America."

It was Mike's voice. What were they doing out there?

Lip smacking and a murmur of pleasure drifted through the window.

Oh. That's what.

"Romance doesn't build ratings the way drama does. I want the viewers to want to keep me in the house. So, I tell them that Jen is bullying me and trying to steal the man I have all these feelings for, and they see her sucking up to him, and then they vote to send her home. It's perfect."

I KNEW IT!

I'd never forgiven Ariana for making me look like the bad guy at dodge-ball, and this was my chance to get even. Finally, America would recognize my nemesis as a vindictive liar.

In my excitement, my back straightened, and my head snapped up. I wasn't in the best position to adjust my position. The foot I'd braced against the wall slipped. I teetered on top of the tank before finding myself hanging by my fingertips from the window. My toes smacked against the toilet bowl, creating an unfortunately loud clanging.

". . .hear that. . .?"

Ariana. Crap. She heard me.

". . .nothing. . .don't worry. . ."

For several moments, I hung there, taking deep breaths to calm my beating heart. A door closed downstairs. Footsteps clattered up the stairs. In seconds, a PA would drag me out of the room. I yanked at the ledge, trying to hear more, but gained no ground. Not enough upper-body strength. All that reached my ears was more lip smacking, followed by a low moan. They'd apparently decided to abandon their conversation. I had no reason to hang around.

No pun intended.

I dropped to the ground, determined to get the lying sneak eliminated. Time to find Justin.

But first, the producers wanted an explanation.

Quickly, I relayed what I overheard. The producers understood. It probably helped that Ariana treated them as her personal servants. If I'd needed a reminder in the importance of smiling and saying "please" and "thank you" to people in supportive roles, this was it.

Crossing my fingers behind my back, I swore not to scale any more walls. They let me go.

I tore into the kitchen, praying that it wasn't too late to catch Ariana and Mike together.

Before I found Justin, I ran into Birdie. She was in the kitchen, grinding up vegetables and pounding them into paste. What an interesting way of burning aggravation. I skidded to a halt.

"What on earth on you doing?"

"All these veggies that will go bad if we don't eat them, so I'm making #pasta."

People can do that? I could barely add water to instant soup without help. "Wow. Okay. That's cool. Have you seen Justin?"

Birdie examined my face closely. "What happened?"

After a split second's consideration and a quick glance around, I told her what I overheard. Birdie stopped the grinder, wiped her hands on her apron, and marched toward the back door.

"You, sit. Grab a glass of wine. Not a word to anyone else."

"Where are you going?"

"To have a cigarette, of course." Birdie winked at me.

"But you don't smoke."

"I do now."

The small redhead strode out the door and around the corner of house toward the patio. I was dying to follow her but knew better. Instead, I poured a glass of wine and went to find Ed. If what I suspected was about to happen, I wanted to be far from the patio when things blew up.

Ed, Abram, and Rachel were playing pool while Justin threw darts. I'd barely settled into a chair to watch when Birdie marched in, dragging Ariana by one ear. Mike followed sheepishly.

Lipstick smeared across the side of his face. Ariana's shirt was buttoned crookedly. Her hair was mussed. It was the first time I'd seen her not looking perfect.

Rachel saw them first. "Birdie! What are you doing?"

"#Caughtintheact!" Birdie crowed triumphantly. "I found Ariana making out with Mike on the smoker's porch."

Ariana flushed and glared around the room. "Please. What is this, second grade? We're all adults. I was upset that everyone here always gangs up on me, and Mike stopped to comfort me. It was totally innocent. Nothing happened."

Even if I hadn't overheard the conversation, the state of her clothing belied her words. If they hadn't been making out, Birdie had saved them from a puma attack in the side yard.

As usual when confronted, Ariana turned on the waterworks. "Now let go of me!"

She yanked out of Birdie's grip and ran toward the kitchen. Mike took off after her. I didn't care where they went. Everyone else stared at Birdie in shocked silence.

"Jen, tell them what you heard."

"She was on the back porch, telling Mike about her plan to get me eliminated. She made up having a sick child to get viewer sympathy. And she fabricated a love triangle to create drama."

Justin tilted his head. "She admitted that?"

Across the room, Rachel inched toward the door. Birdie stepped back to let her pass.

"She didn't actually say she has no feelings for you, but she made it clear she's catering to the viewers, yeah," I said.

"Did Birdie hear it, too? Is it on camera?" Justin asked.

Where's he going with this?

Abram followed Rachel. Then, he stuck his head back in and cleared his throat. After a few seconds, a long arm reached back in and grabbed Ed's wrist. As the arm pulled him toward the door, Ed grabbed Birdie and took her with him, leaving me and Justin alone. The door clicked shut.

Palpable tension filled the room. A small, hard pit formed in my stomach.

"No." I stared at my toes.

"So what you're saying is, all we have on tape is you throwing around accusations, and Ariana telling everyone that you've got a vendetta against her?"

Shit. They also have footage of me scaling the wall in the bathroom. For, as far as they can see, no reason.

The pit grew as I wracked my mind for something to say. "Did you know that she's a professional actress? I think she was planted—"

He waved one hand. "What does that have to do with anything? Yeah, she had a couple of bit parts. It doesn't change the fact that you're throwing around statements you can't prove."

"But I heard them talking. And Birdie—"

"Birdie accosted Ariana and Mike after you whispered in her ear. Are you trying to give Ariana immunity for the rest of the summer?"

My knees shook. "I just wanted you to see. . ."

"I know what she is. Do you think I have feelings for her?" Justin shifted the darts from one hand the other, staring at me intently.

"I didn't know. When we were both up for elimination—"

"She stuck to me like glue, followed me around, and wouldn't let me have a single second alone. I swear, I think she would've jumped in the solo shower with me if I'd let her. She's got a crush on me, yeah—or she says she does—and I'm trying not to encourage her without looking like an ass."

For a split second, my hopes rose. I wanted so much not to like him, but my knees still went weak every time our eyes met. And those dimples. Sometimes, I would say anything to get a glimpse of his dimples.

"You may not have noticed, but I sought you out the other night, remember? I went to sit outside with you. I pulled you aside after the elimination. Does none of that mean anything?"

I started to speak, but he cut me off.

"But that doesn't make it okay to set her up and do this whole big scene just to get a reaction out of me. If you wanted to know if I liked her, you should've asked. I don't appreciate being played. By either of you."

My heart plummeted to the tips of my toes. I was such an idiot.

Justin threw the last dart, avoiding my yes. Then he strode out of the room as it hit the bull's-eye.

I sank to the floor, head in my hands. Even when Ariana was wrong, she made me look like the bad guy. And I fell for it every time. Stupid.

* * *

Justin avoided me for the rest of the day. To keep busy, Ed and Birdie taught me how to make meatloaf; then we played cards until bed. The next morning, I wanted to go to Justin and apologize, but they persuaded me to give him space.

"He can't have too much space, you know. We live in a tiny house together. And plotting is part of the game."

"You can talk to him about the game," Ed said. "And the vote."

Birdie said, "Talk about other things. Let him calm down. He'll forgive you when he's ready."

I opened my mouth, but Ed jumped in. They were tag-teaming me. No way to get a word in edgewise.

"Then, you apologize when he seems open to it. If you push him now and force him to talk before he's ready, when you leave this house, you'll never talk to him again. Trust me—I know men, and I know relationships."

"You're probably right," I grumbled.

"Of course we're right! Always listen to the queers on matters of the heart. We know everything: what to wear, how to do your makeup, who to—"

"I think she's got the 'who' down, Ed," Birdie interjected. "We know why. Let's work on the how and when."

"After breakfast?" I asked. "Is it ready? It smells awesome."

Birdie carried a platter of steaming home fries to the table in one hand and a bowl of scrambled eggs in the other. She nodded toward the coffee pot. "It's ready once you pour everyone's coffee."

By the time I finished serving, everyone sat around the table. My heart leapt as I realized the only empty seat was across from Justin. I eased myself into it, half-afraid he would get up and go eat somewhere else.

After a moment, I peeked at him cautiously. “Hi.”

Those piercing green eyes held mine briefly, and hope surged before he looked away.

“Hey,” he mumbled, picking up his fork.

It wasn’t much, but it was a start. At least he was speaking to me. Now, if I could just get him to show me those dimples, I’d know I was on the right track.

Chapter 17

More scenes from the School Room, Week 5:

Ariana: *I didn't know Mike was going to stick his tongue in my mouth. I shoved him away immediately. I can't believe Birdie and Jennifer ganged up to try to make me look bad. It's bad enough that Jen keeps talking *beep* about me to Justin when she knows how much I like him, but this is ridiculous.*

Rachel: *You know, it's really tacky to spend most of your time stalking and making eyes at a guy who's into someone else while secretly getting it on with another man. Do what you want, but be honest about it.*

Justin: *I don't know how many more times or ways I need to say I don't care who or what Ariana kisses. I'm here to win cash, remember? I have student loans. I don't need a girlfriend.*

Friday afternoon, Bella announced the results of Thursday's challenge: Abram and Rachel had the best overall score and were both immune from elimination. I didn't even know that was possible. I shrugged it off, though. Justin and I played our best. Knowing about dual immunity wouldn't have changed anything.

"Birdie and Mike," Bella said. "I'm sorry to inform you that your team had the lowest overall score. As a result, both of you are up for elimination. Abram, Ariana, Ed, and Jennifer, on Monday morning, we'll let you know who the voters chose. Any one of you might be eliminated this week."

Thanks. That's comforting.

The moment the doors closed behind Bella, Mike turned on Birdie. "You threw the challenge to get me sent home."

Birdie, who had been sitting on a beanbag chair, shot to her feet, hands on her hips. "What are you talking about? You're #losingit."

Mike didn't back down. "On the Donkey challenge, you grabbed the tail from me before they blindfolded us. You're way too short to pin it."

"You'd put it between your legs and were twerking it like a rabid penis!"

"Okay, guys." Justin stepped between them. "I'm sure no one wanted to lose. Mike, Birdie knew if she lost the challenge, you would both be up for elimination. How would she benefit from throwing it?"

"She's got it in for me, man. You saw what happened yesterday."

"That was after the challenge," Rachel said.

"She set me up!" Mike whined. "First, she tries to goad me into untying the scarf."

At that, Birdie made a sound of outrage, but Justin hushed her with a glance.

"Then she throws the challenge," Mike said. "If that's not bad enough, she makes a whole big scene to turn everyone against me."

"Right," Birdie said. "I forced you to maul Ariana's face with your tongue to make you look bad." She stuck her tongue out and wagged her head in a rather unflattering imitation of Mike's kissing abilities. "#Douchecanoe."

As the argument escalated, accusations flew. It became impossible to tell who said what. Finally, an ear-splitting whistle filled the room. Silence descended as we turned toward the noise. Abram stood in the center of the room with his pinkies in his mouth.

"How did you do that?" Rachel asked.

"I have four boys, remember? Everyone calm down. Mike, go for a walk. Take Ariana with you. Birdie, why don't you go upstairs for a few minutes to compose yourself? I'm going to go for a swim. The rest of you are free to join me if you can be civil."

Cooling off sounded like a good idea. I almost said so, but Birdie grabbed my arm and charged toward the stairs. Surprised, I followed, mainly to keep her from dumping me on to the floor. I'd had enough of that during the challenge. She waved her other arm in front of her face as if running through spider webs.

What was she doing? Pointing at the ceiling with both hands? When we reached the top landing, Birdie let go of my arm.

"Sing 'Shake it Off,'" she ordered as she removed her clothes. Under her breath, she chanted, "Fuck, fuck, fuck."

"What—?"

"I need a break from the audience. The show won't pay for the #copyright. They won't air profanity. They won't show me naked. Sing."

I sang with a silent apology to Ms. Swift for butchering both her tune and her words. Birdie sank to the ground, sobbing and swearing. Both hands displayed the middle finger between her face and the cameras. Genius. This particular meltdown wouldn't be broadcast to all of America. At least not without blurring her and silencing me.

If only I'd done the same after my argument with Justin.

After my third time through the song, Birdie's tears subsided. She sniffled. "Thanks. You're a good friend. Terrible singer, though. #NeedLessons."

I smiled. "You should have asked Mike to sing for you. He's got a nice voice."

"HA!" We dissolved into giggles on the floor.

When Ariana entered a few minutes later, we were still there. Her look of disgust only made us laugh harder.

"Dorks," she mumbled as she grabbed her swimsuit out of a drawer, slammed it shut, and left.

Wham!

Just as we'd nearly managed to contain our laughter, Ariana's thunk against the glass wall at the foot of the stairs, confirmed by her muffled curse, set us off again.

By the time we composed ourselves enough to get downstairs, Mike had calmed down. He sat with Ed in the kitchen, talking about performing live and how stage fright differed from being on TV.

We walked out to the patio where Abram chatted in the pool with Rachel. The hot tub was empty. Ariana laid on a lounge chair, but when she saw us, she jumped up and went inside.

"Well, she's voting for me," Birdie sighed, settling into the hot tub and leaning her head against the edge. I followed suit.

"Of course she's voting for you—it's you against Mike. Let's wait and see who the third option is. But, honestly, after the past few days, Mike's probably going home. He may have just eliminated himself with that stunt."

* * *

For the second time, when they announced the result of the viewer vote on Monday morning, my mouth dropped: the viewers chose to put me up for elimination. Again. What was I doing wrong? We'd done well in the challenge.

Am I not dramatic enough? Even after last week?

I couldn't move off the couch. I just sat there, trying to figure out what happened. Maybe the viewers were so attached to Ariana, they didn't appreciate me showing them what she was really like. I cursed myself for letting her get inside my head.

"Hey," Ed climbed up and put his arm around me. "Don't worry about it. With two people having immunity this week, your odds sucked."

"Besides," Birdie chimed in as the other contestants trickled out of the room, "it doesn't matter. Mike's going to be #eliminated."

"You think?"

"Oh, yeah," Ed said. "The viewers cemented it. Mike was trying to convince people to vote for Birdie. Now, you'll split the vote, because you've got the same friends here."

"But—" I protested weakly.

"Look at the numbers: there are eight of us left." He ticked off names on his fingers. "Ariana would've voted for Birdie, but Jen, she hates you. So that's one vote. Then, we've got four guaranteed votes for Mike: me, you guys, and Abram. If Ariana, Mike, Rachel, and Justin all vote together, they'll force a tie. But what are the chances?"

I thought about what he said for a minute. "I bet Rachel will vote for Mike. Justin's hard to read, though."

Birdie chuckled. "He's only hard to read if you're secretly in love with him and won't admit it. He's an open book to everyone else."

I stuck my tongue out at her. "Cut me some slack. I've had exactly one boyfriend, and he turned out to be secretly married. I'm in uncharted waters here."

"You're a grown woman, Jen. It's time to chart those waters."

Before I could respond, Ed interrupted. "The point is, Mike's got at least five out of eight votes against him."

"Fine. I'll check with Rachel. Someone may need to talk to Justin."

Birdie said, "No. You need to talk to Justin."

"And not about the vote," Ed said.

A groan escaped me. I hated when they were right.

* * *

At the end of the day, I decide to take the straight approach with Rachel. If I buttered her up or flattered her, she'd see right through me and be annoyed.

Because fate has a sense of humor, Rachel sat in the hot tub with Ariana. Of course. Steeling myself, I eased down the steps and let the warm water envelope me. I leaned my head back and closed my eyes, wanting a moment to relax and compose my thoughts before I said anything. Maybe Ariana would leave, so I wouldn't have to have this conversation in front of her.

After a moment, water splashed. I cracked one eyelid. Rachel swam away from the hot tub, toward a raft.

That wasn't part of the plan. I'd have to follow her without making it obvious.

Ariana noted the direction of my gaze. "Don't bother. She knows Birdie set up Mike to fail. She's not likely to vote to send him home. Besides, he's the only unattached, straight male left."

Well, now, that didn't sound right. "Isn't Mike attached to you? No offense, but I don't think Rachel wants your sloppy seconds."

"Why not?" Ariana smirked. "They're good enough for you."

I blinked at her. "I have no idea what you're talking about."

"Oh, come off it," Ariana said. "Everyone sees you panting after Justin. It must kill you that I got there first. I don't blame you for still wanting a piece, though. He's got very talented hands. Oh, and that tongue. Mmmmm."

My blood ran cold. I forced myself to breathe. *She's lying. Has to be. She's an actress.*

"What are you talking about?"

"The night after the audition, we hooked up. He couldn't keep his hands off me." Ariana shrugged. "Don't believe me? Ask about the birthmark on his shoulder."

It's a glass house. We swim every day. I've seen that birthmark a hundred times.

As the wheels turned in my head, Ariana smirked and crossed her arms. "We had a good time. When we first got here, I hoped we could pick up again, but I'm over it. There are plenty of men who appreciate me."

Oh, God. I saw all her movies. She's a terrible actress. She has to be telling the truth.

I didn't listen to another word. Instead, I dove across the barrier into the pool, swimming violently from one end to the other.

She slept with Justin. How? Why? How?

Is that why he ignored me in the shower when we were tied together? Why did he pretend he wasn't interested in her? Was he one of those guys who ditched a girl the second they had sex? Did he want to seduce me and dump me, too?

And why did he act like he has no idea why she hangs out with him?

Another thought hit me: Had he had sex with Ariana on national television?

Ew. In that case, he wasn't who I thought at all.

When I arrived at the other end of the pool, I stomped up the steps. Water flew around me as Ed and Rachel moved out of the way. Rachel reached out one hand. "Hey, Jen? Is everything. . .?"

In my rush to get to Justin, I didn't even slow down. "Later, Rach."

He sat with Abram and Birdie, sipping a beer. I had the tiny sliver of presence of mind I needed not to call him out in front of the others.

"Hi, Abram. Birdie." I unclenched my jaw enough to sound casual. "Justin, can I talk to you for a minute?"

I stalked toward the maze without waiting for a response. When I was far enough away to avoid eavesdroppers, I whirled around. "Did you have sex with Ariana?"

Whatever reaction I'd expected included large doses of denial and disbelief. Part of me thought his jaw would drop and his eyes would bug out, like in the movies.

That's not what happened.

Justin turned beat red and dug at the grass with one toe. He stuffed his hands into his pockets. My gasp of denial swallowed his mumblings. Nauseated, I sank to the ground, my head between my knees.

A moment later, hands rested on my shoulders. "Jen. No. I'm sorry. Please look at me."

"Go away," I mumbled. "I'm going to throw up."

"No. You don't get to ask and not give me a chance to explain." He settled on to the grass beside me. His hand touched my knee, but I jerked away.

"I'll listen, but don't touch me."

"Fair enough. The whole point of trying out for the show was to do something cool with my sister. The night after the audition, she told me she quit. I was bummed, because I need this to help pay for law school. She distracted the PA at the end of the hall, and I snuck down to the hotel bar."

Something he said tickled the back of my brain, but I couldn't grasp why it mattered.

"Ariana was there. I don't know how she got out of her room, and I don't care. I drank too much, got stupid, we made out a little. That's it. A little kissing and then my sister came down and dragged me back up to the room so we didn't get caught."

Finally, I looked at him. "That's it? A little kissing?"

Justin put one hand on his heart. "I swear. Clothes on, hands above the waist. I regretted it as soon as I sobered up. When I saw she made the show, I was hoping we could pretend nothing happened, but. . .I'm not that lucky."

I stood, brushing myself off. "You lied to me."

He avoided my eyes. "You never asked. I said I didn't have feelings for her, and I meant it."

"But you made it seem like she latched on to you for no reason. You acted like you had no idea why she thought you might like her. And, clearly, there's a very obvious reason for both those things."

Justin's jaw tightened. "I'm sorry, Jen. I was hoping I wouldn't have to say anything. I mean, are you going to tell me every mistake you made before you got here?"

"None of my mistakes are in this house." I pointed out. "Except you."

His face turned red. "You're not my girlfriend. We're not even dating."

"There's something between us. I know you've felt it. During the archery?"

"There's an attraction, yeah. But there's also drama and the game and trying to win. How can I trust any of it?" A tinge of queasiness hit me. It never occurred me that he had the same insecurities I did. That maybe he had a reason for being so hot and cold. We should've had this conversation weeks ago.

He said, "I don't know what we are. If we can be anything or if we could've been. All I know is, I don't owe you an explanation."

I started to respond, but he was right. We weren't dating. We'd never kissed. We'd technically never been "alone," since millions of people theoretically watched the show. He didn't owe me anything.

"You're right," I mumbled, turning away. "You don't owe me anything. I guess we'll never know if we could've been anything. From now on, leave me alone."

I stalked back to the house without waiting for his response, tears of disappointment blurring my vision. Were all men liars? Justin was no better than Dominic. I couldn't believe I'd allowed myself to trust him.

I still needed to talk to Rachel about the vote, but couldn't bring myself to care. Maybe getting eliminated now would be for the best.

Like a zombie, I trudged up the stairs, not really paying attention to where I walked.

Wham!

A glass wall clipped my shoulder as I turned toward the upper staircase.

Clearly, this wasn't my night. Instead of going to bed, I went into the bathroom and turned the dual shower on as hot as I could stand. Then, I let the water wash away my horrible day.

* * *

The next morning, I awoke before the others, as usual. Still agitated, I went through my Pilates routine twice. By the time I finished, Ed had stumbled bleary-eyed into the kitchen.

"No coffee yet?" he asked.

"Sorry, no. I got caught up in my workout. I'm on it."

"Hey, what's going on? What did Ariana say to you last night?"

"She told me she had sex with Justin," I said.

Ed reached for the on/off switch on the coffee maker and missed. The pot clattered off the burner. I caught it, barely, before it smashed on to the floor.

A snort of derision sounded from the doorway. Rachel stood, wrinkling her nose.

"And you believed her?"

Not wanting to meet their eyes, I replaced the pot and started the coffeemaker. "I asked him. It's not true, but they fooled around at the audition."

"Before he met you?" she asked.

I nodded.

Rachel poured a glass of orange juice and sat at the bar. "Then who cares? Does he have feelings for her?"

I bit my lip. "I don't think so. They were in the same place at the same time, drunk. But he lied."

"Did you ask him about it?" Ed asked.

"Not specifically, but all those times he acted like he didn't know why she was into him. . ."

Rachel nodded, but Ed snorted at me. "If you didn't ask, he didn't lie."

"It still feels like a lie."

"I understand, but it wasn't. If you like him, you need to get over it."

I started to point out that it wasn't that simple, but Rachel cut in. "I know it's hard, but he's right."

Ed asked, "Did you ask him if he likes her?"

"He says he doesn't, but what if he's lying?"

"Then he's not the person you thought, and you're better off finding out now."

I smiled at him. "Are you always the voice of reason?"

"Usually not before I manage to get some caffeine. You're lucky you were able to get such brilliance out of me at this ungodly hour. I accept thanks in the form of hot, naked men dancing around me."

"I can offer you coffee." I waved an empty mug tantalizingly just under his nose. "It's almost ready."

"Deal. Gimme." Ed grabbed the mug.

I air-kissed him. As I headed upstairs to shower, I called over my shoulder. "And breakfast better be ready when I get back!"

* * *

When I returned, everyone sat around the table. Rachel had made something called the "the Wife Saver," which she swore was an old farm recipe. After catching whiffs of maple, cinnamon, and ham, I dug in.

I had no idea how to approach Justin, or even if I wanted to. Instead, I stayed in the kitchen after breakfast to help Rachel with the dishes.

"You cooked," I reminded her as I grabbed a dirty plate away from her outstretched hands. "That means someone else cleans."

"Well, I won't argue with that." Rachel dropped the handful of silverware she had gathered and picked up her mug instead. She refilled her coffee and sat at the bar. "You want to know who I'm voting for, right?"

"Yeah. I did the math, and Mike could force a tie if he gets everyone to vote for either me or Birdie. If that happens and the viewers get a say, I'm out."

"That's not going to happen. For one thing, Mike's not that smart. Also, Justin and I are voting for Mike."

"You're sure?"

"Positive. We talked last night after you stormed out."

"Really? Oh, that's fantastic!" I gave her a soapy hug. "Thank you so much. I feel much better."

"You're welcome. Now stop stomping around. America isn't going to like that."

"Deal."

* * *

After dinner, we gathered in the living room for the results. Instead of climbing the tower where I'd be exposed, I sat in the middle of the couch. Birdie squeezed between me and the corner. Ed sat on the other end. I had no illusions that, after voting to put me up for elimination, the viewers would save me. That math didn't make sense. But I also hoped Mike didn't have enough of a fan base to be saved.

"Good evening, Fish!" Bella entered the room with her trademark smile. "Well, this has certainly been an interesting week. First, you were tied together for an entire day. Then, you engaged in a series of tasks while tied to a partner. Abram, Rachel, you did an excellent job, and the two of you received immunity."

She surveyed the room while she spoke. "Birdie, Mike, you unfortunately had trouble working together and are therefore both up for elimination. Jennifer, the viewers spoke, and you, too, are up for elimination, despite getting along with your partner and doing well in the challenge."

It didn't sound like she was going to say anything to shed light on why the viewers nominated me. I had a growing feeling that, if the fans ever had more of a say in the outcome of things, I couldn't win this game. As Bella met my eyes, I pasted a brave smile on my face and nodded.

"Jennifer." Bella held my gaze, and I wondered if the others heard my heart beating. My eyes widened; my breath caught in my throat. "I'm very sorry, Jennifer."

I'm out.

I looked down to hide my disappointment, trying not to cry.

Bella said, "The votes have been counted, and you're going to have to find a way to get along with Ariana for a few more days. Jen, you'll be spending another week in the Fishbowl."

Oh. My. God. I couldn't believe my ears. How cruel of her to give the results that way. But I made it! How? Did that mean—

Bella continued. "Congratulations, Birdie! You've also earned another week in the Fishbowl. And that means, I'm sorry, Mike, but it's time for you to pack your things and go. You will be leaving *The Fishbowl* immediately."

I whooped and hugged Birdie. It probably wasn't appropriate, but I was too relieved to worry about censoring myself.

After we finished our celebration, everyone gathered in the hall to say good-bye to Mike. He came down the stairs carrying his suitcase. Ariana followed, remaining on the top step.

When he reached the ground, Mike gave Ariana a big hug, spinning her around in a circle. He whispered something in her ear I didn't catch. Then, without acknowledging the rest of us, Mike walked out the front door.

Chapter 18

Jennifer in the School Room, Week 6:

No, I'm not sorry to see Mike go. He caused a lot of unnecessary drama. I realize this is a TV show, but we also have to live here, and it's easier on everyone if we can at least try to get along.

Ariana? Well, no, I'm not having much luck getting along with her. But in my defense, she's awful.

It feels fantastic to have survived five weeks in the Fishbowl. I came seeking adventure, and I'm having a great time. The challenges are fun, I'm learning how to cook, and I'm making some lifelong friends. Even if I'm voted out tonight, I wouldn't trade this summer for anything.

Before anyone could react to Mike's departure, the producers gathered us in the kitchen. When we got there, they'd given us champagne and cake to celebrate making it halfway through the summer. Halfway? I hadn't realized it had been so long.

Wow. Good for us.

The practical part of me wondered if they'd brought in extra alcohol because the producers were tired of watching us play cards all day. I couldn't blame them—most of us were tired of that, too. Or maybe they just wanted to do something to get away from the palpable "everyone against Ariana" vibe in the hall.

I poured glasses of champagne while Ed cut the cake. When I handed Justin his glass, our fingers brushed. A jolt went through me. God, he was gorgeous. Why did he have to be so good-looking? And funny? Easy to talk to? Why couldn't he just be a good-looking jerk? Why did it all have to be so confusing?

He's no better than Ariana. He lied. Ignore him.

Even though I needed to forget about our connection, to focus on the game, I didn't want to be angry with him.

Trying to keep my jumbled emotions off my face, I smiled at him. "Congratulations on making it through the first five weeks!"

In response, I received a full-on double dose of his dimples.

Anghgnag nah gah. What was I saying?

"Thanks," he said. "You, too. Did you think you'd make it this far?"

At that moment, Ariana stepped between us, pouring a clear liquid into two shot glasses. "I certainly did. I said from the beginning I have what it takes to win this thing, and I meant it. I plan to go all the way. A quarter mil, baby! Woo!"

She handed Justin a shot and raised her glass into the air.

"I'll drink to that." He laughed.

The rest of us raised champagne glasses. "To two hundred fifty grand!"

Our glasses clinked.

Justin winced and stuck his tongue out, shaking his head from side to side. "What is this? I thought it was vodka."

"Everclear." Ariana winked at him. "I thought we could have some fun."

"Yikes." He dropped the empty glass on the counter. "Too much for me."

With a smooth gesture I'd never be able to duplicate, she linked her left arm through Justin's right and transferred a champagne glass into her left hand. She grabbed the full bottle in her other hand and waved it above her head as she turned, moving Justin with her. "Come on! Party in the hot tub!"

For a moment, I watched them walk away. *He's certainly making it easy to be upset with him.*

Ed poked me.

"Don't just stand there," he hissed. "We're all going in the hot tub. I'll distract her so you can talk to him. You can work this out."

"Am I that obvious?"

He didn't bother to answer. He sauntered on to the patio carrying his glass and two more bottles of champagne.

Ed gathered everyone in the hot tub and settled himself between Ariana and Justin. He looked at Ariana and issued the twenty-first-century equivalent of an invitation to a duel.

"The Yankees' rotation is crap this year. The Red Sox are going to trounce them."

I hadn't realized Ariana cared about baseball, but the New York City/Boston rivalry apparently trumped petty things like having an interest in sports.

"Are you mental? The Red Sox lineup is so pathetic they have to spout nonsense like 'Fear the Beard' in hopes no one'll notice the team sucks. The Yankees will absolutely take the division this year."

"Right. I guess it's good you're locked up in here so you don't have to cry every morning when you look at the standings."

Ed caught my eye and winked as Ariana gasped in outrage. What a star. He'd hooked her into a conversation without half trying.

Once Ariana's attention focused on the debate, I inched closer to Justin. He'd somehow made it outside without a glass; he sipped directly from the bottle. I'm not much of a seductress, and I hadn't had time to think of a good opener.

Even though I was still upset about the Ariana thing, Ed and Rachel were right: I needed to get over it. I wasn't prepared to throw away what I felt every time Justin came near me. I thought I'd been in love with Dominic, but my day never brightened like this when he entered a room. I didn't lie in bed planning our next interactions. Even the sex paled in comparison to thirty seconds of Justin explaining how to shoot a bow and error. That kind of chemistry needed to be explored.

"Hey."

Brilliant, Jen. Next, try talking about the weather.

"Hey," he said. Awkwardly, we listened to the debate rage beside us. "You a baseball fan?"

"Not really. I used to go to games sometimes for work, before I got laid off. Sitting in the corporate box was fun, but it's not the same experience."

Really? I spent all this time trying to get this guy into a conversation, and this was the best we could find to talk about? If he had been into me, the conversational abilities I displayed might change his mind.

Hoping for some liquid courage, I drained my glass.

"Can we talk? Somewhere. . .away from all this?" I caught his eyes and tilted my head at Ariana, hoping he understood what I meant.

His Adam's apple traveled up and down his throat before he nodded. Pitching his voice toward the others, he said, "Need a refill, Jen? I'll get that for you."

Justin lifted himself out of the tub.

For the benefit of the others—well, Ariana—I spoke before following. "Hold on. I'll come with."

Was it my imagination, or did the corners of Justin's mouth turn upward as he walked into the house? I suppressed a giggle when Ed's voice boomed behind me.

"Here, Ariana. Let me fill that for you. There's no need to go into the house."

I closed the patio door behind me, wanting a barrier between me and her, even if it was see-through and easy to move. Justin stood next to the cake slices that had been ignored in favor of the champagne, filling two shot glasses.

"Care to join me?"

What the hell? Can't make this conversation any more awkward.

I'd never tasted Everclear. As it burned down my throat, I swore never to taste it again. It felt like my eyeballs burst into flames. I coughed, swiped at my throat, and chugged half a glass of water.

"Sorry. I should've warned you. Want some cake?" Justin asked.

"Hold that thought. I have to make a quick trip upstairs."

And try not to barf up my insides.

After splashing a bit of water on my face, I left the bathroom and stopped short. Justin sat on the couch in the small sitting room. Two plates of cake and two glasses of champagne waited on the table in front of me. An unopened bottle stood nearby. I hadn't noticed before, but there wasn't a ton of light in this room, which was much smaller than the downstairs living area. Cozier. Almost romantic.

My heartbeat sped up a notch.

Calm down, I told myself. *Nothing is going to happen.*

Oh, yeah? Then why did he set this up? Awfully intimate, isn't it?

War raged in my head. Part of me still wanted him to apologize for earlier. I needed more than his "I don't owe you anything." On the other hand, I was so tired of arguing. So tired of the drama.

Couldn't we have this one moment?

I sat on the couch, trying to find a happy medium between close enough to be enticing and plopping myself into his lap. God, I wanted to plop myself into his lap. Maybe I shouldn't have taken that shot. Justin handed me a piece of cake, and I thanked him.

"How is it?" I asked.

"It's pretty good. My sister's cakes are better. She works in a bakery. She'll own it someday."

"Oh, yeah?" I asked. Justin rarely talked about his personal life, so I seized the opening. "You've mentioned your sister a few times, but never said much about her. Older or younger?"

"A twin, actually. She tried out for the show with me." He shrugged and swallowed his champagne. "I don't think she was into it. She just did it because I wanted us to do something fun together."

Wait a minute. Why did that sound so familiar?

Think, Jen. I had heard this information before.

As I puzzled it out, Justin tilted his head and studied my face. "What's wrong?"

"Nothing, it's just—what you said is so familiar. It's like déjà vu or something."

"I don't think we've had this conversation before. I remember most of our talks."

He did? A wave of pleasure washed over me. I took in his green eyes, the soft-looking blond hair. Then, with a start, the answer hit me. "You're Sarah's brother!"

A look of confusion passed over his face. "How did you know? Wait. You're the girl from the bathroom!"

"Yes!"

"Cheers!" He clinked our glasses together, then took a long swallow before looking at his now-empty glass. I wondered how much he'd had to drink.

"She told you about that?"

Justin reached for the bottle and refilled both glasses. "Well, she said she had a minor breakdown in the restroom, and some girl talked to her until she felt better. Jennifer is such a common name, though, and she didn't say anything when the contestants were announced."

"That's not surprising. We only spoke for a few minutes."

"Yeah, but you made an impression on her. She thought I'd like you."

At that point, my hopes skyrocketed. He wouldn't say these things just to shoot me down, would he? I took another sip of champagne and shifted a bit closer to him. "Really? And what do you think?"

My fingers itched to stroke his hair. He sat so close. I leaned toward him.

"I. . .I think." Justin inched closer to me at an agonizingly slow pace. "I think. . .I'm going to be sick."

At that, he set his glass down hard on the table. It clanked over on its side, pouring champagne on to the floor. He stood, swayed, and vomited on my feet.

* * *

The next morning, I stared miserably up at the ceiling, flipping the prior night's events over and over in my head. Sarah's once-forgotten words from the audition rang in my head. *My brother's so driven. He'd do anything to win.*

At the time, I hadn't known she was talking about Justin. But would doing anything to win involve participating in a fake romance for the ratings? Flirting with me so I'd vote for him and he'd get to stick around longer? It was hard to believe a guy who really liked me would puke rather than letting his lips touch mine.

"So, what happened?" The next morning, Ed pounced on me as soon as I ventured into the kitchen. I'd gotten up later than usual due to all the time I spent lying in bed, refusing to face the day.

"Yeah. So, he threw up on me."

"Oooooh, he *threw* up on you! I bet he *did*." Ed winked at me. "You go, girl!"

"No, really. That's not a thing. Actual vomit. From his mouth. On to my bare feet."

His face fell. "Damn. I thought that was a metaphor. I mean, sure, a freaky one, but you can make anything sound dirty if you try hard enough."

"Not this. It's dirty in a 'covered in vomit' way, which isn't sexy at all. No, I tried to kiss him; he puked."

"Ew."

"Right. I have no idea how to react to the man of my dreams blowing chunks all over me."

"What did you do?"

"Stared with my mouth open. Got a towel. Cleaned up. Looked for a trash can or bucket to leave by his head. Couldn't find one. Showered. Cried. End of story. I don't want to talk about it, especially not if there's any chance *she'll* overhear." He didn't have to ask who "she" was. "I'm going for a run. Maybe I'll feel better after a few miles."

The first lap around the house did nothing to make me feel better. The second wasn't much better. I forced myself to keep going. By the time I hit the fourth or fifth lap, I got into a rhythm. During my seventh lap, I saw some humor in what had happened. If it had happened to someone else, I might've laughed.

Somewhere around my tenth lap around the yard, I made an important decision: I needed to focus on my end goals. The chase wasn't getting me anywhere. It was time to give up.

I wanted to win $250,000. I wasn't here to find a boyfriend, and I certainly wasn't here to throw myself at someone who'd drink to the point of throwing up rather than talk about his feelings. Or who was possibly repulsed by the idea of kissing me.

Did I want to start another relationship so soon after Dominic, anyway? Especially when I didn't know if I could trust Justin? Hell, were we even in relationship territory? Brandon tried so hard to talk me into a break-up fling last spring, and I hadn't found the right opportunity. National television didn't seem like the way to go.

My eye needed to stay on the prize, or I'd be going home with nothing: no money, no boyfriend, no job, no place to live. Nothing but pending bankruptcy or a future hiding in the Peace Corps. I couldn't afford to take that risk.

By the time I finished my run, showered, and re-entered the kitchen, Birdie was helping Ed make breakfast. I poured myself a cup of coffee and sat at the counter. "What are you making?"

"Hangover special," Birdie winked at me. "Eggs and cheesy hash browns."

I turned on Ed. "You told her!"

"Of course I did," he retorted. "You had to know I would."

"But, also, Ariana and Rachel are in the living room moaning about their headaches, and Abram said Justin can't get out of bed."

"Here, make yourself useful." Ed handed me a package of bacon. "I pre-heated the oven."

Obediently, I got up and pulled two cookie sheets out of the cupboards, then laid bacon in rows. "He's sick? Is it bad?"

Ed shrugged. "It might be if Ariana goes in to offer a sponge bath. Luckily, she also had a lot to drink. I don't think she's feeling too hot, either."

I slid the cookie sheets into the oven. "I mean, not that I care."

"Riiiiiiiiight," Birdie smirked at Ed, who winked at her.

"Seriously, guys, I'm done," I insisted. "All this back and forth is too much. He lied about Ariana. He'd rather get shit-faced than have a conversation with me about everything. I need a quarter of a million dollars more than I need some guy. I hardly know him. I'm focusing on the game. Someone else take him breakfast. I'll stay here and get everything on the table."

"Keep telling yourself that, sweetie," Ed said.

In the end, he took a tray upstairs and brought it right back down. The production team took Justin to the doctor to make sure he didn't have alcohol poisoning. The rest of us ate silently, either nursing our own hangovers or lost in our thoughts.

When Justin came back to the house a couple of hours later, I was so engrossed in conversation with Rachel and Abram I almost didn't notice.

Chapter 19

Scenes from The School Room, Week 6:

Ariana: *The Yankees are way better than the Red Sox. I can't believe Ed was arguing with me. I don't get why he hasn't been voted out yet. Him and Jennifer are so boring. I can't even.*

Rachel: *It was great for the producers to throw us a party, but, um, can you maybe turn down the lights in here? They're awfully bright. I need a nap.*

Justin: *How exactly do you apologize to a girl for throwing up on her? She wasn't wearing shoes. Ew. This has never happened to me before. Is there a way to get flowers in here?*

Ed: *No, I don't care about baseball. I care about keeping nice guys away from snaky bitches.*

"Hello, my little Fish!" Bella greeted us warmly after lunch. "Today's midweek challenge is an endurance test. The winner will receive an advantage in tomorrow's elimination challenge."

Endurance, huh? Like long-distance running? I could probably outrun Birdie, Ariana (propelled by sheer animosity), and maybe Justin. Then again, I may have been the least hungover of everyone, which gave me an advantage.

They herded us outside. Someone had set short, different-colored pedestals in a ring around the pool. Each stood about a foot tall and eighteen inches wide. Squinting into the sunlight, I located the green one near the deep end.

"Each Fish stands on his or her pedestal. Whoever makes it the longest wins. Easy, right?"

Right. Easy. What's the catch?

"Of course," Bella said, "there is one more thing. You'll each have to balance a plate on your head. Once it falls, you're out."

Abram and Rachel had both been looking confident about this challenge. Upon hearing that last part, their smiles faltered. Still, everyone lined up to grab our plates. No one wanted to lose the possibility of an advantage that could save us from elimination—especially after what happened to Maria.

We climbed on to our pedestals. I held my plate in place with my fingertips while I steadied myself. I took a couple of deep breaths and pushed my shoulders back. I could do this.

Bella said, "Ready? One, two, three!"

I'd barely removed my fingertips from my plate when something crashed against the concrete.

"Awww, crap!" Birdie yelled. "I knew I should have taken ballet classes. #Clumsy."

My lips clamped together to keep a laugh from escaping. My head remained steady. Still, I couldn't keep an amused smile off my face. Others were not so lucky. Seconds later, glass shattered against the ground a second time.

"That's not fair!" Abram said. "Birdie made me laugh!"

"Sorry, guys," Bella warned. "One chance. Your plate falls, you lose. And no distracting the remaining players. Go wait over there."

I couldn't see where "over there" was. I didn't dare look.

Two down, four to go. This was easy. I'd been doing Pilates since high school. I just needed to focus. Eyes closed to avoid distractions, I focused on my breathing. In, out. In, out. I was so deep in the zone I almost jumped when Bella's voice informed us we'd been standing there for five minutes.

Apparently, I wasn't the only one she startled. Two plates crashed to the ground. Bella called Justin and Rachel out. The competition was down to me, Ed, and the person who'd scrambled up a thirty-foot fireman's pole to avoid being eaten in *YetiNado: Snow Drifts Back.* After her legs were bitten off. Brandon and I watched that scene six times. Ariana was in excellent shape. (It had to be her; the film didn't appear to have a stunt budget.)

I gritted my teeth, determined to beat Ariana if it killed me.

At around the eight-minute mark, Ed's plate fell. "I think I could've won if I hadn't fallen asleep," he complained.

Now it was a grudge match. I closed my eyes, resisting the urge to look at Ariana. No way I'd let her win this.

Bella called, "Ten minutes!"

Ariana whined, "Bella, I have a leg cramp. Can we pause?"

Maybe it was a trick. *Don't open your eyes.* I told myself. *Don't move.*

"Sorry, Ariana. If you're having problems, you can take yourself out. But Jennifer wins."

No way she would do that. Ariana didn't respond.

Sweat trickled down my back as the sun beat down. My nose itched. I ignored it. And then to my horror, something gurgled deep in my belly.

Oh, no. No, no, no. I can win this! My body ignored my brain. But still, I wouldn't let Ariana win. Even if that meant pooping my pants? In front of everyone? Crap.

No pun intended.

Just as I was about to panic with my need to get inside, I heard the sweetest music that has ever touched my ears.

Crash!

Ariana's plate hit the ground!

A second later, Bella said, "And the winner is Jen! Congratulations, Jennifer!"

With a whoop, I grabbed my plate and flung it into the pool. Then, I jumped off the pedestal and raced into the house. Laughter followed in my wake.

* * *

"This week's challenge is a timed obstacle course." Bella explained the next morning. "How well you did in yesterday's challenge determines your starting order. Jen, since you won, you get a thirty-second head start."

An extra thirty seconds? Awesome! Especially since I'd been about a quarter of a second from dropping my plate when Ariana's fell. More importantly, if I had to compete in a physical challenge against people in excellent shape, I seriously needed the edge. After all, Ed told me Abram did one-armed push-ups in their room every morning before breakfast.

"Jen, you'll enter when the first whistle blows. We'll blow the whistle again for the rest of you at the right time."

The producers led us down one side of the property. The starting line hid behind one corner of the maze, so we couldn't see what awaited us on the other side. To hide my nervousness, I knelt to tie my shoes. When I stood, Curly Beard settled a bright green helmet on to my head, pulling the straps tight under my chin. He shook my head a bit, then tapped the top.

"You're good to go. Head right over there."

Once I reached the starting line, my knees bent into a runner's crouch. Bella blew the whistle, and I tore around the side of the house. My head start gave me an edge, but Ariana had strength and agility.

About fifty yards in, logs covered a huge tract of mud. I jumped from one to the next.

A whistle blew behind me, signaling Ariana's entry on to the course. The logs wobbled, and I ordered myself to focus. Sounds of relief escaped me when I jumped off the last log on to solid ground.

That relief ended when the next obstacle loomed: a giant wall. It must've been twenty-five feet tall. Knotted ropes hung from the top about a foot apart. I grabbed the green rope and began to walk up the wall.

Immediately, my feet slid out from under me. I landed in a heap on the ground. Then I realized the bottom five feet or so of the wall were a shade darker than the rest. Cautiously, I reached out one hand and touched it gently. My fingers slipped in something oily. What was that? It smelled familiar. Thoughtfully, I rubbed my fingers together. Olive oil?

I'd have to get up in the air on my own. I jumped and grabbed the rope as high as I could. My feet groped for a knot. If only I were seven feet tall, this would be much easier.

When I was about a third of the way up, a few feet away, Ariana scrambled up the rope as easily as if it were a ladder. Stupid upper body strength. She trained to do that for a movie. How was that fair?

It doesn't need to be fair, Jen, I reminded myself. *It needs to be entertaining.* Hopefully, America enjoyed watching me struggle up the wall.

All too soon, another whistle blew. Ed was on the course.

Finally, I hauled myself on to the top of that stupid wall. Behind me,

Ed had already started to climb. I'd lost my head start. If I managed to survive another week, push-ups would have to become part of my routine.

Stairs at the end of the wall made it easier to get down. I sprinted to the next challenge. When I saw it, I nearly doubled over laughing.

We each had a large toy box, crammed full of stuff. On top of mine, I spied dress-up clothes, Operation, blocks, and a stuffed horse. A sign located near a few feet away informed me that we had to remove each item and carry it to a rotating platform ten feet away. When the trunks were empty, we'd have to retrieve the items from the platform and repack everything so the box closed.

I smiled as a memory hit me.

"How on earth did you do that?" Dominic asked.

I stood in front of the open freezer, empty grocery bags strewn about the floor. There wasn't a single square inch of space left, but, somehow, every last item fit in there.

"It's a gift," I laughed. "Just don't touch anything or it will all come falling out."

"I can't touch anything?" Dominic wiggled his eyebrows at me. With a seductive smile, he reached out with one arm and grabbed me around the waist, pulling me close—

Spurred by the memory, I grabbed the top item from the green trunk and began trotting back and forth. Just as I finished emptying my toy box, a triumphant shout arose from Ariana's direction.

"I got it!"

Already?

I swiveled around to see how she'd done. The lid hovered several inches above the top of the box. Several items teetered on the lid, and a strand of costume jewelry dragged on the ground.

Ed worked on the black trunk next to me. He also stared at Ariana's overstuffed toy box.

"Do we tell her she didn't do it right?" I asked.

"Leave her," Ed suggested. "She won't come back, and Justin and Rachel are right behind us. We need to keep moving. Either the producers will penalize her for not completing the challenge, or we'll know the show is rigged because she's prettier than we are."

"Well, that's certainly comforting."

When I finally closed my lid, Ed was trying to figure out what to do with a child's fishing pole, and Justin and Rachel had started restocking their trunks. No sign of Birdie or Abram. I hoped Ariana hadn't already won.

The next station involved huge tires to flip, end over end, across a length of grass roughly the size of a football field. At one point, Justin passed me. Slowly and steadily, I plodded along, trying not to admire the view of his butt moving down the field.

Next, we used magnetic fishing poles to locate colored "fish" in the pond. As I scoured for green fish, I spied one of Ariana's silver fish floating near the bottom.

She was definitely going to finish first, but would she win?

When I crossed the finish line, sweat poured down my back. Breath escaped me in pants, and my knees felt ready to collapse. Ariana sat in a lounge chair with her feet up, sipping something with an umbrella in it. She'd already changed into clean clothes and redone her makeup. She could have been Queen of the Yard.

If I hadn't seen her out there on the course, I never would've guessed she'd done an obstacle course. How long had she been finished? Did she complete any of the tasks? Or did she head back to the house as soon as we couldn't see her?

I stepped out of the way just as Ed barreled across the finish line behind me. Accepting a cup of water from the producers with a grateful smile, I walked in a circle, trying to bring my heart rate back to normal. Justin paced nearby; I'd never managed to catch him. Rachel was nowhere in sight. We'd been neck-and-neck near the end of the fishing challenge, but she'd gotten completely stuck trying to get her last fish, so I raced ahead.

A moment later, Justin noticed Ariana. The look on his face must have mirrored my own. He walked over to me and spoke in hushed tones.

"She didn't get all her fish."

"I saw that! Do you think they'll do anything?" I asked, meaning the producers.

He shrugged. "It creates drama. They like drama. They'll wait to see if someone calls her out. I know you hate her, but don't do it. The fans love her."

"And they hate me," I said miserably.

"We don't know that. But for some reason, you're not a fan favorite. If you want to win, you don't necessarily want to be the one throwing drama at her all the time. Leave that to someone else."

My mouth opened to argue with him, but movement over his shoulder caught my attention. I squinted into the sunlight.

"Is that them?" I trailed off, uncertain of what I was seeing.

One hand shading my eyes helped a little. Although still about twenty feet away, the silhouette could only be Abram's large frame. He walked funny. No, it couldn't be.

What's going on? Is he carrying something?

Justin turned to see what had distracted me. One hand also went up to his forehead. "Is Abram—?"

"He's carrying her," Ed said from a few feet away. "Abram is carrying Birdie across the finish line."

Abram walked toward us, dirt smeared across his face. Birdie lay in his arms. With her eyes shut, it looked like Abram cradled a large doll. She wasn't moving. Abram's lips moved as he trotted toward us, but I couldn't make out his words. He might have been talking to Birdie or praying.

Tall and Curly Beard raced across the field toward them (probably to remind Birdie she agreed not to sue). I followed, but Overalls called me back.

"Let the professionals handle this."

A couple of the paramedics who were always on the scene during challenges were already in motion. They'd get to Birdie and Abram before me, and they were trained. The paramedics whisked her away from Abram and put her into a waiting ambulance.

Ariana's treachery was temporarily forgotten. We stood in shock, watching the ambulance take Birdie away. Silent tears streamed down my face. No one moved until the flashing lights disappeared around a corner, taking my friend away.

Chapter 20

More Scenes from the School Room, Week 6:

Abram: *It was awful. We entered the course seconds apart. My legs are much longer than hers, so I was way ahead when I got to the logs. I'd made it to the top of the wall when she screamed.*

No, I didn't see what happened. Birdie lay on the ground, clutching her ankle. It was awful. She couldn't walk. I picked her up and went to get help.

Elimination? It never entered my mind that I might be eliminated, but if it had, I still would've done it. If my competitors want to vote me out for helping someone in need, I'm not sure I want to be here. But I have faith in most of them.

After Birdie left, the producers fussed over the rest of us. We had to assure them we weren't injured. Aside from some bumps and bruises, everyone else was fine. The whole thing shook us up, though. Instead of scattering into small groups like we usually did after challenges, the remaining contestants gathered in the kitchen to wait for news.

"What happened?" I asked Abram.

"She said she slipped on one of the logs in the first obstacle and twisted her ankle in the mud. She kept going. Then, at the big wall, she fell off the rope and landed on it again."

"Is she going to be okay?"

"She'll be fine. I'm no doctor, but I think her ankle's broken. It swelled up as big as her head."

A couple of hours later, everyone welcomed Birdie back into the house. When she entered the front hall, she showed off a bright pink walking cast on one ankle. We cheered. Birdie twirled clumsily on her good leg, then bowed deeply. Abram picked her up and carried her into the kitchen. Everyone except Ariana and Justin followed. I refused to speculate on whether they were together. Ariana was probably in the School Room bragging about how she "won" the challenge.

I took Birdie's place behind the counter, chopping and assisting while Ed made dinner. Birdie sat at the bar with her ankle propped up on a stool.

"So #stupid!" Birdie moaned. "I should never have tried to keep up with the athletic kids."

"It's not one hundred percent your fault. When they advertised the show, they asked for smart people," I said. "It didn't mention running obstacle courses."

"Wait a minute—what?" Rachel said. "That's not the ad I saw. Mine was all, 'Are you the life of the party? Do you get invited everywhere? Do people want you around to liven things up?' Nothing about smart people."

Huh.

It made sense the producers posted different ads, although I hadn't considered it, even after realizing Ariana wasn't the brightest crayon in the box. She lied about everything, so I'd assumed she lied during casting. It made more sense if she wasn't expecting to meet anyone on the show with brains. She thought she'd get away with it.

"C'mon," Ed said. "You can't think Joshua responded to a 'smartest person in the room' ad and got cast on that basis. Dude is not smart. If he was, he could've been the bad guy without being a complete ass. And let's not talk about someone else."

I smiled.

"My ad wanted athletes who enjoy pushing themselves," Abram added.

Ed thrust a serving dish into my hand and handed Rachel a bottle of wine. "Doesn't matter now. Food's ready. Someone go find Justin and Ariana?"

Rachel handed me the wine and headed into the living room. As I served, Abram picked Birdie up effortlessly. She giggled as he spun her around and deposited her at the head of the table. Was she drunk, or just enjoying the attention? Maybe both.

Even if he was married, it must be nice to have someone muscular, nice, and reasonably attractive carry you around all day. I didn't blame Birdie for basking in the attention. Heck, a traitorous part of me wanted to "accidentally" break an ankle to see if I got the same treatment from Justin.

But I wouldn't. Probably.

After dinner, I changed into my swimsuit and went to enjoy the hot tub in the setting sun. It was odd they hadn't announced the results of the challenge yet, even though we all knew Ariana and Justin finished first and Abram and Birdie had been last. Would they penalize Abram for helping an injured player? Would Birdie be eliminated for getting injured? That didn't seem fair.

The warm water soothed my aching muscles. Too bad it couldn't do the same for my racing mind.

The water splashed as someone eased into the other side of the hot tub.

Please don't be Ariana, I prayed before opening my eyes. *Let it be Justin or Ed or Birdie—or one of the production assistants. Joshua. That guy from One Direction. Anyone but Ariana.*

Whichever deity received these silent prayers apparently wasn't listening. I cracked one eyelid enough to get a view of silky black hair, then slammed it shut.

"I saw that," Ariana said. "You can't pretend I'm not sitting here."

"Just enjoying the quiet," I mumbled. "It's nothing personal."

"You're a terrible liar."

I shrugged, but sat up and opened my eyes. "I was trying to be polite. You should look into it sometime. Did you need something?"

She smirked. "I heard you're trying to get me eliminated."

"I want to win. For me to win, I have to get *everyone* eliminated. As far as I know, you're not up for elimination this week. You should be."

"What? In case you didn't notice, I won the challenge."

"You finished first. You didn't win."

"Finishing first *is* winning. I thought you were supposed to be smart."

"It wasn't a regular race, or I'd have skipped the obstacles and run straight for the finish line. Unless you have different rules that don't apply to anyone else?"

Ariana flipped her hair and smirked again. God, I wanted to slap that look off her face. "I have no idea what you're talking about."

I'd had enough. I walked toward the stairs. "You do realize we're being videoed, right? And other people saw you cheating?"

Without waiting for a reply, I climbed out of the tub. I found an empty lounge chair next to Birdie and flopped on to it, calling myself a thousand kinds of idiot for letting Ariana get to me. Again.

She nodded toward the hot tub. "What did the bitch want?"

"Nothing, really. To crow about winning the challenge. To pretend she didn't cheat. To remind me why I hate her, maybe."

Birdie raised an eyebrow. "Were you likely to forget?"

"Nope."

We both laughed. Then, Birdie's expression changed. All traces of laughter vanished.

"Listen, Jen, I need to ask you a favor. Vote for me this week. Send me home. Tell the others."

"What? Why?"

"Half the show is based on physical challenges. I've got a broken ankle. I can't even participate. Even if the show doesn't send me home this week, I'll be out as soon as there's another physical challenge."

"We don't know what the remaining challenges are."

"Doesn't matter. Really, the show should send me home."

"Will you even be up for elimination if you were injured?"

"I already talked to the producers. They promised. But no matter what, I'm leaving."

"Oh, Birdie! No!"

"It's fine. Listen, I'm the least athletic of those of us left. Most of the challenges require some physical ability. I'm not the most likable person here. I like to think I'm kooky, but let's face it, I'm an odd duck."

"You're quirky!" I protested. "Also, sweet, funny—"

"No, I'm weird. It's fine. I like who I am. But America doesn't like weird. Abe's a nice guy, and he has a better shot at the grand prize. Vote for me. I had a good run, but I'm ready to go home."

She'd never spoken that much without throwing in a hashtag. For a moment, I wondered if she lost her mind due to Twitter withdrawal. But, deep down, I knew the things she said made sense.

"You're absolutely sure? You've made it so far!"

"I only joined the show in the first place because I was pissed. My ex broke up with me for spending too much time online. She swore I'd lose my mind if I lost Wi-Fi for a day. A friend told me about the show, and we agreed if I won I'd use the money to write 'Suck it, Tara' in the sky above her house."

I burst out laughing. More than once, I'd wondered what she was doing here. The explanation was so simple, yet perfect: revenge.

"Okay, I'll vote for you." I pulled her into a hug, trying not to cry.

* * *

Something was up. No one gave us the challenge results. It was Monday morning before the producers called us into the living room.

"We have a bit of a wrinkle this week, my little Fishies." Bella stood before us, beautiful as always in a gauzy light blue dress.

"One of you took it upon himself to quit the challenge to help a friend in need." Everyone looked at Abram, who blushed and hung his head. "And one of you, unfortunately, did not fulfill the requirements of each station."

Ariana tossed her head and glared around the room. Sometimes, I wished I had her "Go fuck yourself" attitude. Being able to make other people feel bad for noticing when I did something wrong was a good trick.

"As a result," Bella said, "The producers granted Abram immunity. The two official losers of this week's challenge are Birdie and Ariana. Both of you are up for elimination, along with the viewers' choice."

YES!

I wanted to jump up and down, screaming. My enthusiasm, however, was short-lived.

"I'm sorry, Jennifer, but the viewers voted for you again. You will also be up for elimination this week."

My shoulders slumped. No matter what I did, it wasn't good enough for the audience. Were they mad I mentioned that Ariana cheated? I hadn't said anything until she brought it up. Were the only viewers her friends and family? Wouldn't they at least miss watching the way she manipulated me if I left?

God, I hated her. I hated myself for letting her get to me, every time.

I bit my lip and looked down, blinking back tears of frustration.

Birdie leaned close and patted my knee. "Don't worry, Jen. I'm going home, remember? You're #safe. Everyone will vote for me."

I lowered my voice. "Ariana won't. She doesn't care what you want. She'd rather send me home now and focus on you next week. But everyone else might."

The glass walls closed in on me. I couldn't stand to be in the room another moment. What a stupid, crappy situation. I got up and walked toward the stairs. Birdie pulled me back.

"Where are you going?"

"To change. I need to go burn some energy. I'm going to go for a run."

Birdie hesitated, as if she wanted to say something else, but let me go. "Okay. Enjoy your run. Wish I could join you." I smiled, because we both knew she would never have offered to run with me if she hadn't broken her ankle.

"Thanks. I'll be thinking of you."

Later, I went looking for my friend. Suspecting I wasn't the only one who wanted some time alone, I started in the laundry room. Sure enough, she sat in the hidden corner with her leg propped up on a stack of dirty towels.

"Do you need anything?"

She eyed me warily. "You're not here to try to talk me out of leaving, are you?"

"Nope. Just here to hang out."

"In that case, sit with me?"

I sat. For a long time, we said nothing. We knew this was one of the last times we'd get to hang out until after the show. Beyond that, there wasn't much to say.

After a while, Ed found us. We filled him in on Birdie's plan. The three of us stayed up late, sipping drinks by the pool. One by one, Rachel, Abram, and Justin stopped to chat. They all agreed to send Birdie home.

When Ariana slipped into the hot tub, Ed joined her. I couldn't hear the conversation but presumed he filled her in. Part of me expected her to argue. But she cocked her head to one side, listening. Finally, she nodded.

A moment later, Ed sat on the edge of the pool, swinging his legs into the water. "She's in. That's everyone."

There wasn't much left to say.

"I'm going to miss you, Birdie."

"I know, Jen, I'll miss you, too. Come visit me. You, too, Ed."

"Nashville in summer? Ha! You should both come to Boston before it's cold and gross. We'll visit Nashville later."

"Well, I have nowhere to live. Be careful what you wish for. I may not leave." My smile fell, and I hid a sniffle behind one hand.

Eventually, when the moon rose high in the sky and empty wine bottles littered the patio, I helped Birdie hobble up the stairs to bed.

On Tuesday morning, I voted with a heavy heart. As much as it killed me to vote for Birdie, I had to let her go. She couldn't do the challenges, her ankle hurt, and she wanted to sacrifice herself.

I really wanted to dump some glitter in Ariana's bowl, even if I knew it would be a wasted vote. It would've been so satisfying to watch that smug smile drop off her face when Bella announced that she had been eliminated. I desperately hoped that, when the moment eventually came, I would see it.

And not from Brandon's living room.

As I turned to leave, some of my glitter sparkled where it had spilled on to the table. Absent-mindedly, I swiped at it with one hand, pushing most of it on to the floor. Then I paused thoughtfully, looking at the glittery emerald on my forefinger. After a moment's consideration, I wiped my finger across Ariana's smiling face, gloating from the front of her bowl.

Yes, I knew it wasn't a vote against her. Still, I held my head higher when I strutted out of the room.

After dinner, Birdie and I went upstairs to pack her stuff. When Bella came with the results, she was ready. I carried the suitcase down to the entryway.

Even with all that preparation, I cried when Bella announced the results. One by one, Birdie said her good-byes, leaving me for last.

"Don't cry," Birdie said as she hugged me tightly. "I'm glad to be going. They're taking me to a get some real painkillers! None of this Tylenol 3 garbage."

She paused, pulled me closer, and lowered her voice. "Now, make a move on Justin already! Give me something to watch when I get home. #showmance." I giggled.

"I'll do my best," I promised. "Bye, Birdie."

Chapter 21

Jennifer in the School Room, Week 7:

Voting for Birdie was hard, but what else could I do? She can't keep competing, and she wanted to go home.

I think the only reason she wasn't taken out when she got hurt is they didn't plan to lose two people in one week. From what I've seen on other shows, if she left before the vote, they'd have to bring back the last eliminated player to take her place. Maybe they didn't want to bring Mike back.

I'm so lucky to still be here. I wake up every morning grateful for this opportunity, and I'm glad to have another week on The Fishbowl. *I can't wait to see what happens next!*

The Fishbowl felt much bigger without Birdie. She may have been small, but her presence took up a lot of space. Ed and I rattled around the kitchen. Even though Birdie's elimination put me one step closer to the grand prize, I missed my friend.

While we were preparing breakfast, the producers called us into the living room.

"Good morning, Fish!" Bella greeted us. Our hostess stood before us in a bright yellow sundress and matching heels with a white shrug.

We blinked at her bleary-eyed. Several people grumbled in response. Most of us had been called out of bed, and the coffee hadn't finished brewing yet. I counted two yawns for each mumbled word. Nearly everyone wore wrinkled pajamas. Only Ariana was bright-eyed, waving enthusiastically in her perfect makeup with her hair in braids.

"Good morning, Bella!" She wore a nightie, which looked like it had been ironed. Was there an ironing board in the house? Had she brought one? Did Ariana know how to iron? She couldn't cook, clean, or do laundry.

She hadn't been wearing a red satin slip that barely covered her important bits when we went to sleep. I still hadn't caught her sneaking into the bathroom to put on makeup, then pretending to go back to sleep, but no way she woke up looking like that. In contrast, Abram had a streak of drool on his face, Rachel's hair stuck straight up, and Ed wore thick glasses because he stopped for his contacts. Ariana stood out like a rose in a sea of dandelions.

The midweek challenge was pretty simple, at least in that I didn't have to be tied to anyone or have any forced interactions. Until the end of the day, we were required to speak in rhyme.

Most of us spoke less than we normally would. Or was it only less than we could? Rachel was the first to miss. She realized her errors with a hiss. Then we went to the pool, enjoying our ability to cool. Lounging in our languid way, everyone had little to say.

Dinner was a quiet affair without Birdie there. Ed made a gaff that made us laugh. Then he jumped up with a shout, "Yuck! Suck! Fuck! Muck!" and slumped into a pout.

Finally, the daylight began to wane. The rest of us had won this game. "Good night, sleep tight," I said. I climbed into bed and rested my head.

* * *

Thursday morning, I sat alone in the kitchen after breakfast. I lingered longer than usual over my coffee, thinking about the past few weeks.

Suddenly, the weekly pre-challenge music blasted throughout the house, startling me out of my reverie.

"Ack—I'm late!" I raced toward the stairs.

This was our one chance all week to let it all hang out. Since the songs were copyrighted, they couldn't air the footage. We took full advantage of this reprieve. I sang at the top of my lungs into a curling iron, jump and danced across the couches, twirled around on the stairs, and tangoed back and forth across the main floor with Ed. We rocked out as they piped in "Rockin' Robin" in honor of Birdie. By the time the music stopped, my soul felt lighter.

Hopefully, none of the pre-challenge footage ever surfaced online. It would make great blackmail material.

When my turn came to start the challenge, I squeezed Ed's hand and smiled. "Thanks." I didn't need to say why.

"No problem. Now, let's go out there and kick some butt! Go Team Get-Ariana's-Obnoxious-Ass-Sent-Home!"

"Go us!" I cheered.

When I got to the challenge site, some sort of giant grid awaited me. Thick white lines composed the outer edges, and thin white lines ran between them. The structure spread about twenty feet up and down and across. Wooden blocks lay scattered throughout the grid, and several bins with more blocks sat off to one side.

Something was written on the blocks. I squinted into the sunlight to see better.

Near the front corner, I spotted a four. The one in the middle said "7". It was a giant Sudoku!

In high school, Adam and I used to play Sudoku Wars. My mom bought two copies of the same book, and we raced to see who finished first. Yes, we were dorks. No, I didn't care. It was loads of fun. I couldn't beat my older brother every time, but I could beat the remaining contestants.

Oh, this was going to be awesome! I danced in place while I waited for them to explain rules I knew by heart.

Just like an ordinary Sudoku, I'd place numbers 1 through 9 in each three by three square on the grid. Each line and column also had to contain numbers 1 through 9. I could only move one block at a time. One block per square.

I've got this. I own this challenge.

"Uh, Jen?"

The production assistant I thought of as Goatee stood a few feet away, looking at me curiously. The question broke my concentration.

"Yeah?"

"Are you humming 'Roar' by Katy Perry?"

Oops.

So what if I was? It's a catchy song. My face grew warm, but before I could answer, the light changed, and I was off.

After I finally dropped the last block into place, I raced back to the starting line and hit the button, panting. There were thirty-two minutes, forty-seven seconds showing on the timer. That was it? It felt like the challenge took at least an hour. Sweat dripped from my brow, and I could barely hold myself upright.

"Wow." Goatee stood behind me, looking at the course.

"What?"

"Oh, sorry. Nothing. I shouldn't have said anything."

"What? You can't just leave me hanging like that!" I laughed. "Was it 'Wow, you look great for someone who just had thirteen hernias?' 'Wow, I've never seen someone sweat so much?' 'Wow, you got the entire puzzle wrong?' What did I do?"

He gestured at the grid. "The puzzle. I'm not allowed to share results, and maybe some of the others carried them more easily, but you did well. Good for you."

"Thank you!"

Not everyone had gone yet, but the fact that my time impressed him gave me hope. With a spring in my step, I headed back inside the Fishbowl.

Turns out, I didn't need luck. I *crushed* them! Justin came in second, and I beat him by more than five minutes. All that time playing Sudoku Wars with Adam paid off.

I couldn't believe my good fortune. Not only did I win, but my biggest competition failed miserably, taking almost an hour to complete the challenge. The viewers couldn't nominate me for elimination, because my time gave me immunity. I was guaranteed another week in the Fishbowl! With luck, maybe Ariana wouldn't be part of it.

* * *

"So," Ed smirked at me from across the kitchen counter the next morning, "you'll never guess what I heard."

"Kevin Spacey is gay?" I guessed. "We're all pretty sure of that one."

Ed blew a raspberry at me. "Oh, way better. Apparently, Ariana dropped the blocks wherever. She didn't solve the puzzle."

"No way!"

"Yes! She grabbed the blocks and dropped them wherever, but the PAs made her redo it."

With a glance around the room, I learned forward. "How do you know this?"

Ed shot a meaningful look at the camera in the corner. Instead of answering he said, "Phew! Do you smell that? What's in the disposal?"

He grabbed a handful of ice and chucked it into the sink. His back to the camera, he beckoned with one finger. As I learned forward, he flipped the switch on the garbage disposal and turned on the water. His lips touched my ear.

"Let's just say that Rachel and J-dawg aren't the only ones who can play fifty-nine seconds in heaven late at night."

Curiosity filled me, but there was no reason to get anyone in trouble. I'd seen the way Curly Beard and Ed eyed each other. I could wait until the show ended for details.

I settled into my stool with a grin as Ed shut off the disposal. "Yes, that smells much better. Thanks."

"Did Ariana know we had to solve the puzzle?"

Ed shrugged. "Probably. I got instructions. Didn't you?"

"Yeah, but I recognized it. Who else was in the bottom?"

"Abram. He's probably got enough good will from last week to keep him around." He grinned. "And we know the viewers can't vote against you."

That was a relief—especially since I wasn't a fan favorite. "But what if it's you?"

He gasped in mock surprise. "Me? How could it be me? Surely, the viewers love me! I'm fabulous!" He gave a wry smile. "Besides, now that Birdie's gone, I'm the only one who cooks. The viewers will only vote for me if they want to spend the next three weeks watching you all starve. Unless one of the coming challenges is a fight to the death over the last bowl of cereal, Gladiator-style? That might be interesting."

I laughed. "In that case, they better not nominate Rachel, either, or the show may turn into a battle for the last clean plate. Ariana certainly isn't going to do dishes."

After breakfast, we headed out to the pool where Ed practiced his material on us. At one point, he flexed his muscles, pumped himself out, put a baseball cap on sideways, puffed out his cheeks, and swung his arms while jerking around the backyard.

"Yo, yo, yo, jerks! Don't get mad cuz the truth hurts!" Ed bellowed, striking his chest. "Y'all think I'm a sinna, but you hate me for being such a winna! Y'all can't keep the J-dawg down, not even with a frown!"

He spread his arms and threw his head back. Everyone cracked up. My sides hurt before I got control of myself. Even Rachel's eyes danced with amusement, although she hid her smiles behind one hand.

No one mentioned the elimination.

Later that afternoon, I peered down from the top of the couch tower at everyone sprawled around the living room. It was a hot day, even for Southern California, and we'd chosen to cower in the air conditioning rather than bake in temperatures over a hundred degrees. Even the pool was uncomfortably warm with the sun beating down. The thought of sitting in a hot tub curdled my insides.

I directed my question at the entire room. "So, what would you do with a quarter of a million dollars?"

"Pay off my student loans," Justin said. "That's why I'm here. It may not be exciting, but it beats spending the next thirty years paying a mortgage on my brain."

I respected that. "Rach?"

She waved a hand half-heartedly in my direction from the lower levels of the tower. "Too hot. No talk."

"Well, I know what I'd do," Abram said. "I'd donate ten percent to my church, and I'd put the rest away for my boys' college. I never went because we couldn't afford it. I want them to have better opportunities than I did."

"That's admirable," Ed told him. "I had different plans when I auditioned, but I want to move to Los Angeles and try the comedy scene. Boston is dead. The money will support me until I get my big break. During the day, I'd like to mentor gay kids. Life's hard. It's harder when you don't have anyone who understands you."

"Christ! You're all such boring do-gooders," Ariana groaned. "Really? Churches? Helping gay kids? College educations? What a snooze! *When* I win a quarter of a million dollars—not if—I'm renting a private plane and flying all my friends someplace amazing. We'll party as long as I want. If there's anything left when I go home, I need a new wardrobe."

"You'd blow it all? What about your daughter?" Abram asked.

Ed reached up and squeezed my hand. We both knew she didn't really have a daughter. I only wished there were a way to call her out—again—without looking petty or jealous. Again.

"Naturally, I'll take her with me. My daughter is the center of my world." She added with a sneer, "Not that it's *anyone's* business how I raise my child."

"Of course not," Ed said. "You clearly know how to have more fun than the rest of us. What about you, Jen? Parties and private planes? Or school and charity work?"

"Hmmmm." I'd wondered earlier how much of myself to reveal on TV. If I wanted the viewers to identify with me, there was no benefit to holding back, especially now that I wasn't a fan favorite. Maybe showing them a little more of the inner Jen would help them connect with me more.

"Things have been rough. I've got a medical bill that's been killing me since I broke my leg last year. My landlord condo-ized my apartment at the end of May, so I'm living on a friend's couch when I get home. Then I caught my boyfriend cheating. And I got laid off. Worst year ever—until this summer, I mean.

"When I go home, I'm single, unemployed, and homeless, with some big debts. The money would give me some breathing room until I get back on my feet."

"Wow," Justin said. "I had no idea you'd been through all that. I'm sorry."

"Thanks. At least I'm here. Things could've been worse—"

"Is anyone hungry?" Ariana stood. "Food will energize us. Maybe the producers will bring us ice cream." She wandered into the kitchen.

I stayed put. I couldn't stop her from changing the subject every time I got two seconds of positive attention, but I wasn't about to play into it by following her.

Rachel sat up and hollered toward the kitchen. "I WOULD USE A QUARTER MIL TO START A CHEERLEADING CAMP FOR UNDERPRIVILEGED CHILDREN!"

Oh, that was amazing. I smothered a giggle until I made the mistake of looking at Ed. His face contorted with barely controlled laughter. Justin snorted as a sound of disgust rolled back from Ariana's direction. After a moment, Abram sat up with a sigh.

"I guess the Christian thing to do is go see how she's doing."

Below me, Rachel said, "As soon as she wants to start acting in a Christian manner, I'll consider giving her the same courtesy."

Abram was right, but I agreed with Rachel. Ariana had been too horrible for too long to give any credence to her staged hissy fit. Attention would only encourage her.

Low voices traveled out of the kitchen. It was impossible to make out the words, but it didn't matter. Leaning against the side of the couch, I closed my eyes and napped.

When I woke, the sun had set. Goose bumps dimpled my arms. The spot on top of the couch tower was cozy and had a great view, but it sat directly below the air conditioning vents. Earlier, that had been a bonus, but they must not have turned it down when the outside temperature dropped.

"Hey, there," Justin's head poked up over the edge of the tower. "You awake?"

"Mmm-hmm. Sort of," I mumbled, sitting up. I hugged myself and rubbed my arms, trying to get the blood flowing. "How long have I been out?"

"I'm not sure. I fell asleep, too." He shrugged. "Probably somewhere between fifteen minutes and three hours."

"Thanks, that's super helpful."

"I know, sorry," he said. "Anyway, Ariana got the producers to bring us ice cream and stuff. Ed's declared that sundaes and leftovers can be dinner for one night."

"He's getting tired of cooking for everyone, especially now that Birdie's gone. I don't mind giving him a night off."

"Need help getting down?" Justin held out a hand, which I took. Goosebumps rippled up my arm at his touch.

Getting to the ground was awkward, not difficult. Unfortunately, I hadn't noticed that my left foot fell asleep while I napped. As soon as I put pressure on it, I fell—and tumbled into Justin's arms.

The universe enjoyed testing my resolve to get over this guy and focus on the competition. Stupid universe. Stupid, wonderful universe.

I closed my eyes and inhaled, savoring the feel of his hard chest pressing against me. Maybe I could just stay here. One of his hands cupped the back of my head, and I thought I heard him swallow.

"Careful." Justin moved backward, helping me stand on my own.

I swore internally. Was it my imagination, or did his hands linger on my waist for just a second longer than necessary? His face was so close to mine.

"You don't want to have to leave due to injury. I think one of those per season is the network's limit."

His lopsided smile awoke the butterflies in my stomach, and my shiver had nothing to do with the cold.

Calm down, I told myself. *This is the guy who puked when you puckered up at him. And, after sleeping all afternoon, your breath must be terrible.*

Justin lowered his voice. "Look, I never got a chance to say anything. I know you've been avoiding me, and I understand if you never wanted to talk to me again, but I'm so sorry about that night. I woke up hoping it was a nightmare. You're the last person in this house I'd choose to throw up on."

"I didn't think you did it on purpose. I just worried your body's natural reaction to being so close to me was to. . .well, you know." I chuckled to act like I was kidding, but it sounded hollow to my own ears. I couldn't meet his eyes.

Focus on the money. Forget the illusion of romance. It's all part of the show. He'd do anything to win.

Justin put one finger under my chin and forced me to look at him. "No." His words were soft, yet firm. "When I haven't been doing shots of Everclear, vomiting is the opposite of what I want to do when you're around."

He still stood very close. The heat of his body called to me, a siren song I didn't want to want to answer.

Think about the money, Jen.

A two-bedroom one-bath condominium I'd seen when I'd first found out I had to move swam before my eyes. I grasped for that image.

Think of the open floor plan and stainless steel appliances. An easy walk to the Metro. Only two hundred thousand. All you need is to win.

Justin gazed into my eyes. "What are you thinking about?"

When he gazed into my soul like that, distracting myself didn't work. Visions of hardwood floors were replaced with the way we'd laughed together that first night. Our late-night Speed tournament. His—

Oh, God. What about my breath? My tongue felt thick and fuzzy as I ran it over my teeth. *Can the guy who threw up on my feet complain about my breath?*

Yes, he can.

It took every inch of willpower I had not to lean forward. *Anything to win, remember? Anything.*

This was hopeless. No matter how much my brain screamed to walk away, the rest of my body wouldn't listen. I craved more of him with every fiber of my being.

"Hey, guys! The ice cream is—oh, sorry."

A voice in the doorway caused Justin to drop his hand. We both jumped backward. Ed stood in the doorway looking sheepish. I blushed and examined my toes.

"I didn't mean to interrupt, but the stuff is here. The ice cream bar is all set up when you're ready." Ed ran one hand through his hair. "I'll. . .just. . .uh. . .go."

Justin's tomato-colored face must have mirrored my own. He cleared his throat and swallowed hard. "Right. Dinner. Right. Sorry."

He followed Ed out of the room.

Eye on the prize, Jen.

But as I went to brush my teeth, I wondered what the real prize was.

Chapter 22

Scenes from the School Room, Week 7:

Ed: *My kingdom for a television. One little movie? Magazines? A book! Or we could have some paper? We'll write our own books, and read them to each other.*

Ariana: *I couldn't tell them the truth. I really need the money to help my little girl. She's so sick. But I feel like, if they knew, they'd use it against me. It's our secret, America.*

Rachel: *Actually, I was planning to use my winnings to buy my mom a new truck. She needs one. Then I'd buy a house and go to beauty school. But whatever.*

Justin: *I'm impressed with how fast Jen finished the Sudoku challenge. It lessens the sting of second place.*

Abram: *Jesus was nice to the tax collectors and criminals. I can be nice to one spoiled rich girl who doesn't have any friends in the house.*

The heat wave continued on Sunday. The air conditioning helped, but we basically lived in a greenhouse. No one wanted even the minor physical exertion of playing pool or darts. Finally, Ed and I dug out the decks of cards I'd made what felt like a lifetime ago. We stuck to the basics: Old Maid, Crazy 8s, Go Fish.

At one point, desperate for something to do, I cleaned the fingerprints off all of the glass walls in the house. What a stupid idea. After several weeks of people touching and walking into them, smudges on the walls made them much more visible. Now, we were back to square one.

After the sun set, we ventured into the pool. We lazed for quite a while before Rachel swam over to test the hot tub.

"Oh, guys! It's nice!" she exclaimed, pulling herself over the wall. "Kind of like a warm bath!"

"I'll enjoy my raft, if it's all the same to you," Ed said. "I'm not moving until I fall asleep and roll into the water."

"You better not splash me when you do," Ariana said, floating nearby. "I finally got comfortable."

The cool breeze brought the temperature low enough to make the hot tub seem tolerable. As I settled myself across from Rachel, she glanced at the pool.

"Just so we're clear," she said in hushed tones. "We're voting for Ariana, no matter who the viewers pick, right?"

Her question surprised me. "Are you worried, Rach? You and Ed are the only ones who've never been up for elimination."

"I know, but I didn't do great in the challenge. Ed and Justin both beat me. I can't stay safe forever. Sooner or later, my luck will run out."

I settled back against the edge of the tub and tilted my face up to the stars. "Well, I'm not choosing between you and Abram. I'm voting for Ariana, even if that ultimately means she'll be choosing who goes home."

"What do you mean?"

"If five out of six of us vote for Ariana, and the viewers save her again, then the person leaving is whoever gets that final vote. It will all come down to who Ariana picks. Who knows what she's thinking? You may have to apologize for that cheerleading camp comment."

"Like hell!" Rachel said. I raised my eyebrows at her. "Okay, maybe after we see the viewer vote. No way I'm sucking up to her unless my life depends on it."

"Of course not."

I'd never been happier to have immunity than when I realized I'd unquestionably be going home without it. The viewers had nominated me for elimination the last two weeks I hadn't won my safety. If Ariana's vote had been the deciding factor, I'd have been on the first flight back to Seattle.

The next morning, we gathered to hear the results of the viewer vote. As usual, Bella greeted us as enthusiastically as if we were giving her a quarter of a million dollars.

"Good morning, Fish! How was your weekend?"

"Boring," I grumbled.

A chorus of, "hot," "long," etc., echoed my sentiments.

Ed piped up. "I think I perfected my Joshua impression! That was the highlight."

Bella gave us a withering look. "Can we try that again for the viewers?" Then she plastered her trademark perfect smile back on to her face.

"Good morning, Fish! How was your weekend?"

I felt like when I was in school and the teacher chastised us for not enthusiastically responding with "Good morning, Mrs. Redding!" But I was here to put on a show, so I responded appropriately with an enthusiastic smile. "Fantastic, Bella!"

With everyone else echoing my sentiments, hopefully the cameras caught something that resembled sincerity. From anyone but Ariana.

"Well, I'm glad you enjoyed it. For one of you, unfortunately, this was your final weekend in the Fishbowl. Ariana, Abram, as you know, are up for elimination based on last week's challenge. Jen, you won immunity." A smile split my face in two until Bella continued. "The viewers have spoken. I'm sorry, Justin, but you are up for elimination."

Oh, God. Not this again. Part of me loathed the viewers. I had to remind myself that the only person I wanted to see leave was already up for elimination. She couldn't be nominated twice, sadly. Still, I gave up on trying to figure out what the viewers wanted.

Before I could speak with the others, the producers called me into the School Room. After I finished my interview, Rachel and Abram lounged in the sitting room with Ariana. I found Justin in the kitchen with Ed and sent him to "confess."

Ed handed me a cup of coffee. "We're pretty sure Abram's going home."

"Yeah, that was more or less my conclusion," I said. "I'm voting for Ariana, but since we can't count on America to actually let her go home, it'll be whoever comes in second."

A platter of eggs and bacon sat on the table. My stomach growled to remind me I'd missed breakfast while giving my interview. I made a sandwich.

"Right. Ariana won't vote for Justin—although, since he couldn't be expressing less interest in her, maybe she should. If the viewers don't have a say in the final winner, he could beat her," Ed said.

"If she thought about it, she'd send him home just to upset me. But she'd rather take another week to make me watch her hang all over him before I get eliminated."

"You don't know you're going home next week."

"True. But let's just say that the odds have *not* been 'ever in my favor.'" I finished my sandwich and stood, brushing crumbs off my fingers. "Ugh. One thing I can say—all this frustration has been great for my health. I'm going for a run."

After dinner, we gathered in the living room to hear the results of the viewer vote. Remembering how packed in we were on day one, I was surprised to realize that the remaining contestants all fit on the sectional.

As soon as we sat, Bella waltzed in, looking perfect as always.

"Good evening, Fish. I imagine you're desperately waiting to hear the results, so I won't make you wait." She opened the envelope she carried and read the contents aloud.

"Ariana, my dear, I'm sorry to tell you that, once again, your fellow Fish have voted to eliminate you."

My ears perked up. *Is this it? Finally?*

"Luckily for you, the viewers have again voted that you should remain in the house. You're safe, Ariana."

ARGH!

It wasn't until everyone turned to look that I wondered if I actually emitted a growl in my frustration. Based on Ed's expression, probably. I forced myself to relax.

"Justin, Abram, I'm sorry, but that means one of you will be leaving us tonight." Bella paused for effect. "Abram, I'm sorry, but you have been eliminated. You must leave *The Fishbowl* immediately."

Tears prickled behind my eyes. I refused to let them fall. I'd known his was coming, and I was glad it wasn't Justin, but Abram was a good guy. He deserved better than to get beaten by Ariana.

"Well, I guess that's it, guys," Abram said. "And just when I managed to snag a seat on the tower."

I grinned at him. I hadn't paid attention to where he sat, but it was unusual for someone else to beat me to my favorite spot. He climbed to the ground and went to get his suitcase as the five remaining Fish lined up in the hallway.

A few minutes later, I hugged Abram tightly. It was like embracing a slab of granite. "It was great getting to know you."

"Thanks for teaching me how to play poker," he said. "Let's keep in touch. I think you'd like my wife."

"Absolutely," I said. "I'd love to take your kids to the Space Needle."

He continued down the row, saying good-bye to the others. A few minutes later, the front door closed, and he was gone.

Bella called us back into the living room. That was new. I leaned against the wall as she spoke. "There are now only five Fish left. And that means something important: no more immunity! It's officially every Fish for himself. No one is safe."

My already low spirits plummeted. The only thing that saved me this week was that the viewers couldn't nominate me for elimination. If I couldn't get immunity, I wasn't sure how to stay another week. When would the rules finally shift away from Ariana's favor?

I wanted to scream. Ed stepped toward me, but I stopped him with one shake of my head.

Frustrated, I headed for the one place I could be alone: the laundry room.

No one ever used this room. I'd grown very fond of almost all the other Fish, but their housekeeping skills left something to be desired. I was still the only one who spent any amount of time cleaning. The work busied my hands but freed my mind, which was exactly what I needed.

A moment later, Justin's voice dragged me away from my task.

"Hey."

He stood in the doorway, leaning against the frame. He must have been on his way to the pool. I dragged my eyes away from his bare chest and up to his face. His tanned, perfect bare chest with the finest sprinkling of golden hair.

Nope, not looking. Not looking at the trail leading from his belly button below his shorts, either.

When I'd been with Dominic, I'd thought a hairy chest was sexy, a sign of virility or something. How naive. As my eyes lingered on Justin's chest, it was his smattering of hair that got my pulse racing.

"Hey," I said. One of these days, I'd figure out a good opening line. If I didn't get sent home.

"You okay?"

"It's just so frustrating," I said. "I do everything to win, to beat Ariana, and the viewers keep voting her back in. If she's predestined to win, why do I even bother?"

"Because we don't know how the winner will ultimately be chosen."

I sighed. "Yeah, I guess. Sorry to unload on you."

"It's okay. I came to talk." He walked farther into the room and went to the back corner. "This is the magic spot, right?"

"Yeah. How did you know?"

"Birdie told me before she left. Said if I wanted a private conversation, to head in here. Ariana won't see me?"

"Nope." I pointed at the camera. "We're being filmed, but she won't know you're here, unless she was in the kitchen when you walked through."

"She's in the School Room." He ran one hand through his hair.

My fingers itched to do the same.

"I've been wanting to talk to you without everyone else around. I'm sorry, Jen. You were right. I should've told you about her."

I shrugged, my eyes on the laundry pile. "Maybe you were right. You don't have to explain yourself to me. We're not dating. I don't know how you feel about me. When I started to ask, you hurled on me."

"You know I didn't do that on purpose."

Purely so he couldn't see my shaking hands, I put a load of wet towels into the dryer and turned it on, refusing to meet his eyes. "I know. But, after that, and knowing about Ariana—it felt like I should give up. I couldn't figure out how to know if I could trust you."

"No one ever knows, Jen. That's why they call it 'trust.'" He paused. "But remember—when you asked, I told you everything. I have no secrets. I made a mistake. I thought I'd never see her again. We were going to go our separate ways and never see each other again. We'd both been drinking. If I could go back and undo it, I would. I hate that this is coming between us."

"It's not just that. When we first met, I thought you liked me, but then when we showered together, you wouldn't even glance my way."

"That shower was amazing. You looked so hot, I was terrified I'd get a hard-on. I spent the whole time thinking about my sister and my grandma so you wouldn't realize how turned on I was."

I laughed.

He said, "And when I had my arms around you during the archery challenge, I just wanted to close my eyes and hold you, timer be damned."

The dryer was loud. That's why I took a step closer. To hear him better. Yup. The only reason. And probably why he stepped closer to me.

"I really like you. Ever since we met. And I thought you liked me, too." He reached out and pulled me toward him, into the hidden corner.

My arms went around his waist as he hugged me. It felt so good to lean into him. I wanted to believe him.

"I like you, too," I said. "Does every relationship have to be so difficult?"

"No. It can be very easy." He whispered in my ear. "I've wanted to kiss you for weeks. It just feels cheap to put something so personal on national television. I want to take you on a real date, walk you to your door, and give you a proper kiss good night with no one watching except your nosy neighbors."

Although every inch of my body screamed that other eyes didn't matter, I understood what he meant. "Want to go into a changing room?"

He laughed. "For fifty-nine seconds? God, that would be awesome. No, let's just sit here for a bit. Let me hold you."

Justin sat in the corner on a pile of clean towels. I sat, snuggled against him, and put my head on his shoulder. He put his arms around me and rested his chin on top of my head. We stayed there, hidden from the other contestants, until the dryer buzzed.

* * *

The next morning dawned bright and beautiful. Justin and I played footsie under the kitchen table while Rachel made breakfast. When the producers called us into the living room to hear about that day's mini-challenge, we held hands.

As we sat on the couch, Ed's gaze went from our still linked hands to our identical ear-to-ear smiles. He winked at me. Blushing, I grinned back at him. Ariana stumbled in behind us, scowled, and climbed to my old spot on top of the tower, her back to us. Rachel arrived a second later, sitting on the couch between me and Ed.

Usually, Leanna explained our mini-challenges, so Justin and I exchanged a glance when Bella entered the room instead.

"What's going on?" he whispered.

I shrugged.

"Good morning, everyone!" Bella said.

"Good morning," we chorused back.

"We're down to the final Final Five Fishes! Isn't that exciting?"

The group cheering became noticeably less impressive each time we lost a Fish. The room felt muted without Abram's booming voice.

"Excellent," Bella said. "To congratulate you on making it this far, the producers have arranged a surprise. We know that you've been cooped up here for a long time, with no access to the outside world. You all miss your friends and family."

Her gaze moved around the room, locking eyes with each of us. One at a time, we nodded.

"Who do you miss the most, Justin?" Bella asked.

"My twin sister," he said promptly. "Being here without her is like half my brain's missing."

"Well, luckily, you might get a chance to see her. Today, you will compete for a chance to have a private lunch with someone very special to you. There are five people, right now, waiting in a hotel room nearby to see who will be chosen—including Sarah."

A huge smile split Justin's face in two. I gnawed my lip, wondering if they'd paid to fly Adam in from Montreal. More likely, though, it was my mom. I missed my mom. All I wanted was to pour my heart out and get some advice. The idea of seeing her again—and introducing her to Justin—sent a wave of excitement through me. Just when I thought things couldn't get any better, the show did something like this.

"Ariana," Bella said. "Your best friend, Veronica, is here, hoping to see you."

She squealed and clapped.

"Rachel, your mother, Jacqueline, is here, living it up in the spa."

"Oh, wow!" Rachel clapped her hands over her mouth, beaming.

"Ed, we've brought out your best friend, Jerome."

"Jerry," he said. "And that's awesome. Thanks."

"Don't thank me yet. You still have to win the right to see him," Bella said. "And last but not least, Jen. If you win today's mini-challenge, you'll earn the right to have a one hour romantic lunch with your serious boyfriend, Dominic!"

My jaw dropped. What the hell? I opened and closed my mouth, but no sounds came out. Someone gasped, and I didn't even know if it was me. Three heads swiveled toward me. But I focused only on the fourth one, the blond head that bolted off the couch at the word "boyfriend" and stormed out of the room.

Justin.

Chapter 23

<u>More scenes from the School Room, Week 7:</u>

Rachel: *Nuh-uh. Nope. No way. She's totally into Justin.*

Ed: *Jen's not a cheater. She was in love with some asshole before the show started, but she dumped him when she found out he was married. How did the show even find him? And why would they bring him here instead of her mom or brother?*

Ariana: *Oh, this is amazing. This is so fantastic! *laughing* This is the best thing that possibly could've happened to me. Thank you so much, producers! Thank you.*

Justin: *I don't want to talk about it. Sorry.*

Ignoring everyone around me, I tore after Justin, Ariana's laughter floating up the stairs behind me. At the top of the stairs, I paused for a split second, trying to figure out where he went. The bedrooms weren't terribly private, so I turned toward the bathroom.

The stall door slammed shut just as I got to the doorway. I banged on the door. "Justin! Come on, open the door."

No response.

"Please talk to me. It's not true."

Silence.

Why would the show do this to me? How had they even found Dominic? Why would they think I wanted to spend an intimate lunch with him? Wearily, I leaned my head against the door, tears sliding down my face.

"I'm sorry, Justin. Please open the door."

I don't know how long I stood there before a hand fell on my shoulder. Rachel stood behind me, concern in her eyes. I fell into her outstretched arms, sobbing. Behind us, the stall door remained firmly shut.

She stroked my hair with one hand. "Shh. It's okay. Let's not spend all day crying in the bathroom."

Like a calf to the slaughter, I followed her to into the sitting room. I didn't notice the School Room door open until Ariana emerged, looking like the cat that swallowed the biggest canary. "Awesome dramatic moment, Jen. Way to go. The viewers are going to love this."

Like hell they would. The viewers would never get a glimpse of Dominic if I had anything to say about it.

"I don't have a boyfriend, and I don't know why he's here. But I'm going to find out." Already calling for Leanna, I raced down the stairs.

She met me at the bottom.

"Can we talk outside?"

Wordlessly, she motioned toward the front door, and I followed. "What's going on?"

"You tell me. Dominic? What the hell?"

Her brow furrowed. "Look, I know you've got a thing for Justin, but you listed this guy on your contact sheet. Said he was your 'serious boyfriend.' Was that not true?"

Oh, shit. I'd totally forgotten. At the audition. One of the stacks of forms they'd handed me. Now that she mentioned it, I saw myself adding "serious" in front of boyfriend, so the producers would know I wasn't just listing a fling. What a naive idiot I'd been.

"It was true at the time," I said. "We broke up the next day."

"You never updated your contact sheet."

"I didn't know I was supposed to!"

"Well, I'm sorry to hear that, but when we called, Dominic went on and on about how you're the best thing that ever happened to him. Sounds like he wants to get back together. Doing it on the show would be great for ratings."

For a long moment, I forgot how to speak. My mouth opened and closed, but no sounds came out. "Nope. Nope. Nope. He can't come here."

"It's too late. He's in town," she said. "If you don't want to see him, lose the challenge."

"What?"

"Let someone else win. I'm sure Rachel would love to see her mom. Or Ariana her BFF."

Although my natural competitiveness screamed at her words, I couldn't deny the beautiful simplicity of it. Lose the mini-challenge, don't see the douchebag who ruined my life, make up with Justin. Simple, right?

If only I had any idea how.

* * *

When Leanna gathered everyone to explain the rules of the mini-challenge, I remained on the bed in my room, staring stubbornly at the inside of the canopy. They said on Day One mini-challenges were optional; they couldn't make me play their twisted game.

Rachel came back after the game. "Justin won. His sister's coming."

"Thanks." For almost a heartbeat, that lifted my spirits, until I remembered that only the winner got to see the guest. Not that Sarah would want to see me once Justin told her what happened.

"Ariana's down there right now, sinking her hooks into him. You should go talk to him."

I shook my head, even though she couldn't see me through the curtains. "It doesn't matter anymore, Rach. I can't fix this if he won't talk to me."

She sighed. "Well, at least I'll try to keep Ariana away from you. You'll figure something out."

"Thanks."

A member of the production staff popped by to tell me not to venture into the second floor sitting area until Sarah left. Briefly, I dreamed of bursting in to say hello, to make them both listen, but the PAs had eyes and ears everywhere. Still, they couldn't stop me from using the bathroom, and we only had one.

On my way past the changing room door, an arm snaked out and dragged me inside, slamming the door shut. I swallowed a yelp as I stumbled over my own feet.

Inside, I found myself nose-to-nose with Sarah.

"We've got to stop meeting like this," I joked.

"We need to talk," she hissed. "We've got sixty seconds?"

The steely look in her eyes made me swallow my laughter. Nodding, I moved farther into the cubicle, pulling the door shut behind me. All the times I'd dreamed of locking myself into a tiny room with a hot, green-eyed blond, and not once had I imagined it would wind up like this.

"What's going on?" I kept my voice low, mimicking the urgency in Sarah's voice.

"Are you toying with my brother to win the game?"

Her words sent a shockwave through me. It never occurred to me that Justin had the same doubts I did. "No! If I'd known we'd get a second alone, I'd have asked you exactly the opposite question. Remember when we met? You said he'd do anything to win."

"Oh, hell." She ran her fingers through her curly hair. "I just meant he'd have no problem streaking or eating bugs or whatever. Not this. He really likes you, but he's worried it's not real. That you're just trying to get more screen time."

I didn't know what to say. Hearing that Justin really liked me made me feel lighter than I had in weeks. But if he didn't trust me, either, how could we make it work?

"Dominic and I broke up weeks before the show started. Right after the audition. I swear I don't have a boyfriend. Serious or otherwise."

She stared into my eyes so long I feared the timer would kick on and we'd be locked in. "I believe you," she said finally.

Relief flooded through me. "Thanks."

"Wait. There's more. But we're running out of time."

"Hold on a sec."

Checking to make sure the coast was clear, I dragged her into the other changing room, buying us another sixty seconds.

"Here's the thing," Sarah said. "Justin had a serious girlfriend in college. They loved each other, or he thought they did. He was planning to propose after graduation, with all our friends and family. Except her family never showed up. She lied about her parents, her siblings, everything, because she was ashamed to come from poverty."

"That's awful."

"He wouldn't have cared that she was poor, but she'd racked up huge debts on her clothes, makeup, hair, etc., all so she could snag a husband from a rich family. Which we're not—except compared to her. It hurts to find out someone only likes you for your money. He hasn't been serious about anyone since."

Poor Justin. My heart bled for him. That explained why he was as hesitant to start things up as I was.

"I'm sorry," I said. "I didn't know."

"That's why I'm telling you. He likes you. Right after the show sequestered you guys, your ex's wife showed up all over the media. Did an exposé for some paparazzi blog, talking about how you stole her husband, you're a home wrecker, etc. It went viral."

I'd never understood what someone meant when they said the blood drained from their face, but I grew lightheaded. Leaning against the wall for support, I clutched my microphone.

"That's why the viewers keep voting against you. Danielle painted a really bad picture."

"Who?" I asked.

She glared at me. "You didn't even know her name?"

Oh. Duh. "She was mostly naked when we met. I didn't stick around for introductions. But I swear, I had no idea. Her appearance came as a complete shock."

"That's fine, but Ariana's fans are playing it up. Say you know how much she likes Justin, and he likes her, too, but you're in the way, trying to make her look bad."

"I knew it," I said. "I mean, I didn't know, of course, but I knew there was something going on. Did you tell Justin?"

A voice sounded from the speakers. "Girls? What's going on in there?"

We ignored them. Sarah started speaking faster, leaning closer to me. "I tried, but the producers warned me not to tell him anything about the outside world, so he wouldn't hear it."

"So why are you telling me?"

"I've been reading the forums. You're probably going home soon, and I wanted to give you a chance to tell Justin the truth."

"About Ariana?"

She snorted. "He knows what she is. Tell him how you feel, dummy."

Feet pounded up the stairs.

Sarah flung the door open and greeted the production staff at the top of the stairs. "I'm so embarrassed! I thought that was the bathroom. Scared the hell out of poor Jen by walking in on her changing."

"Uh-huh," Curly Beard said.

He winked at me and ushered Sarah back behind the curtain where

Justin presumably waited. She grinned and waved at me over her shoulder.

Back upstairs, I spent a long time thinking about Sarah's words. Justin liked me. Not show-liked me; he liked me, liked me. Doing "anything to win" didn't mean exploiting me. And no matter how much I swore I wasn't going to develop feelings for my competition, I liked him. A lot.

Before I got eliminated, Justin needed to know the truth.

* * *

The second Sarah left, I made a beeline for Justin. I found him in the kitchen with the others. My heart plummeted.

"So sorry you didn't get to see your *serious boyfriend*," Ariana said.

"Leave her alone," Justin said before I could reply. "They broke up."

Our eyes met, and my heart lifted. This wasn't the time to talk, but we were going to be okay. He believed me. I poured myself a drink and sat at the counter, joining the conversation.

"Hey, guys?" Ed said some time later. "What's going on outside?"

The kitchen had been growing steadily darker, which I attributed to the setting sun. But now I turned and realized the producers had hung sheets over the kitchen windows.

"An evening challenge?" Rachel suggested.

"We've never done two in one day," Ed said.

"That doesn't mean we couldn't," I said.

Justin went to try the door, but it wouldn't open.

"This is stupid," Ariana said. "I'm going to find someone to tell me what's going on." She strode into the house, calling for a member of the production staff.

"Should we help?" I asked Justin. "The sun is setting. We've never been locked inside overnight."

He shrugged. "I guess it's better than sitting here waiting for the other shoe to drop. I'll go check the front door."

While he did that, I wandered around, calling out to the cameras. "Leanna? Hello? Anyone there?"

Wham!

For what must have been the fifteenth time that summer, a glass wall clipped the side of my foot, smashing my pinky toe.

With a groan, I hobbled into the kitchen and sat on a barstool. Ed made something that filled the room with the scent of garlic and basil.

A moment later, Justin wandered in. "The front door's locked, too."

"I give up, guys. There's no challenge this week. Or, it's a secret challenge, and the one who walks into the fewest walls wins." I picked up a bottle of Cabernet. "I lose. But the one who walks into the most walls get a free bottle of wine."

Justin plucked it out of my hands. "That's Rachel."

"Yeah, good point. But I hurt my foot. Gimme."

He set the bottle out of reach, then brought me a frozen bag of peas and a hand towel. He gently stretched my leg to the adjacent bar stool, then wrapped the peas in the towel and set it on my toes. "Try this."

My hand brushed his when I reached for the peas. My heart beat so loudly he might hear it. Our eyes met, and for a brief second, I knew we thought about the exact same thing. But I needed to clear the air.

"Listen, about before—"

"Don't," Justin said. "Sarah told me everything. I get it."

The spell broke when Ariana poked her head through the doorway. "Leanna's here. Come on."

Justin and I exchanged a look but followed her. Our fingers brushed as we walked, sending tingles up my arm.

"Hello, my Fish!" Leanna said. "Interesting day, huh? This week, we're doing something different. The challenge for the Final Five Fish is a temptation."

What did that mean? Were they going to show us delicious food we couldn't eat? They should have done that before dinner. Or maybe I'd have to sit inches from Justin without being allowed to touch him. I'd fail that temptation.

"As you know, the winner of *The Fishbowl* will win $250,000. And as you may also know, there is *no prize* for second place." She paused to let that information sink in.

"Or is there? We've placed a television screen outside by the pool. Outside, you will find five bowls, each containing a fish with your name on it. For the rest of the night, we will flash prizes on the screen: Trips. Cash. Cars. It could be anything. The first person to take his or her fish and throw it into the pool wins that prize. You will also leave *The Fishbowl* immediately."

They would pay one of us to quit? Would it be enough to make it worth leaving?

"If none of you succumbs to temptation, Rachel, Ed, Justin, Ariana, and Jen will complete a challenge tomorrow, and the game continues. If one of you leaves, a former contestant will take your spot."

She gestured toward the large glass doors. The sheets covering them inched downward as she spoke.

"We asked America to choose which eliminated Fish they most wanted to see come back to *The Fishbowl*. And they voted for—"

The sheet dropped, and the outdoor lights blazed. Sitting in the hot tub was—oh, no. Not him. Bring back anyone else.

"Joshua! Welcome back, Joshua!"

Fuck.

"Everyone, go outside and get your fish. It is now exactly eight o'clock. I'll be back at midnight, or when a fish hits the water, whichever comes first." She waved far too happily for someone who had just dropped such a bomb on us.

No. No. Nonononono.

America wanted to see more of that jerk? Really?

Rachel, of course, beamed and smoothed her hair. I'd almost forgotten they'd been friends. She walked right past the big pink fish with "Rachel" on the side, stripped off her sundress to reveal her bikini, and jumped into the hot tub.

A speaker crackled overhead, and Overalls spoke from the control booth. "Rachel? You're not allowed to interact with Joshua unless he re-enters play. And you can't touch him. Move to the other side of the tub."

"Okeydoke. Sorry." Rachel dutifully shifted a couple of feet to her left.

The speaker crackled again. "Thank you, Rachel."

She gestured to indicate she'd heard.

At the moment, the screen said, "Please stand by."

"Hey, Ed," I said. "Do you want to quit the game in exchange for some 'Please Stand By?'"

He tilted his head to one side and rubbed his chin. "A very generous offer, Jen, but I think I'll have to pass. Now, if you had some 'Hold on a Minute,' we'd be in business."

As I hobbled to the lounge chairs farthest away from the hot tub—and, more importantly, Joshua and Rachel—I realized I still held my wineglass. On one hand, the idea of letting the cheating jerk back into the game made my entire body tense, and wine relaxed me. On the other hand, I didn't want to agree to leave for a party hat and a slice of pizza because I got drunk.

The screen changed. "Please Stand By" vanished, replaced with "$500." Did they think any of us would sell our opportunity to win a quarter of a million dollars for a mere five hundred bucks?

After a few minutes, Justin and Ed came to sit with me, carrying their own wineglasses, plus a fresh bottle. Ariana had gone back into the house. No way would she leave. The fans loved her.

"What do you think?" Justin asked.

I gestured at the screen. "I'm not sure. Some of the prizes aren't bad. I mean, I'd love a trip for two to Hawaii. But with $250,000, I could buy about sixty thousand trips to Hawaii. I could go every week."

Justin nodded.

"The thing is, I'm unemployed. My severance package barely covers this summer. I need first and last month's rent and security for a new apartment. And I've got some bills I'd love to pay before I'm fifty." I sipped my wine and sagged back into the chair. "I don't know."

The screen behind me offered a brand-new Toyota Prius. Now *that* tempted me, if only because of the resale value. I didn't need a new car; public transit took me everywhere. Also, I didn't actually possess a driver's license. Living downtown meant never needing to learn how to drive.

"I guess it comes down to two things," Ed said. "Do you think you can win, and how much would it take for you to accept the sure thing?"

"But those aren't the only considerations," Justin said. "Only one person can accept the offer, so you also need to think about who else wants it."

"Do you want it?"

"No," he said. "Maybe I won't win, but I at least want to know I gave it all I had."

I turned to Ed. "What about you?"

"Oh, I want to win," Ed said. "The gay guy never wins these things."

The screen now read "$10." They weren't giving us much time to think. Of course, ten dollars wasn't a real offer. The amounts would have to increase significantly to make it worth giving up my last week with Justin.

"There's no way Rachel will leave if Joshua might come back. She's the only one he was ever nice to, and for some reason, she likes him."

"Right," Ed said. "He was only a jerk to everyone else. What about Ariana?"

"No way. America likes her: She's already been saved. Twice. No one else can say that. If the viewers have a say in the finals, she'll win."

"You never know," Justin said.

"That's the problem. What I do know is America put me up for elimination three times, and never put Ariana up for elimination at all. They saved Ariana twice. The other people they wanted eliminated are almost all gone. If it comes down to a viewer vote, I'm out. So, I need to consider what offer I'd accept."

The board changed again. "Trip for 2 around the world."

Now, that sounded nice. Briefly, I let myself picture me and Justin in a sailboat in the Caribbean. Hiking up the Andes. Climbing the Eiffel

Tower. But a dream vacation wouldn't pay my bills, and I couldn't pay the taxes on it.

What would they have to offer me to leave? Ten thousand dollars wasn't enough, although it would be better than nothing. I would absolutely leave for seventy-five thousand, but there's no way they would go that high. If they did, no matter what anyone said, I'd be tripping over the other players on my way to grab my fish.

I leaned back and watched dark clouds gather overhead as I sipped my wine, thinking.

* * *

Three hours later, I knew exactly two things: One, I did not want to spend another second of my life in the same room as Joshua (who at that moment stood gyrating his hips on the top steps of the hot tub with his arms waving over his head). Two, I couldn't afford to go all the way to the end of the game and leave with nothing. The problem was, without knowing how the show picked a winner, I couldn't calculate my chances. But if the fans had a say, I wouldn't win the grand prize. Sarah confirmed all my fears: the viewers hated me, and there wasn't much I could do about it at this point.

If the producers crowned the person who solved the most quadratic equations in under five minutes, I was in a great position. Unfortunately, the final challenge would most likely mix strength, intelligence, and viewer loyalty. Like everything else. And the viewers hated me.

Rachel had changed into blue plaid pajama pants and a white tank top. She laid next to the hot tub with a starfish pillow, waiting to see what happened. Ed had gone inside to play pool with Ariana. None of them displayed any interest in being tempted. Justin had left for a while earlier, but he now sat on a nearby chaise. I wondered what he thought. Law school cost a lot of money. He owed a considerable amount, too.

I got up and went to sit next to him. "Okay, seriously, what do you think? I know you said you're staying, but did you mean it?"

I'd kept my voice low. So did he.

"There's no way I'm taking any offer," he said.

"What about your loans?"

"I'll get a job and pay my loans, like everyone else. I can make it on my own. You need the money more than I do."

"Don't stay because you want me to have the money."

"How much would you need to go?"

"Well, they did thirty grand earlier. It takes me almost nine months to make that much. I think if they go back up in that area, I'll take it. Even after I pay my debts, I'll have enough to live on while I find a new job."

"Yeah." Justin's expression was inscrutable.

In that moment, I would've given all the money to know what he thought about me leaving. Or about me staying with him. Or about the two of us running away together. Thunder rumbled in the distance.

"Either way, you better decide soon. They may call the whole thing off when the rain starts."

I hesitated, then asked the question I needed him to answer. "Do you want me to stay?"

"Don't stay for me, Jen. If you want to stay, do it because you think you can win."

He was right. In my heart, I knew if I stayed at this point, he would be the only reason. Was a guy that I'd yet to kiss worth potentially tens of thousands of dollars? Was any guy worth that much money? Or, more accurately, was he worth walking away from the ability to pay off my debts?

It didn't sound like he wanted me to stay. If he didn't want me to stay, staying for him would be a huge mistake. I should go. My heart ached with indecision.

Seeing the anguish on my face, Justin opened his mouth. Then, whatever he'd been about to say died in his throat. He pointed at the screen behind me. "Holy shit."

I turned around. "$50,000."

Fifty. Thousand. Dollars. That would pay off my bills, plus cover first and last month's rent and security on a new apartment. It might give me a down payment on my own (tiny) place. It was more than my annual salary at my old job. It was a year's salary for a lot of people. With fifty grand in the bank, I could take my time, figure out what I wanted to do with my life, and find my dream job.

The producers were offering me the answer to my prayers. All my prayers but one.

"That's an incredible offer, Jen." Justin said.

"I know."

"Take it."

I prayed for a sign he wanted me to stay with him. That our moment in the laundry room hadn't been for the ratings. That Sarah had been right and he liked me but was just as scared as me. In that moment, I didn't care about the show, the money, or anything but getting to spend more time with him.

But he'd said I should go. He didn't want a few extra days with me.

I knew what I had to do. Any fool could see what was best, and I wasn't a fool. "I have to take it."

"I know."

Overhead, the clouds broke. Thunder rumbled, closer now. Before it faded, lightning split the sky in two. Fat raindrops dotted the pavement.

Rachel tore into the house with only a glance in my direction. She didn't even look at the screen. A comical look crossed Joshua's face as if he couldn't decide whether he was allowed to follow her.

Letting the storm drench me, I searched Justin's green eyes, willing him to ask me to stay. He swallowed, but said nothing. The silence grew into a canyon between us.

I bit my lip, hoping he couldn't see how badly I wanted to stay with him. "Good-bye, Justin."

Quickly, before I changed my mind, I leaned over and planted a quick kiss on his soft lips. Then I stood, grabbed my fish, and tossed it into the pool. I was going home on my own terms.

Chapter 24

Jennifer in the School Room, Week 8:

How, exactly, did Joshua get chosen to come back into the house? I'm having trouble believing the viewers chose him over, say, Abram or Maria. Unless they just want to make us suffer. I wouldn't think it was that interesting to watch someone walk around calling everyone ugly, fat, and stupid. Did the producers pick him solely to increase the drama?

. . .If it would keep me from having to live with Joshua again, I would do just about anything. What do you want? Naked dancing? My first-born child?

The second my fish hit the water, Joshua whooped and leapt from the hot tub. He waved his arms, twerked, and pranced around the yard, doing his own version of a rain dance.

I turned away, ignoring him. Tears prickled my eyes. I couldn't look at Justin. He wanted me to go.

Through the loudspeakers, Overalls directed us to gather in the living room and wait for Bella. I stayed where I was, my brain not yet processing the consequences of my body's actions. Had I just done this? I had. And I knew, deep down, it was the right decision.

Lightning tore the sky in two, illuminating the backyard. I saw only Justin, standing in front of me for the last time.

"You're really going?" he asked.

Not trusting myself to speak, I nodded, my eyes glued on his. My breath hitched at the emotion reflected there.

"You said you wanted me to leave," I pointed out. The words stuck in my throat.

Tears blurred my vision. A raindrop landed on my eyelashes.

Justin smoothed a now-dripping lock of hair away from my face and kissed my forehead. "I said you should take the offer. Not that I want you to leave. Taking the money is the right decision for you, but this isn't the end for us."

My hands found his. I took a deep breath before Justin crushed me against his chest. I hugged him close, my face buried in his shoulder. He smelled like coconut sunscreen and Dreft laundry detergent, just like everyone in the house. Beneath it, I found the sweet musk that was uniquely Justin and imprinted it on my memory.

After a moment, someone tapped my shoulder. Curly Beard stood beside us, motioning toward the door at the rear of the house. It was impossible to finish this conversation now. Maybe we never would. Hanging my head, I followed the producers woodenly to the School Room for my final interview.

When I returned to the living room, I stopped dead at the emptiness. Where was everyone?

Someone entered the room behind me, but I didn't turn to see who it was. A few minutes later, Ed moved beside me and squeezed my hand.

"Hey," he whispered. "I packed all your stuff for you. Your suitcase is in the hall."

I smiled gratefully. "You're a good friend, Ed. Good luck." He hugged me tightly as Bella entered.

She explained the next steps, but I wasn't listening. This whole thing felt so surreal. It was all happening so fast. Was I leaving? Voluntarily? I barely noticed when Leanna came in until she touched my shoulder.

"You have a few minutes to say good-bye," she told me. "Then, there's a car waiting outside to take you to the hotel."

Saying good-bye was not easy.

Rachel hugged me. "It was great to meet you."

"You, too, Rach. I'm glad I got to get to know you. We should keep in touch." I was more surprised by my sincerity than by hers. Over the past few weeks, I had come to like and respect her.

"Absolutely," she said. "I'll follow you on Instagram."

I smiled. No matter what, I'd always have the friends I made on this adventure. Even if I couldn't have Justin.

Ariana leaned against the wall. "Bye! So sorry to see you go! The driver's waiting," she sang.

What a bitch. I was not the least bit sorry to realize I never had to see or think about her again. Unless, of course, I watched the finale to see who won. God, I hoped she didn't win. If America voted and she won, I have would have to seriously consider moving to Canada.

Leaving Justin for last was a mistake. I couldn't speak when I got to him. I just hugged him tightly and blinked back tears. I'd never known I could feel this strongly about someone. Before Bella mentioned bringing Dominic back into the house, I'd nearly forgotten him. That was a stupid infatuation. This was the real thing.

For me, anyway. Not for Justin. The only thing to do now was go home and try to get over him.

When we pulled apart, his hands cupped my face. He lowered his voice in a futile effort to stop everyone around us from hearing. "I will see you again, Jen. I promise."

I wanted to believe him, but then why tell me to leave? I couldn't stand the thought of risking my heart to another man, only to have it trampled again. "I'll miss you."

Blinking furiously, with one last glance around, a smile, and a wave, I turned and left the Fishbowl forever.

* * *

Five minutes later, my stuff was loaded in the limousine and the car pulled away from the house. I stared straight ahead, trying not to cry. I had certainly made the right decision, but—what if I never saw Justin again?

I couldn't think that way. There was never any reason to think I might see him again after the show ended. Worse, I had no way of knowing how much longer it would be before one of us would have been eliminated. I had always known our time together was limited.

Ending it on my terms was the smartest move.

So, really, there was no reason to cry. Things turned out okay. Second place was a pretty good place to be. I won an awesome prize. Fifty thousand dollars is a lot of money. Yup. I felt fine. Yay for my prize!

It just wasn't the prize I really wanted. A tear trickled down my face. I let it fall, sliding down my neck and disappearing into the top of my T-shirt.

As the car picked up speed, I let out a sob.

Before we made it to the end of the driveway, the car stopped abruptly. What the heck? The driver lowered the barrier between us and smiled at me in the mirror.

"Turn around, Jennifer."

Surprised, I looked out the back window. In the distance, I heard a voice. It sounded like someone calling my name.

Lightning flashed overhead, lighting up the dark driveway.

Justin was racing down the driveway in the pouring rain, yelling my name. Water drenched him from head to toe. Not quite daring to believe this was really happening, I threw the door open and leapt out of the car.

"Jennifer!"

"Justin!"

He ran toward me and grabbed me in a bear hug. I threw my head back and laughed as he swung me in a circle. After that first, exhilarating spin, he set me down and wiped a now dripping lock of hair out of my face.

"What are you doing?" I asked.

"I left. I'm coming with you."

I shook the water out of my ears. He was picking me. He chose me! Our connection wasn't just part of the game, some role he played for the cameras. Justin felt the same way I did.

"I thought you wanted to give it all you had."

"As soon as you walked out that door, I realized I want to give *us* everything I have instead."

My heart lurched, and my brain scrambled to think of the right thing to say. "But you could have won the grand prize!" That wasn't right, but I couldn't take the words back.

Justin smiled his slow, lazy smile that made my stomach flutter and my insides melt. Then, he cupped my face with both hands, leaning toward me. "I already have. I love you, Jen."

"I love you, too."

As he closed the distance, my lips met his halfway. Justin's hands went into my hair, pulling me close. My lips parted as he deepened the embrace, and his tongue found mine. I wound my arms around his waist, pulling him closer. Actually kissing Justin felt a hundred times better than all the times I imagined kissing him. I would've been perfectly happy to stand there all day.

Around us, rain continued to pelt the pavement. Lightning split the sky, but none of that mattered. All that mattered was this moment: Justin kissing me like he never wanted to stop.

Funny how, sometimes, second place feels better than winning.

Epilogue

<u>Scenes from the School Room, Week 8:</u>

Ariana: *I CAN'T BELIEVE HE PICKED THAT MOUSY KNOW-IT-ALL OVER ME!*

Joshua: *Yo, yo, yo bitches! The J-dawg is back, baby! I'm gonna rock this competition, yo, and I don't mean maybe! It's gonna be TIGHT! Just wait and see! Long live the J-dawg, right?*

Ed: *It's about time those two got it on! I was starting to worry I'd have to tie them together and sit on them. Hey, Jen, if you're watching, you go, girl!*

Rachel: *I fear the sweet Joshua I met at the audition is gone forever. That's okay, though, because it'll feel good to beat this jerk twice.*

SHOCKING ENTERTAINMENT NEWS ONLINE

BREAKING NEWS: THE FISHBOWL STAR A HOMEWRECKER

"Jen slept with my husband," grieving wife moans

by Stephen Taylor, July 3, 2016

Reality television fans have been avidly following the path of Washington-native Jennifer Reid, who introduced herself as a twenty-four-year-old marketing assistant. With her girl-next-door good looks, witty personality, and effusive charm, Jen looked like an early favorite.

On June 14, Seattle resident Danielle Rossellini stepped forward, presenting an alternate view of the wholesome, fresh-faced girl.

"Jennifer had sex with my husband. I caught her waltzing around my house like she owned the place. For more than a year, she tried to talk him into leaving me for her." The 32-year-old redhead paused, dabbing at her eyes with a silk handkerchief. "My marriage was solid, and then she just swooped in. Dominic told her no, over and over, but she kept after him. They both went to the same school. No matter how he avoided her, she was there. Finally, she wore him down."

A producer for *The Fishbowl* declined our request to interview Jen. Dominic Rossellini did not return several e-mails and telephone calls requesting comment. A search of public records revealed that Danielle filed for divorce only days after *The Fishbowl* premiere aired.

Click here for rest of article.

Related Stories:

Meet the Fish: Seattle's Own Jennifer Reid Makes Reality Debut

Former High School Classmate Speaks Out: Joshua Nice Guy, Bad Actor

See *The Fishbowl* Star Ariana's Audition Video LEAKED!

SHOCKING ENTERTAINMENT NEWS ONLINE

J-Dog: "ARIANA'S A LIAR!"

Eliminated player returns to The Fishbowl *with shocking truths*

by Monica Summers, August 15, 2016

Many analysts theorized early on that the beautiful, devious Ariana would waltz away from ABC's new hit reality show with the grand prize. An early fan favorite, Ariana presented herself as a sympathetic figure: she claimed to have been raped, leaving her a single mother at 14. Worse, a genetic condition endangered her daughter's life.

However, everything changed when Seattle's Jen took the temptation to leave the show early, paving the way for J-dawg's return. Readers may remember that J-dawg left *The Fishbowl* after the second week amid allegations of cheating in a contest that required the contestants to disclose information about themselves (See story here).

Upon his return, however, J-dawg revealed that he wasn't the only contestant who had been less-than-honest with the fans. Only moments after he officially re-entered the competition, J-dawg told America that he'd done some research at home.

The other contestants were shocked to learn that Ariana never had a child. Her entire backstory was taken from a character she played in a movie. (See video)

Ariana attempted to convince the others that J-dawg was lying, until he began to repeat her lines from the film. Her resulting meltdown garnered four million views on YouTube within an hour after the show aired on the East Coast. (See video)

She spent the rest of the week trying to recover, but Ariana's fate was sealed. For the first time, the viewers nominated to put Ariana up for elimination. Viewers may remember that Ariana was previously the only

Click here for rest of article.

Related Stories:

Tell-All: Eliminated "Fish" Gives Sneak Peek Behind the Scenes

Abram: How to Keep the Faith Inside *The Fishbowl*

Maria Hernandez Favorite Mrs. Texas Contestant

Network: *The Fishbowl* Renewed for Second Season.

SHOCKING ENTERTAINMENT NEWS ONLINE

FORMER CHEERLEADING CHAMPION CROWNED THE FISH-BOWL *WINNER*

Sioux City native takes $250,000 prize

by Ted Hernandez, August 22, 2016

It's been a roller coaster of a season. With love triangles, backstabbing, cheating and more, the debut season of *The Fishbowl* has been anything but dull. Sioux City-native Rachel Sorenson flew under the radar early on. However, after the weakest competitors were picked off, the former cheerleading champion revealed herself as a force to be reckoned with.

Readers may remember Ariana's shocking meltdown after J-dawg revealed she'd been lying to the viewers. (See video) With the main obstacle between her and victory removed, Rachel settled into her role as front-runner.

The week after Ariana's starling elimination, Rachel shone during the Murder Mystery challenge. She not only figured out the clues before the other two players but managed to masterfully weave false information to lead J-dawg on a wild goose chase, thereby ensuring his elimination. Rumor has it that members of the production scoured the property for hours before the previously eliminated contestant was located.

The show's finale featured Rachel up against the handsome Ed Silva in a race for survival. With nothing but a compass and some basic provisions, the producers deposited the final two Fish in the desert outside of Las Vegas. It

Click here for rest of article.

Related Stories:

Ariana Sassani Cast as Bond girl

Ex-Wife Scorned for Reality Star Negotiating Own Series with Fox

Former Reality Contestant Joshua Adams Charged with DUI

Shocking Reality TV Meltdown Gets 20m Hits on YouTube

Ed Silva Named Fan Favorite

About the Author

Photo Credit: Andrew Heffernan

Laura Heffernan is living proof that watching too much TV can pay off. When not watching total strangers participate in arranged marriages, drag racing queens, or cooking competitions, Laura enjoys travel, baking, board games, helping with writing contests, and seeking new experiences. She lives in the northeast with her amazing husband and two furry little beasts.

Other random facts from Laura: "I make stuff up and write it down. Some of my favorite things include goat cheese, Buffy the Vampire Slayer, Battlestar Galactica, the Oxford comma, and ice cream. Not all together."

If you enjoyed Jen and Justin's story, the adventure continues in the next Reality Star novel. . .

SWEET REALITY

by

Laura Heffernan

Available in fall 2017 from Lyrical Press

Read on for a preview. . .

SHOCKING ENTERTAINMENT NEWS ONLINE

Runaway *Fishbowl* Couple Returning to TV?

Jen and Justin to appear on upcoming new series

by Talky Ted, Nov. 1

During the first season of The Fishbowl, Seattle's Jen Reid shocked viewers across the nation by accepting a $50,000 payout to leave the show and allow previously-eliminated contestant J-Dawg to take her place.

The brown-haired, blue-eyed former marketing assistant admitted earlier in the show to mounting money problems, including homelessness. Many viewers thought she'd stick around to seek the grand prize. However, after viewers repeatedly nominated her for elimination, Jen wisely decided to take the money and run.

But that wasn't the end. Seconds after Jen announced her decision, her on-again, off-again love interest announced that he, too would leave the show. Despite being what many considered a serious contender for the grand prize, Justin Taylor of the startlingly green eyes and fabulous dimples followed Jen's limo down the driveway. The two shared a thrilling kiss before driving off.

Jen and Justin returned to their respective homes in Seattle and Florida. After the holidays, Jen moved to the Sunshine State where she invested her winnings in a bakery co-owned with Justin's twin sister. In May, Justin graduated U. of Miani Law third in his class.

Sixteen months after their famous departure, America's most well-known reality couple may be returning to primetime. The Network recently announced a new show. *Reality Ocean: Caribbean*, which takes a boatload of former reality stars and their guests to the Bahamas, Jamaica, the Cayman Islands, and Mexico. The show begins filming next week.

Jen, Justin, and a spokesperson for the network refused to comment, leaving this reporter hopeful the hunky blond law student will be reappearing soon on a television near you.

Related Stories:

Shocking Reality TV Meltdown Gets 20m Hits on YouTube

***America's Next Drag Suppermodel* winner donates winnings to anti-gay-bashing organization**

***Deaf Teen Mother* finale shocking, poignant**

I craned my neck, seeking any speck of light, but the makers of this blindfold should be proud of their craftsmanship. My roommate, Sarah, helped me out of her car and led me away, but I hadn't the faintest clue where we were going. Honking cars and street noise suggested we'd driven to somewhere in the city. The cool breeze and taste of salt in the air suggested we'd stopped near the beach, but in Miami, those clues told me little about our actual location.

"Jen, stop. You're peeking." At Sarah's order, I halted.

"I am not peeking. I can't see a thing." I could smell though, so I sniffed the air again, seeking other clues. Beneath the salt, the city odors, and the fabric of the blindfold lingered something else. Something not quite identifiable, but enticing.

"Then why do you keep tilting your head back?" Even with the blindfold, I could perfectly imagine Sarah's hands finding their way to her hips as she glared at me.

"Because I'm *trying* to peek," I admitted. "But I can't see a thing. Also, something smells amazing." The farther we walked, the stronger the scent became. Wherever we were, something edible lurked nearby. Something *delicious* and edible.

"I'm glad you mentioned that. Stop here."

A lock clacked open, and a wave of cold air hit my face—air conditioning escaping from whatever building we stood in front of. It seemed strange when people used the A/C in the fall, but October was oddly stifling in Florida this year. Oddly to me, anyway, since this would be my first winter living in the South. Fall in my hometown of Seattle usually brought some clouds, some rain, some temperatures below one hundred degrees. Not in Miami, though.

That's what I got for falling in love with a soon-to-be lawyer. Thanks to state licensing laws, my boyfriend, Justin, couldn't exactly pick up and move to Seattle as easily as my unemployed, couch-surfing self had moved to Florida and found a two-bedroom apartment with his sister.

His sister who was currently leading me into a place full of enticing aromas. Cinnamon, chocolate, butter, vanilla. . . I couldn't even identify all the components. While I waited for her to tell me what was going on, I lowered my head and wiped my chin in case I'd started drooling.

It wasn't my birthday, so a surprise party didn't make any sense, but I smelled cake. Justin and I were leaving for a cruise in a few days, but a surprise Tuesday morning bon voyage party seemed out of place. Maybe the cloak and dagger routine meant she'd come up with a surprise for our upcoming business venture, opening next year.

When I left *The Fishbowl*, I didn't have any more idea what to do with my life than before I started, but I did have more money. The producers paid a per diem: a cash stipend for every day on the show. After eight weeks on the set, I walked away with almost seventeen hundred dollars. Plus my fifty thousand dollar cash prize. Even after taxes, not bad for less than two months' work.

With no job, a boyfriend in Florida, and no place to sleep other than on my friend Brandon's couch, it didn't take long to find the perfect solution: co-owner and manager of the bakery Sarah planned to open in Miami. My marketing background would help us promote the shop, and I loved talking to people, so the customer service aspect would be a breeze. Plus, being my own boss at least ensured I wouldn't get another crappy mass email if I ever laid myself off.

Starting a business is easier said than done, but while I gained experience working nine-to-five behind the counter of the grocery store's bakery, Sarah came up with the perfect idea: *Sweet Reality*, a bakery offering a variety of desserts inspired by reality shows and contestants. I'd act as the face of the company, hopefully bringing in fans of *The Fishbowl* and similar shows. Sarah had already designed fishbowl-shaped cookies and cupcake flavors inspired by the personalities of several first season contestants.

"Are we doing a secret taste test of a bakery to scope out the competition?" I asked

"Not exactly. Hold on a sec."

Somewhere, a switch flicked, and light appeared beyond the blindfold. I still couldn't make out any shapes, but we no longer stood in darkness.

Finally, Sarah said, "Okay, take it off."

A sign reading "Sweet Reality" hung across the far wall, with little television sets on either side and clapper boards in place of the E's. The sign jumped out from a wall covered with glittering stars, both of the astrological variety and from television.

"OMG, it's our bakery! I love it!"

"Isn't it amazing?" Sarah asked.

"It really is." A framed poster of me and Justin sharing our first kiss, which happened to take place on national television, hung near the front door where passersby could spot it. "Wow, that's a huge picture of us."

We'd no idea the limousine driver taking me away from *The Fishbowl* carried a handheld camera, even though it made perfect sense in retrospect. Nothing we'd done during those eight weeks was private, why would our final good-byes be? They wanted to catch the good stuff, and Justin chasing me down the driveway after I took a cash incentive to leave the show certainly qualified as "good stuff."

The poster brought a smile to my face. That kiss had been pretty good stuff, too.

"You're the draw," Sarah said, breaking into my memories. "We need to bring people into the store, and they want to see you and Justin kissing."

"And you're okay staring at a picture of me and your brother making out all day?"

"I'll be in the back, baking." She winked at me. "Besides, I like to think I had a hand in you two getting together, so why not profit from it?"

I laughed. Sarah and I first met in the bathroom at *The Fishbowl* audition, where we'd bonded instantly. When Justin said she was his twin sister, I'd been ecstatic at the thought of seeing her again after the show. Then, during a surprise family guest appearance on the show, Sarah had been the one to help me and Justin realize that we were both being idiots, letting a miscommunication and our fear of getting hurt overwhelm our feelings. We grew closer every day, and she'd become the sister I'd always wanted. No offense to my brother Adam who was lovely, but not quite the same. Sarah never once gave me an atomic wedgie.

"Thanks," I said, "but I think the show also helped a little bit. Not to mention, the two of us."

"Maybe. Anyway, I'm preparing recipes for opening day. Come see what I've made."

A row of cupcakes, cookies, brownies, lemon bars, and more filled the counter behind the display cases. My mouth watered in anticipation. "When did you do this? And how? I thought the contractors wouldn't be finished until the fifteenth?"

"They called yesterday to say they finished early. You were at Justin's, and I wanted to whip up a few recipes before bringing you in to see it. Surprise!" Her eyes danced. "We can open as soon as you get back!"

"That's amazing! I can't believe you made all this stuff for me. It looks fantastic. Although I hope you don't expect me to eat everything before I leave."

"No, Justin will help. I'll take a few things over to Mom's later. But also, we can freeze most of this so it's ready for the grand opening. I'm baking and freezing all this week and next."

"*Our grand opening!*" After months of working for this moment, I could almost taste it.

Unable to wait another second, I reached around Sarah and snagged a chocolate cupcake with chocolate hazelnut frosting. I bit into it, moaning as rich, nutty sweetness exploded across my tongue. "This is fantastic, Sarah. We're going to sell a mill–"

All the color drained from Sarah's face. She choked on her words, sending a chill down my spine.

"What's wrong?"

Soundlessly, she pointed over my shoulder. I spun around, expecting to see the drug store taking up most of the block across from us, and the silver slats and padlock barring the recently-vacant store beside it. A store that no longer sat vacant or empty Someone had raised the metal slats, the front door stood open, lights filled the front window, and the sidewalk bustled with people going in and out. All within the few minutes since Sarah led me in here.

A sign hung off the store front, just barely visible out of the front corner of our shop. "GRAND OPENING! 10% OFF CUPCAKES TODAY ONLY."

No wonder Sarah's face had taken on the color of flour. Patty's Cakes, one of the most popular bakeries in Miami, had set up shop across the street from us. I could almost see our profits racing from our shop to theirs. How could we possibly compete with Patty's? How could we even stay open?

"What the hell is going on?"

Sarah's mouth opened and closed, but no sound came out. Oh, this was bad. So, so bad. The location, the timing, everything.

Patty's Cakes' namesake was legendary, as much a fixture of this city as Disney World was in Orlando. Well, okay, maybe not quite that much. But they were huge, and amazing cakes filled their windows already. And they'd opened before us.

A line of people already wound down the block and out of sight.

* * *

My mouth dropped and my hand opened involuntarily, sending chocolate cake and hazelnutty goodness to the no-longer pristine white and silver tiles.

The store across the street sat on a corner, where it would get the pedestrian traffic we needed to bring in. It also sat directly in front of a bus stop. The same bus stop we hoped would bring customers to Sweet Reality, not to our competitor.

Patty's Cakes looked quaint and inviting, with its flowery pink and purple decorations. Worse, it was open *now*, whereas we wouldn't have anything to sell for at least two weeks. Even with the shop all set up,

Sarah couldn't exactly throw out the open sign and start selling goods at a moment's notice. The cash register wasn't even online yet, and we'd been counting on the free press from *Reality Caribbean: Ocean* to start some buzz. We couldn't throw away all our plans for a grand opening now.

"How did this happen? Why didn't we know about it?" I asked.

Sarah narrowed her green eyes, and her nostrils flared. "I don't know! They weren't there when I leased this space in June. The storefront wasn't even for rent—it was a cell phone store or something."

"What about when you were setting up, checking on the construction?"

"No! Don't you think I would have mentioned if I'd seen the sign? It's not like I forgot to say, 'Hey, Jen, we're going out of business before we even open!" Her voice rose with each word, quickly trending toward a frequency that only dogs could hear. This wasn't helping anything.

"It's okay. Calm down. I'm sorry. That's not what I meant. Just. . . You didn't see anything?"

"There's been activity over there," she said. "But with shutters over the windows and no sign, I didn't think anything was opening for months. And I never thought it might be another bakery. Are they allowed to put a competing store across the street?"

I tapped furiously on my phone. "I don't know, but I'm texting Justin. There are perks to dating a lawyer."

My phone buzzed less than a minute after I hit "send." *It's legal unless you have a non-compete in your lease. I'm on my way. Will be there soon.*

Sarah fell into a chair behind the glass cases, burying her face in her arms on the counter. Her shoulders heaved. Not knowing what to do, I patted her shoulder, trying to seem more calm than I felt.

Renovating and redecorating this shop used up most of the last of my *Fishbowl* money. If we didn't succeed, I'd be left with nothing. Sarah's baking skills grew more impressive every day; she'd get another job as a pastry chef or in a bakery in a heartbeat. Her former boss would probably pee herself in excitement if Sarah called asking for her job back.

But I'd been laid off a month before going on the show, and I didn't know anyone looking to hire a washed-up reality TV star who once worked in marketing. Justin's temporary job become permanent as soon as his bar exam results came in next week, but he wasn't going to support me. Not that I would ask him to. I needed to make this bakery work so I could support myself long-term.

"It's going to be okay," I said. Even to my own ear, it sounded unconvincing. "We've got a unique hook, right? It's not just a bakery, it's Sweet Reality. People who eat here get baked goods to remind them of their favorite TV personalities. *Delicious* baked goods."

"What if it's not enough? They've got name recognition. We can't compete with that."

"Of course we can! They only make cakes and cupcakes. We make everything. Besides, you've got great recipes."

She didn't answer, absorbed by the scene outside. There wasn't much we could do until Justin showed up with more information, so I went into the kitchen for a broom to sweep up the mess of crumbs I'd made. If possible, it smelled even better in here than in the main room. Following my nose, I quickly found the source: four giant cupcakes, much bigger than the samples sitting by the display case.

Strawberries peeked over the top of each white dome, and the bowl in the sink held the remnants of what turned out to be whipped cream , not vanilla icing. She'd made strawberry shortcake cupcakes! Judging from the little white cake bits on the counter beside the plate, the strawberries weren't only on top: Sarah stuffed these babies. It was just like her to hide the best treats for last, to completely floor me after I finished raving about everything else she'd made.

My mouth watered. If I wasn't careful, I'd gain three hundred pounds working here. Unless Sweet Reality turned enough profit to buy me a whole new wardrobe in the next few months, I should talk to Justin about signing up for a joint gym membership before Sarah and I opened. Or maybe I should plan to walk to and from work every day instead of taking the bus.

I promptly abandoned my plan to find a broom. We could clean up later. Instead, I ripped the wrapper off one of these amazing cakes, grabbed another with my free hand, and backed into the swinging door leading back to the main room.

"Look what I found." I called.

Sarah stood at the front of the shop, peering out the window and nibbling her thumbnail. "You got a broom?"

"Better! Why didn't you tell me you'd hidden strawberry shortcakes back there. They look amazing!"

Sarah whirled around, her face white. I bit into the first cake, holding the second out to her.

"Wait!" she said at the same moment.

Too late. My teeth sank through the whipped cream and vanilla cake, closing in on the sweet, sticky strawberry goodness. I savored the flavors in my mouth for a moment, eyes closed. Then my tooth hit something hard. A foreign object flew down my throat. I choked. The other cupcake tumbled to the ground, exploding at my feet.

"Oh, shit!" Sarah said. She ran toward me. "Are you okay?"

Unable to answer, I coughed and spit. Something hard lodged in my throat. Tears poured down my cheeks.

"Water," I croaked. "I think I lost a filling."

Spinning around, I tore back for the sink, one hand over my mouth to catch the crumbs spewing everywhere. Running my tongue around my mouth, I didn't find any holes, so my dental work remained intact. What I choked on remained a mystery.

What the fuck was in these things? How did strawberries and cake get so hard? And why would anyone put them in food if they did?

When I reached the sink I leaned over, hacking until I feared a lung might come up.

Something shot out of my mouth, clattering against the sink. I shut my eyes, sagging against the counter for support.

Sarah appeared at my side. "Jen! Can you breathe? Talk to me."

"I don't think those are going to be a bestseller," I said when I finally got control of myself. "One of them cut me. My mouth tastes like metal."

I was reaching for the faucet to get some water when Sarah's hand closed over mine, staying it. Her green eyes were huge. "Listen to me. Did you swallow the ring?"

Did I what the huh?

I stared at her at her for what felt like a full minute. "The. . . ring?"

"My grandmother's diamond ring. I hid it in your cupcake. Where did it go?"

Made in the USA
Middletown, DE
07 August 2018